D0720568

LORI WICK

A Texas
Sky

HARVEST HOUSE PUBLISHERS

EUGENE, OREGON

Scripture references are taken from the King James Version of the Bible.

Cover design by Dugan Design Group, Bloomington, Minnesota

This is a work of fiction. Characters, places, and incidents are products of the author's imagination or are used fictitiously. Any resemblance to actual persons, living or dead, or to events or locales, is entirely coincidental.

A TEXAS SKY
Copyright © 2000 by Lori Wick
Published by Harvest House Publishers
Eugene, Oregon 97402
www.harvesthousepublishers.com

ISBN-13: 978-0-7369-2241-8
ISBN-10: 0-7369-2241-5

The Library of Congress has cataloged the edition as follows:

Library of Congress Cataloging-in-Publication Data

Wick, Lori.
    A Texas Sky / Lori Wick
        p. cm. — (Yellow Rose Trilogy ; 2)
     ISBN 0-7369-0187-6
        1. Texas Rangers—Fiction. 2. Kidnapping—Fiction. 3. Texas—Fiction. I. Title.
  PS3573.I237 T49 2000
  813'.54
                                        00-028127

Printed in the United States of America.

08 09 10 11 12 13 14 15 16 / BP-MS / 10 9 8 7 6 5 4 3 2 1

Acknowledgments

I had such fun with this book, during which many lives touched my own. This page is to thank…

Merry Hahn. Thank you for letting me borrow the spelling of your name. You, Norm, and the kids are so precious to our family. We thank God for you. May we long serve Christ together, honing and sharpening each other as the Word commands.

Mary Vesperman. This is the one that fell apart, Mary. Thank you, dear friend, for giving me permission to start over. When all is said and done, I think this was the best work. God bless you.

Diane Barsness. It's so fun to have a friend who loves a good romance and laughs in all the right places. Thanks for being there on days when I wonder if I'm going to survive parenthood. Our friendship is such a good reminder that through God's help, our mothers did.

The Caminiti kids. Thank you for being great friends to our gang. Your examples do not go unnoticed. No matter where your paths lead, I pray that all of you will walk strong in obedience and trust in our saving God.

My Bob. The vocabulary lessons never end. From *constabulary* to *coffers*, from *tertiary* to *tributary*, thank you for always bringing in new words, explaining them with clarity and patience, and expanding my world in this small way. Of all the things you say, however, my favorite is about your love for me. We don't live under a Texas sky, but my Wisconsin sky would be very small without you.

Prologue

❦ ❦ ❦

June 1882
Wellsville, Texas

"HOW IS HE?" MARTY BRACEWELL ASKED anxiously as he entered the bedroom, not remembering to remove his hat or offer any of the standard greetings.

"Doing a little better," Desmond Curtis said. "Slate and Cash were just here, and although Dakota's as weak as a girl, he's in a good frame of mind." Desmond, knowing how Brace would feel if he knew the whole truth, did not elaborate, but he knew that Dakota was doing as well as he was because of how significant his brothers' visit had been.

"Hey, Dak," Brace said softly, watching the Ranger's eyes come open a little. As a point in fact, all three men were Texas Rangers, but only one of them had nearly bled to death from numerous gunshot wounds, and he was still very injured.

"Hi, Brace," Dakota tried to say, but his mouth was too dry. Desmond helped him with a drink, but they had to go slowly—they would probably have to go slowly for a long time.

"Sorry I took so long. I was up north and just got back."

"It's all right," Dakota managed.

"What happened out there?" Brace asked, not really expecting an answer. Dakota tried anyway.

"I thought I had the jump on them, but there were more men than I figured. I went down fast. Had no choice."

Brace felt his throat close. This man was one of his best. To see him shot-up and helpless was hard. He cleared his throat, telling himself this was no time for tears.

"You'll be back soon, ornery as ever."

"No doubt," the man in the bed agreed, a small smile coming to his lips. "I'll see you in a few weeks."

Brace was suddenly angry. That this would happen to one of his best infuriated him!

"If you so much as show your face near my office inside of six months, I'll shoot you myself," Brace warned. "And I mean it!"

Dakota could only nod. Right now six months sounded too soon. Sleep was coming in again, but that was all right. For the first time in his life, Dakota James Rawlings had Someone he could talk to.

☙ ☙ ☙

Dakota heard gunshots a few days later, as real as the ones that had taken him down. His eyes flew open and he gasped, remembering with painful clarity where he was.

"Easy..." Desmond's voice came softly to his ears, and Dakota turned to find him sitting next to the bed.

Dakota tried to tell Desmond he was thirsty but couldn't manage it. Thankfully the older Ranger knew the signs. He lifted a cup for the injured man. Dakota thanked him with a slight raise of his hand, amazed at how spent he was.

"Better?"

"Yeah. Is it hot in here, or is it me?"

"Both I would guess. It is June."

Dakota nodded a little, and Desmond thought he would fall right back to sleep. Drained as he seemed, Dakota's eyes stayed on a faraway spot on the wall, and he began to speak.

"Do you know what I thought of when everything started to go black?"

"No. What?"

"Something Slate said to me," Dakota said as he licked his lips. "Of all the things to remember, I recall something he said when I was angry." Dakota's mind went back to a cloudy day in Shotgun. As the result of a senseless shooting, a woman had just been buried. At the funeral Dakota thought they should have talked about the woman and not about God.

"What did you want Pastor Caron to say, Dak?" his brother asked him. "What would you have deemed appropriate?"

"A little more about the woman herself, for starters. He turned it into a sermon!"

"She was a changed person because of her faith."

Dakota's eyes narrowed, telling Slater he was not happy with that answer, but his brother went on anyway.

"If I'm a different person because of my beliefs, Dakota, and if I were to die, I would want other people to know they could have the same hope. Maybe you should be listening instead of criticizing."

"My life is fine!" Dakota did not hesitate to clarify.

"If that's true, then why does this have you so upset? If everything is fine, you should be able to shrug this off and go on with your life."

Dakota's eyes now met Desmond's.

"In so many words, Slater said it shouldn't bother me if I didn't believe as he did—but it didn't work that way. It bothered me so much, I left angry."

"So the turning point came when Slate and Cash were here?"

Much as it hurt, Dakota's chest lifted with his sigh. "My very last thought before I lost consciousness was that I had waited too long. When I woke up and they were sitting here, I knew I'd been given a second chance." Another sigh escaped the injured man. "As you well know, I've been a fool many times, but not this time. I grabbed that second chance."

Desmond had a comment on his mind, but he could see that it was going to have to wait.

"Do you think he can eat something?" Geneva Curtis asked from the doorway.

"No," her husband answered with a shake of his head. "He just slipped back out."

Geneva came and stood close, her hand on Desmond's shoulder.

"He will make it, won't he, Des?"

"I think so," that man replied with his eyes on Dakota's face. "As Dak just put it, he's been given a second chance. I've been wrong before, but something tells me he'll get out of this bed and want to know everything God has ever said—and in the first hour, if I can tell him."

Geneva chuckled softly and exited the room ahead of her husband. Her only thought was *Look out, Texas, Dakota Rawlings is nearly on the loose.*

One

IF YOU SO MUCH AS SHOW YOUR FACE NEAR my office inside of six months, I'll shoot you myself.

Sitting alone by the window, Dakota Rawlings remembered the words of his supervisor from just a month earlier and sat back, a thoughtful frown between his brows. He didn't know if he could stand five more months of inactivity. When Brace had first uttered these words, it had been an emotional time. Dakota had been certain he hadn't meant a literal six months, but his first letter—telling Brace when he thought he could come back—was hotly returned in a no-nonsense way.

Dakota's hosts, Desmond and Geneva Curtis, were out at the moment, so the house in Wellsville was quiet. Their home sat right in the middle of town, but the street was not a busy one, and for a moment, Dakota thought he was very much alone. He'd just eaten a large lunch and still had half a cup of coffee to drink, but he was not particularly eager to continue sitting at the window.

As a new believer in Jesus Christ, he'd spent almost two hours studying the Bible that morning and had understood some new truths. Desmond had been a great help in this area, and Dakota was still amazed at how pertinent the Bible was to his life right now. Not many months back, he

9

would have said that old Book was outdated and unrealistic. He was learning every day just how wrong he'd been.

Knowing he did not want the rest of the coffee, Dakota went to the sink, rinsed out his mug, and wandered onto the front porch. It was blistering hot, much as it was every day at this time. That was Texas in July—something they all had to live with.

He wrote a quick note and took himself out for a walk. It was too hot to be out for long, but he had to stretch his legs. He hadn't planned to feel this good. Only five weeks ago he'd been shot so badly they thought he would die, but God had had other ideas.

"I shot you first," a child's voice yelled from nearby. Dakota turned to see two little boys scoot up the alley, firing sticks at each other. Though he hoped they would never actually experience that pain, he nevertheless found himself smiling at their antics. He continued slowly up the street and turned right onto the main street of town.

Interesting as the storefronts were, Dakota was beginning to sweat. He thought he might have overdone and should turn back, but his sister-in-law had celebrated a birthday a few weeks ago, and he hadn't sent her anything. Not that he'd been in any shape to do that.

"What are you doing out here?" Desmond suddenly spoke as he came up behind Dakota.

Dakota turned with innocent eyes. "Just strolling."

Feeling like a father, Desmond pointed back up the street. "Get home!"

Worried as she was to see Dakota's pale face, Geneva laughed from her place beside her husband.

"You sounded as if you were scolding the dog."

Dakota laughed as well, but he did want to shop for Liberty, who was married to his younger brother, Slater. He said as much to the Curtises.

"As if Libby will be expecting anything with the way you were hurt," Geneva said with a mild shake of her head.

"Even a firecracker would do the trick, Gen. She was born on the Fourth."

"And she'll enjoy a late gift," Desmond said, his hand to the younger man's arm as he turned and directed him back up the boardwalk.

Dakota wanted to argue, but he was suddenly feeling very warm and weak. By the time he reached the house, he was sweating profusely, and two of the bullet wounds were starting to burn. Geneva brought him a cool drink of water and waited for him to lie down on the sofa.

"It looks as though you need to give it more time, Dak. I'm sorry."

Dakota sighed. "I guess I could write to Libby."

"She would probably enjoy that, but even as little as I know her, I can't think she would expect anything from you at this point."

Dakota nodded and thanked his hostess, who returned to the kitchen, and then let his mind drift backward to when Geneva had met Liberty Drake, now Liberty Rawlings.

The wedding had been on Saturday, April 22. The whole family had gathered, including his parents, who had come all the way from St. Louis. Special friends like Desmond and Geneva Curtis and Marty Bracewell had also been invited. Closing his eyes, Dakota could still see how pretty Liberty looked in her dress, her eyes shining with love for Slater as her stepfather, Duffy Peterson, walked her down the aisle.

He and Cash, Dakota's older brother, had both known that Slater would be the first to fall. They were only thankful that he'd found a girl like Liberty. Dakota thought that if another Liberty could be found, he too might be tempted to marry. Almost as soon as the thought materialized, he pushed it away. His was not a job that was suited to family life. Hours on the trail, uncertain pay, and the dangers of being a Texas Ranger played hard in his mind. Desmond had made it work, but a career in the Rangers had its drawbacks. The fact that the Curtises had never been able to have children had been a factor.

Suddenly Dakota wanted to get up. He felt lazy, as though his not trying hard enough was slowing the healing process. But wanting to get up and actually doing it were proving to be two different matters.

Just help me, Lord, Dakota prayed. *Just help me to rest and give it some more time—even a few weeks.* Dakota fell asleep while still wondering what he would do with himself in the months to come.

$$\text{❧ ❧ ❧}$$

August

Dakota could not believe the difference just four weeks had made. He was feeling very strong. His last little escapade had set him back, but as he left the church with Desmond and Geneva for the second week in a row, that incident was already receding from his thoughts. His mind was on the sermon for some of the ride back to the house, but Dakota waited only until they sat down to eat Sunday dinner to tell his hosts what was really in his thoughts.

"I need to thank both of you for your care and hospitality, but I have some good news for you."

Desmond looked up from cutting his meat.

"A statement like that could mean only one of two things," the older Ranger began. "Either you're pulling out soon, or one of the women who were falling over themselves to catch your eye this morning did in fact catch your eye, and you're getting married."

Dakota had a good laugh before saying, "The first one is correct."

"Where are you headed?" Geneva wished to know.

"Back to work," Dakota replied calmly while buttering a piece of bread with complete ease.

"I thought you said Brace didn't want you for the full six months."

"That's right.

"But you're going anyway?"

"Yep."

"And what of Brace?" Desmond asked.

Dakota smiled his slow, warm way. "He'll get over it."

Knowing how much Marty Bracewell liked to have his own way, Geneva enjoyed a good laugh over this.

The next morning, however, her laughter was not to be found. Tears welled in her eyes as she hugged their guest. Dakota had come to Christ under their roof and grown so much in the few months they'd had with him. She could have easily had him stay on.

"Thanks, Gen. Thanks, Des."

"You know the door is always open" were Desmond's parting words to the young Ranger.

Husband and wife stood together as he rode away, Geneva with a hankie to her face and Desmond watching for signs of hurt or discomfort. Not that he actually expected to see any—Dakota was as tough as they came—but he was concerned too, and missing him already.

"Will he be all right?" Geneva asked, her eyes still on the dark figure as he rounded a corner and moved from sight.

Desmond slipped an arm around her.

"Don't forget who indwells him now, Gen. He'll be more all right than he's ever been before."

🎗🎗🎗

Austin, Texas

Marty Bracewell entered his office as he did most mornings, sat at his desk, and began to open the mail; it was always a large stack. As a Ranger, Marty had traveled extensively for many years, but now he kept the home office fires burning. He kept track of new men, deaths, countless details, and payroll for the area. It wasn't that he never went out on patrol, but most weeks he was needed at the office.

"What in the world?" Brace was muttering over some confusing correspondence when the door opened and someone stepped inside. He looked up to see a familiar face and smiled in delight.

"You must be feeling better," he said as he stood and came around the desk.

Darvi Leigh Wingate warmly accepted her uncle's embrace and smiled into his eyes when he stepped back.

Darvi was a smallish strawberry blonde who appeared more frail than she actually was. However, this time she had been very ill. She had come by train and stagecoach all the way from St. Louis, and had picked up an illness en route. For the first few days of her visit she had been laid up in bed, miserably achy and sick to her stomach.

"I do feel better," she admitted with conviction, taking a chair when the Ranger returned to his desk. "For a few days there I was dreadfully sorry I had come, but now I'm raring to go."

"Where are you headed first?"

"To the bank and then to see Merry. Did you need anything? I'd be glad to pick it up." Darvi had asked the question, but Brace didn't answer. He sat staring at his niece for several seconds, his face uncertain.

"What is it, Uncle Marty?"

"She's married now, Darv. Didn't you know that?"

"Merry? Of course I knew. She was engaged when I last saw her."

"She's also moved away. She and the doc moved about six months after the wedding."

Now it was Darvi's turn to stare.

"She doesn't live in Austin?"

He slowly shook his head. "Up in the hills. A small town outside of Blake called Stillwater."

Darvi continued to stare, her mouth slightly agape. This couldn't be true. She'd been dying to see her friend for close to three months and only now was able to make time to come to Austin. How could this have happened?

"I can't believe it," she muttered softly.

"It's been four years since you've visited, Darv. A lot can change in that time."

Her shoulders drooped a little.

"Yes, they can, and we never tried to stay in touch outside of my visits. There was never a need. We were always able to pick up right where we left off."

"I'm sorry, Darv. I wish you had known."

It took Darvi only a moment to see the sadness in his eyes. In the next instant her chin tipped up. "I'll just go to her," she said, standing up as though leaving on the spot.

Brace was already shaking his head. "I don't have time to take you, and you—"

"You don't have to," Darvi cut him off. "I can get there; you know I can."

"Don't even think about it," Brace said in a voice he'd have used with his men. "I won't even discuss it."

"Uncle Marty, when are you going to realize I'm not 16 anymore?" She threw her arms up and flopped back down on the wooden seat. "For that matter," she muttered, "when are you going to face the fact that I'm not 20 anymore?"

But Brace was still shaking his head no.

"You know I can make it!" she tried again.

"I'm not willing to let you try."

"Why can't you take me? I'll just make it a quick visit. We can't be talking about more than two days on the trail, if that."

"I don't have time. I wish I did, Darvi, but my boss is coming into town, and I can't be gone when he arrives."

"When is he coming?"

"Sometime next week."

"And that's all the more specific he could be? Men!"

Brace leaned back in his chair, a big smile on his face.

"What is that grin about?"

"Oh, nothing much. Only about a niece who said she was coming back every summer and hasn't been here in four years." Brace nodded sagely. "Yes, indeed, women are much better about saying when they'll arrive and then coming on time."

Darvi stood, working hard to hide her smile.

"I believe I'll be going on my way now, since all you can do is insult me."

"Are you going to be around at lunch?" Brace asked, knowing she was not really angry.

"That all depends."

"On what?"

"On whether I've found someone to take me to Merry's or not."

The smile she gave him could have melted butter in the snow, but he knew the steel in that little backbone of hers—just like her mother's. He didn't let himself laugh, however, until she exited and shut the door in her wake.

❧ ❧ ❧

Dakota hit Austin hot, dirty, and sore. There was no doubt in his mind that his first stop would be Brace's office, but from there he was headed for a bath. The dark cowboy rode easily up the familiar street only an hour past noon, stopped in front of the office, and didn't so much as wince when he climbed painfully from the saddle.

Brace's back was to him when he entered the sparse room, but that didn't change Dakota's routine. He pushed his hat back on his head, turned the chair around as he always did, and straddled it. This done, he waited for Brace to turn and acknowledge him.

Brace knew someone had come in behind him, but he'd lost a file that morning and was determined to find it. He wasn't usually so rude to folks who entered and decided he had best say something.

"I'll be with you in a moment," he called over his shoulder.

"Don't hurry on my account."

The sound of that voice caused the older man to stop. He turned slowly from the file cabinet and speared Dakota with his angry gaze. The seated Ranger looked back with a calm that was genuine.

"*What* are you doing here?"

"Coming back to work."

"I told you I didn't want to see you for six months."

"I don't need six months."

"I say you do."

The old Dakota would have stood and gone back to work without a word of apology. The new Dakota debated his next move. He wasn't certain of too many things right now, but lying low for another four months was not something he needed. He tried a new tack.

"So what you're telling me is that you have so many Rangers that you can let men sit around for months at a time."

Brace came to the desk and sat across from Dakota, his eyes thoughtful as they watched him.

"If you still feel good in another month, I'll put you back on."

"And what am I supposed to do for another month?"

"As a matter of fact, I have a personal favor to ask you. It won't take a month, but it should put you closer to home where you can go and lie low until the end of September."

Dakota was not the least bit interested in lying low, but he figured once he'd done the personal favor, he could talk Brace around.

"What's the favor?" he asked, knowing it didn't matter; he would do whatever Brace needed.

"Can you escort my niece to Stillwater?"

"Darvi?" Dakota guessed, knowing she used to visit every summer. He'd even met her one year.

"Yes. A friend of hers moved, and she wants to see her."

"Certainly. When does she want to leave?"

"Probably next week, but I'll ask her."

Dakota nodded.

"And until then," Brace said unyieldingly, "you can just enjoy the sights of Austin. If I see you working, I'll shoot you myself."

Dakota knew he had no choice, but he didn't like it. Fighting the urge to say more, he stood.

"I'm headed to get a bath."

"All right. Why don't you come to dinner some night? You name the day."

Dakota nodded. "I'll get back to you."

Brace watched him leave, looking for signs of injury. He wouldn't have admitted it for the world, but it looked to him as though Dakota was right: He was ready to come back to work.

☙-☙-☙

Darvi's attempt to find an escort to Stillwater was proving fruitless. For a time she had traversed the streets of Austin, hoping to find an advertisement or anything that might indicate a guide service, but she knew such possibilities were remote.

From her place in Austin's reading room, Darvi looked out the window and told herself this was not going to work. *But I don't know what else to do*, she then answered herself. *I can't exactly walk the streets looking for a man to hire—Uncle Marty would have a fit. But I'm feeling just about that desperate.*

Just about ready to give up and open a book that had caught her eye when she came in, she spotted him. Darvi was willing to bet her grandmother's inheritance that he was a Ranger. She'd certainly spent enough time around her uncle to spot the type. Not even remembering to replace the book to the shelf, Darvi came to her feet as gracefully as speed would allow and made a beeline for the door.

ꢴ-ꢴ-ꢴ

Dakota knew he was being followed, but he wasn't overly concerned. After all, the streets were fairly crowded and the bathhouse was on a main street. Still, there was no doubt that he heard footsteps that matched his own. And unless he missed his guess, it was the light tread of a woman. He let it go a few seconds longer before stopping and slowly turning around. Sure enough, about ten yards behind him, a woman stopped as well.

"Did you need something?" he asked politely, removing his hat.

"No," she answered softly, but everything in her voice and manner said the opposite.

"Are you all right?"

This time she only nodded and looked away, clearly embarrassed.

Dakota studied her for a moment, replaced his hat, and turned back on his way. He nearly shook his head when she continued behind him.

Thinking she was simply going his way, and not wanting to make her feel awkward, he left it alone. Not until he was ready to walk up the steps of the bathhouse did he let himself look again. What he saw stopped him. The woman—quite pretty he could see from this distance—was even closer and staring right at him.

"Are you certain you're all right?"

"You are a Texas Ranger, aren't you?" the woman suddenly blurted.

"Yes, ma'am. Is there something I can do?"

Dakota watched her composure slip a little more before she visibly gathered her courage and went on.

"Do your duties happen to take you into the hills very often?"

"The hills, ma'am?" Dakota asked, completely at sea.

"Yes. I have a need to go to Stillwater, and I'm looking for someone to escort me."

Dakota had all he could do not to react, asking himself if this could actually be Darvi. Gone was the child he'd met years ago, and Dakota was left wondering how long it had been.

"You see," she tried again, this time catching herself and now standing like a woman in command, "it's rather important that I go to Stillwater. I'm terribly sorry to accost you on the street in this way, but I thought if you were to be traveling in those parts, I could accompany you and give my family ease about my travel."

Dakota was on the verge of telling her exactly who he was and that he had already been asked to see her there when gunshots were fired down the street.

"Will you excuse me a moment?" he said to the woman without hesitation as he turned and ran that way.

Gun pulled and ready, Dakota hurried toward the sound, which took him between two buildings and onto a side street. He heard shouting as he moved and sure enough, as soon as he spotted the commotion, which appeared to be a woman with a shotgun, he also spotted two officers. Even though the woman still had the gun, the men seemed to have the situation under control. Glad not to be pressed into duty just then, Dakota holstered his weapon and walked back toward the bathhouse.

Long before Dakota reached his destination, he could see that the street was empty. He debated getting back to Brace right then so that he could get word to his niece, but a spark of mischief lit inside him. He would certainly have to let Brace know that he *would* be coming for dinner. The sooner the better.

Two

DAKOTA THOUGHT HE MIGHT BE MORE comfortable at the boardinghouse, but if he wasn't going to be working for another month, he would have to be a little careful with his money for a time. That determined, he rolled out his bedding and prepared to sleep under the stars for the fifth night in a row. He could have made it to Austin in less time, but he'd taken it slow. As he now shifted around for a position that would not aggravate his wounds, he knew why.

I may not be as ready for this as I thought, he told the Lord. *I was pretty upset that Brace didn't want me back right now, but I think You must have had a hand in that.*

For a moment Dakota lay very still and wondered at this miracle that had happened in his heart. He knew God could have closed the book on him so easily; his wounds still ached in reminder, but here he was, alive and able to do things differently.

How many people get a second chance? I don't know why You think me worth it, but I'm grateful, God—more grateful than I can say.

Hot days on the trail were catching up to him. Dakota fell asleep still praying for his parents' salvation and then for Desmond and Geneva, asking God to help him remember all the things they had shared with him.

❧-❧-❧

"I have a surprise for you," Brace told Darvi on Saturday as they sat down to lunch.

"What is it?" Darvi asked, trying to show interest when all she could do was think about her friend. She could write, she realized, but it wouldn't be the same.

"I can't tell you. It's a surprise."

Darvi didn't like surprises, and she suspected her uncle knew this.

"Just give me a hint."

"All right. Let's just say that someone is coming for dinner tonight."

Suddenly things made sense. Milly, the woman who kept house for her uncle a few days a week and started his meals, had put a large roast in to bake that morning. With Darvi in the house, she had been leaving a little earlier in the day, giving the young woman leave to change anything she wanted on the menu. But today she had told Darvi exactly how she wanted the meat finished and what she'd wanted to go with it.

"Someone as in a family? Or someone as in one person?"

"I think I've told you enough."

"A man or a woman?"

Brace went on eating.

"What if I have plans for the night?" Darvi now tried. "What would you say to that?"

"I'd say I'm surprised. I thought you were here to visit me."

Her sharp tongue getting her into trouble in the usual way, Darvi didn't reply.

"I think that might be why I'm confused about your being in such a hurry to rush off to see Merry. You only just got here."

"I'm sorry, Uncle Marty," Darvi whispered in true repentance, her heart seeing how insensitive she had been.

"Oh, Darv," he laughed, "I'm just teasing you. You know I would wish for you to go. I'd take you myself if it were possible."

Darvi smiled at the warmth in his tone, but her head was having a little talk with her heart.

You're going to have to drop it, Darvi. He's right about this. You came to see him. Now accept that and enjoy your visit here.

Not one to feel sorry for herself, Darvi forced herself to accept the situation. She would write to Merry in the morning and be done with this plan.

❧-❧-❧

"You look like a pincushion," the doctor said mildly as he examined Dakota's torso. "Oh, yes, I see what you mean. This one is rather red and nasty."

Dakota took a breath as the man probed around his side but didn't cry out as he was tempted. He'd woken that morning feeling warm and uncomfortable and knew it was more than the weather. He'd tried to ignore it for most of the day, but the pain had grown worse. With just two hours before he had to be at Brace's for dinner, he stopped in to see the doctor.

"I've got some powder I want you to put on this, and sleep on your other side for a while."

Dakota nodded, not bothering to mention that he'd been shot in the upper arm on the other side. It wasn't any wonder that sleeping without a mattress was fitful these nights.

"If you don't see vast improvement by Monday, get back in here."

"All right. What do I owe you?"

The doctor named a price so low that Dakota looked at him.

"My nephew's a Ranger," the man said with a sigh. "You're a breed apart—there's no denying that."

Dakota smiled a little and thanked the man. Once outside, he could tell evening was on its way; the temperature had dropped a little. A cool evening and a home-cooked meal—Dakota could hardly wait.

ༀ·ༀ·ༀ

"Are you about ready to come out?" Brace had found Darvi in the kitchen and asked her for the second time.

"Almost," she said, knowing she wasn't going to have any other excuses.

"I thought you'd be more excited," he teased.

Darvi looked him in the eye, her hands going to her waist.

"I'm expected to be excited about someone I've never met?"

"I didn't say you'd never met him, but it's been a long time, and I would especially want you to be excited when I've asked him to take you to Stillwater."

Darvi stared at his mischievous eyes. "Do you mean it?" she asked, afraid to hope.

"Indeed, I do. Now come on. He's in the living room."

Darvi was suddenly all aflutter. Hair she didn't care about before was checked with careful attention, and she wiped perfectly clean hands two more times. Brace watched and waited patiently for her to join him.

"Now?" he teased again.

"Yes."

Brace let her precede him but was talking as they approached.

"Here she is, Dak. You can ask her yourself what day she wants to leave."

Darvi, whose heart had been pounding with excitement, felt the pit of her stomach plummet as they entered the small living room and the cowboy from the street the day before rose to meet her. Darvi's face flamed with mortification even as he came toward her, a kind smile on his face.

"It's nice to see you again, Darvi. You've done some growing up."

"Yes," she barely managed and then realized she did not want to explain this strange reaction to her uncle.

"You've changed a bit too," she said honestly, trying to act naturally. "I wouldn't have known you."

Dakota smiled then, a full-blown work, but Darvi was still a little too tense to join him.

"So, what day do you want to go?" he asked after reading the hesitancy in her eyes.

"What day is good for you?"

Dakota's hands came out. "My schedule is very open."

"May I think about it then, and let you know?"

"That's fine."

"Let's eat then," Brace declared, feeling he'd successfully pulled off his surprise, not to mention the fact that he was famished.

Dakota was hungry as well. He remembered his manners, but Geneva's cooking seemed much longer ago than a week. Darvi, he noticed, was not very hungry. Dakota wished he could ask her if he was causing the discomfort, but it looked as though they were going to have several days of travel where he might do that.

Partway through the meal, Brace began to tell Dakota about some cases and episodes from the last several months. Some Dakota knew of; others were new to him.

"I've got a photograph I need to show you. I think it's up in my room. I'll run up and get it, and you can tell me if you've seen this man before."

When Brace left, the dining room suddenly became very quiet. Dakota was almost through eating, and Darvi had given up pretending to eat. Dakota studied her from his seat, thinking that she had been something of a hoyden when he'd met her originally and that she had certainly grown into a refined young woman. She was poised and graceful; the only things out of place were the short curls that refused to be caught back in the elegant chignon she wore.

And that mouth! Dakota had never seen the like. Her upper lip protruded past a small shapely lower lip, giving her one of the most unusual looks he'd ever seen. In the strictest sense, she wasn't a beauty, but the soft curls around her face and those large brown eyes above her small, turned-up nose were all very eye-catching. And because she was looking everywhere but at her guest, Dakota went ahead and watched her. The moment she brought her eyes to his, however, he spoke.

"So tell me, Darvi, does your uncle know you were asking perfect strangers to escort you around the state?"

"I could tell you were a Ranger," she defended herself.

"Not all Rangers are trustworthy, and you know it."

Darvi was silent at this, her eyes moving back to her plate.

"So I take it Brace knows?"

Darvi was suddenly interested in the things on the table, straightening them just so and smoothing the already-perfect cloth.

"I didn't exactly mention it to him," she admitted. She glanced over to find those dark eyes leveled on her and asked herself if he'd always had such a powerful presence. "Are you going to tell him?"

"It's not my place, but I think you know how dangerous that could have been."

Darvi was only just able to nod before Brace came back to the table and the conversation turned to the man in the photo.

Darvi began clearing the table for dessert, thinking Dakota was right: It had been dangerous. But there was more to it, something neither man would understand. She *had* to see Merry.

❦ ❦ ❦

Desmond had not had an extra Bible to give him. Dakota had read from Geneva's when he had studied with Desmond, but when he left Wellsville there was no Bible in his gear. He'd had time the day before to look for one, but because he had woken with pain and some fever, it had completely slipped his mind.

Now Dakota sat in church wishing he had a Bible he could refer to. It wasn't that he doubted what the man was saying, but he thought if he could read it for himself, he would remember it better. Off and on each day he went over the things Desmond had told him, still somewhat amazed over how much made sense to him.

"Let me read verse 13 to you," the pastor was saying, referring to the fifth chapter of Galatians. "'For, brethren, you have been called into liberty; only use not liberty for an occasion to the flesh, but by love serve one another.'

"It sounds to me," the man went on, "as though the Galatian church had become sloppy and willful. Remember how earlier in the chapter Paul had given them the good news that salvation was by grace alone, through Christ alone? Well, it almost looks as if they were taking this freedom, 'liberty' as the verse calls it, and treating it like an old shoe. It seems as though they no longer treated this freedom with the respect and hard work it deserves.

"Do you see how he commands them to love each other? I think selfishness has reared its ugly head. Paul is calling these believers to love each other because they were doing anything but. Verse 15 uses words like 'bite,' 'devour,' and 'consume.' Not exactly what we picture in a church family where love leads the way."

Dakota had leaned forward in his seat. He knew from his brothers that coming to Christ did not make everything perfect, but seeing that one of the churches from the Bible—one that had to be very new—had experienced these types of problems took a little getting used to.

"So what does Paul tell them to do instead?" the pastor asked. "Look to verse 14. Love your neighbor as yourself.

Have you ever known someone who hated himself? We don't usually meet people like that. I can tell you that I don't do things to hurt my own body. If I so much as stub my toe, I sit down and rub it until it feels better.

"So, I have to ask myself, 'Jake, do you love your neighbors like you do yourself? Do you care for them in the careful way you look after yourself? Or are you devouring and biting?'"

This was heavy stuff for a man whose salvation was so new and who had no one with whom he could discuss what he was hearing. Dakota had seen many ugly things in his life, but he wasn't sure he could picture people in Desmond's or his brother's church acting this way. He didn't think the Bible would cover such a thing for no reason, but he was going to have to do some thinking before he made up his mind.

Getting yourself a Bible would certainly help, Rawlings.

"Let's stand for our final two hymns."

Dakota had not seen that coming. Where had the time gone? The Ranger hadn't known any of the songs at the beginning of the service or the ones they closed with, but he did his best. He didn't even take notice of his surroundings until people began to move from their seats. He was still taking in the simple wooden pews and small pulpit when from the periphery he caught someone approaching. Dakota turned to see the doctor from the day before.

"How are the wounds?" that man held his hand out and asked.

"Better, I think," Dakota answered with a return shake. "I used the powder last night and again this morning."

The older man nodded. "That's just what every doctor wants to hear—that people are taking their medicine."

Dakota smiled a little but didn't say anything else.

"Do you have someplace to eat lunch today?"

"As in the form of an invitation? No."

"Well, consider yourself invited. I'm Marcus Scott, by the way."

"Dakota Rawlings, and thank you."

"Let me give you directions to the house."

Dakota listened to the simple explanation, but before the doctor could finish, he was joined by Mrs. Scott and their two grown sons. Dakota ended up meeting them and simply following the Scotts' wagon home.

"Are you just passing through Austin, Mr. Rawlings?" Mrs. Scott asked after her husband prayed and the dishes were passed.

"In a way, ma'am, I am. I just came into town to tell my boss I'm ready to go back to work."

"And where will you go from here?"

"Just on a short jaunt into the hills, not actually working at all."

"I was going to ask," the doctor cut in, "does your boss know you're not back to strength?"

"No, but he didn't want me going back to work anyway."

"Where do you live?" one of the sons now asked, and the meal progressed in companionable conversation, doctor and Ranger taking measure of each other. Finally, near the end of the meal, Dakota found the courage to ask some questions.

"Have you gone to the church very long?"

"Years and years. Have you ever visited before?"

"No, I haven't," Dakota answered and then plunged in with what was on his mind. "Do you happen to know whether the pastor is open to questions? I have a few."

"Indeed, he is," Marcus answered as he stirred the coffee his wife had just brought to him. She returned to the kitchen to finish cutting pieces of cake. "Is there anything I can help you with?"

Dakota frowned down at his plate for a moment before admitting, "Were those verses this morning saying that the church was having problems?"

The doctor nodded. "Earlier in the chapter, Paul warns the people about the seriousness of adding anything to the gospel. Do you know what I mean by 'gospel'?"

"Salvation?"

"Yes. Their big issue was circumcision."

Dakota's brows rose on this, but he stayed quiet.

"Some people were still insisting that the men be circumcised, though Paul made it very clear that salvation comes by faith alone through Christ alone. Pastor mentioned the freedom this gave them, but they started to treat that freedom carelessly and were falling into sin toward each other."

"But the church was new! How could there be that many problems so quickly?"

Marcus smiled. "I don't know too many people who don't have problems or past experiences that affect the way they think and act. These people were no different. They had been used to blood sacrifices and circumcision. Now Christ had come along and taken all that away. And that was wonderful for these folks, but old habits—especially ones that make us feel comfortable—can die hard."

"So what type of sins are we talking about? I mean, how were they treating each other?"

"The verses that are coming up have a pretty serious list. Paul calls them the works of the flesh, and they include adultery, fornication, hatred, and much more. Maybe this was what they were saved out of, and with the way they were acting, he feared they would go back to this life. At the end of that chapter, he goes on to tell them how important it is to walk in the Spirit and gives another list, this one full of righteous acts for them to practice."

"But these people *had* heard the gospel and been saved?"

"I believe so, yes, and I don't wish to make excuses for them, but keep in mind that salvation does not take all those old temptations and actions away. We still tend to think of ourselves first and want our way much too often."

Dakota couldn't argue with that. Until recently, his own life and wants were his main concern. He cared about his family and his job, but he could now see how self-centered he'd been. At the same time, he had to admit that he was changing. The doctor was willing to talk for hours, and Dakota's questions were not about his own life, but that of Jesus Christ.

ॐ-ॐ-ॐ

Thinking about how good it had been to talk to Dr. Scott, Dakota left their home and headed straight to Brace's small abode. Not until Mrs. Scott had asked if they would see him next week did Dakota realize he had no idea what his plans were. It was time to see Darvi. Because he wasn't staying at the boardinghouse, he realized Darvi had no way to tell him when she wanted to leave for Stillwater. For all he knew, they'd be pulling out of town first thing in the morning.

Dakota arrived at the house about three o'clock, knocked softly on the door, and waited. Dressed in an elegant day dress the color of dark plums, made more elegant by its unadorned lines, Darvi answered.

"Oh, Dakota!" she said in soft surprise. "I wondered when I would see you again."

Dakota stepped inside as she held the door and then understood why she whispered: Brace was sound asleep in the rocking chair.

Hat in hand, Dakota smiled a little before turning back to Darvi.

"What day did you want to leave?"

"Will Tuesday work for you?"

"That's fine. I'll check the stage schedule and get back—"

"I don't want to go by stage," Darvi cut in.

Dakota blinked.

"I thought we'd be going on horseback. I want to go on horseback," she clarified.

Dakota couldn't help the way his eyes moved over her elegant dress. "The stage will be much more comfortable."

"And also more unreliable."

Dakota nodded slowly, thinking that it was her choice but also asking himself what he'd gotten into with this favor.

"I'll check into renting a mount for you."

"Uncle Marty has two horses now. He said I can take one of his."

So Brace knows about this.

Outwardly Dakota nodded calmly, but his mind was already doing mental calisthenics as he went over the route to Blake and then on to Stillwater. The terrain wasn't bad, but it wasn't always the safest. On his own he wouldn't have given it a thought. Taking Darvi put it in a whole new light.

"What if we took the stage to Blake and then rented horses for Stillwater?"

Without so much as a moment's hesitation, Darvi shook her head no. She didn't look stubborn, just certain. Dakota decided to let it drop.

"Okay. How early do you want to leave?"

"I was thinking five."

Again Dakota was surprised but only nodded. Maybe it was for the best. He was coming to see that Darvi Wingate was one classy, sophisticated woman. More than likely they would have to take it slowly. Leaving early would help get them there in a more reasonable time frame.

"I'll see you Tuesday," Dakota supplied.

"Thank you, Dakota," she said, her face no longer businesslike but wreathed in soft, delighted lines.

Dakota couldn't help but respond. He smiled back, replaced his hat, and turned toward the door. He didn't know what the next week would bring, but he was fairly certain it wouldn't be dull.

Three

LIKE A CHILD AT CHRISTMAS, DAKOTA SAT DOWN under the large shade tree, leaned against it for comfort, and opened the package he had just bought from the general store. It had taken some searching, but he finally had it.

Moving as though touching the pages might damage them, Dakota opened a book that boasted the gold-tone title *Holy Bible* on the cover. He didn't read at first but just paged through, recognizing books that he'd discussed with Desmond and realizing he knew just where he wanted to read. He searched for a full five minutes for the book of Galatians before turning to the index in the front. After finally finding it, he settled in to study. So much was unclear to him, but he kept at it until the fifth chapter, where things fell a little more into place.

It was good to recognize things that both the pastor and Dr. Scott had referred to. Dakota read the chapter twice and sat mulling over several problematic issues. Of all the things that suddenly became clear to him, one was the thought he'd had while sitting in church the day before: The Bible didn't talk about things for no reason.

"If Paul talks about this, it must have been a problem." Dakota heard his own voice and stopped. "How did they know the writing was from Paul?"

With that Dakota was off again. He spent the next several hours reading and rereading, trying to get a grasp of the text and suddenly realizing it must have been a letter.

Shaking his head at times in complete confusion, Dakota came away with one certainty: There was a way that God wanted men to act, and it was laid out in this book. It didn't all make sense, but Dakota vowed in his heart to learn that way and do his best to follow it.

❧ ❧ ❧

"Do you want any more coffee?" Darvi asked Brace that night.

"No, thank you."

"All right. I'll go ahead and wash the pot."

Taking her uncle's coffee mug, Darvi made swift work of the kitchen detail. When she came back into the living room, she took a comfortable chair and put her feet up.

"I enjoyed coming, Uncle Marty. Thank you."

He waved at her as if she'd imagined his care of her.

"You'll have a good time with Merry," he said, ignoring her thanks. "But you've got an early morning coming up, so you'd best head up to bed."

"All right."

Darvi stood and went to his chair. She was going to lean down to kiss his cheek but suddenly stopped.

"I'm leaving after such a short time, Uncle Marty. I feel a little bad about that."

There was no ducking the issue this time. Her uncle looked her in the eye and spoke seriously.

"You're doing better, and that's all I care about, Darvi girl. And if things get rough again when you go home after your visit to Merry's, you just come right back here."

With a whispered word of thanks, Darvi did bend and kiss him. No other words were shared as Darvi left the room, mounted the stairs, and readied for bed. Tired as Darvi was, she lay awake until her uncle came up those same stairs, the sound of his steps a comfort to her. Praying for him as she felt herself relax, she drifted off to sleep some time after she heard his boots drop to the floor.

ॐ-ॐ-ॐ

Dakota was glad that Darvi wanted to leave early and take it slow. He was still rather tender in spots and had even bled some in the night, and although he no longer wanted to sit around Austin, it was nice to know he was going to have an easy day.

All this he had decided before he saw Darvi. She and Brace were in the front yard when he arrived, and Dakota thought he'd never seen anyone so loaded for bear. Gone was the frilly dress and elegant hairstyle. In the morning light he could see that she was dressed for the trail. Darvi wore a brown dress he could only term "serviceable" and had her hair and neck covered by an all-consuming hat and handkerchief. It was such a contrast to the day before that Dakota had all he could do not to stare.

"Here's some money," Brace said the moment Dakota dismounted.

"I'm doing all right," Dakota replied, not taking the bills that were being held out to him.

Brace stuffed them in Dakota's vest pocket.

"Be that as it may," he said rather softly, "you never know what's going to happen with Darvi, and I didn't mean for you to do this without some compensation."

Dakota opened his mouth to start to protest, but Brace cut him off. "I mean it!"

Dakota watched him turn back to his niece. The two hugged.

"Have you got everything?" Brace asked.

"Yes. I'm sure I do."

"All right. Have a good time. Tell Merry I said hello; Calder too."

"I'll do it."

"And when you get home, tell your mother she hasn't written in weeks."

Darvi's brow lowered. "You said you just got a letter."

"I know, but your mother always expects me to complain about something, and I don't want to let her down."

Darvi gave him another hug and turned to the horse called Finley. With a boost she didn't need, Brace had her in the saddle in the blink of an eye. Dakota waited to shake Brace's hand and thank him before gaining his own saddle, and a moment later he and Darvi were on their way. Dakota glanced back just before they were out of sight to find Brace reaching for his handkerchief, causing something to trigger in his own heart. It was a good reminder that Darvi was precious cargo.

"Hey, Darvi," Dakota called to her as they turned their horses toward the west side of town. "How soon would you like to get there?"

"Soon," she admitted. "I guess I'm not much for dawdling."

"Well, be sure and let me know if we're going too fast."

Darvi glanced at him. "Why don't I set the pace? Will that work?"

"Go to it," Dakota said with easy confidence. He knew Eli was up to anything, and he had strong doubts that Darvi could wear him out. With this thought in mind, Dakota simply heeled his mount to keep pace with Darvi the moment they hit the edge of town.

❧ ❧ ❧

Calling it pride never occurred to Dakota. It was a perfect description, but the word never crossed his mind, nor did it occur to him to tell Darvi they had to slow down.

More than 12 hours after he and Darvi left Austin, they arrived in Blake, a town not far from Stillwater. Dakota was in so much pain that he didn't think he could even speak. All five of his bullet wounds were burning, and he knew the one on his waist had to be bleeding.

"I think the hotel would be good, don't you?" Darvi spoke like a woman in charge, and at the moment she was.

"Fine," Dakota managed, glad that the horses' hooves drowned out the strain in his voice.

At a later time, Dakota would think back on the way God moved to rescue him on this evening, but right now he just knew relief at how solicitous the hotel proprietress was, how swift she was to volunteer her son to take their horses to the livery, and how Darvi told Dakota she was going to eat in her room and turn in early. He fell into bed the moment he shut the door and dropped into unconsciousness for the next ten hours.

೪-೪-೪-

Not feeling what anyone would term "brand new," Dakota was nevertheless at the breakfast table in a timely manner and not looking as pale as he felt. Darvi joined him just ten minutes after he sat down, and Dakota found himself feeling somewhat thankful that she had not seen him nearly swallowing his food whole. He was calmly sipping coffee when she arrived.

"I'll just have a quick bite," she explained and smiled at the waitress when she glanced their way.

"Don't hurry on my account," Dakota said, meaning it with all his heart. He'd used the powder again and tried to patch the wounds, but the job was middling at best.

"I think we're only a half-day's ride now."

Dakota nodded before asking, "How do you know this friend, by the way?"

"She used to live in Austin. We played together every summer I visited." Darvi paused. "I certainly hope she's home."

"She's not expecting you?"

"No. We never kept in touch through the mail, and I didn't even know she'd moved until I arrived in Austin."

They fell silent for a moment, and then Darvi looked at her companion.

"Did you hear any screams out your window last night?"

Dakota could have told her he didn't even remember lying down but only said no.

"I did," Darvi said. "It sounded like a woman was receiving some unwanted attention. I nearly went out to check."

This statement stopped Dakota's coffee cup on the way to his mouth.

"Tell me, Darvi," Dakota said, putting the cup down, his voice mildly curious. "What would you have done?"

"If I'd gone out?"

"Yes, and if the unwanted attentions had been turned on you?"

"With or without my gun?" she asked in all sincerity.

Dakota couldn't stop the smile that turned up one corner of his mouth, but he still managed, "With your gun."

"I'd have shot him in the foot."

Again Dakota wanted to smile but refrained.

"And without your gun?"

"I'd have tried to reason with him, and if that hadn't worked, I'd have screamed myself hoarse and tried to fight."

"It's good to have a plan," Dakota said softly, all the time trying to process whether this woman was safe on her own or not.

You never know what's going to happen with Darvi.

Brace's words from the morning before came floating back to him. Dakota would have enjoyed some time to think on them, but Darvi was pushing her plate away. Within 15 minutes, they were back on the trail.

❧·❧·❧

Stillwater was a surprise. A clean, friendly-looking town that sat in the foothills, it was a good deal cooler than

Austin. Since Darvi had not known of her friend's move, Dakota assumed she also did not know where this friend lived, but he kept his mouth shut and let her lead the way. She took them straight to the general store.

"I'll just be a minute," she said before dismounting and going inside.

Watching her confident stride, Dakota realized that Darvi must have wanted to make this journey on her own. He knew Brace well enough to know that man would not have even discussed it, but Darvi was clearly no stranger to being in charge. Nor did she appear timid in new surroundings.

In the middle of these thoughts, Darvi reappeared. She climbed back into the saddle and turned to him, her eyes alight with excitement.

"We're almost there."

Dakota smiled at her glowing face and said, "Lead on."

The directions Darvi received took them toward the edge of town. She hadn't been in as much of a hurry today, but now she stepped up the pace. Dakota had been on the edge of discomfort all during the day's ride but thought his body might now be nearing the end of its tolerance. His side was starting to burn, and he could only be thankful they were almost there.

"That's the house," Darvi suddenly said, their horses taking a road along the creek.

Dakota feared that she would heel her horse into a run and knew he couldn't take that. Besides, he wanted to give her some privacy.

"Darvi," he said just in time.

She turned to him in some impatience.

"I think I'll sit here by the creek while you go on up to the house."

For the first time Darvi took in his face. It was warm out, but she hadn't really noticed. She didn't think such a thing would bother him, but he looked a little strained.

"Are you certain, Dakota? You're welcome to join me."

"I would think a private reunion preferable, and beyond that, I want to stay here."

She couldn't argue much with that, so with one more glance at the man who was already turning his horse off the road, Darvi went on her way.

Heart pounding, breath coming in small gasps, Darvi rode swiftly toward the house. It was a lovely setting, not far from the creek and not very close to other homes.

"White paint, white shutters, and a large covered porch," Darvi whispered to herself, "just like the man said."

Darvi tied her horse's reins to a corner of the porch railing and went toward the steps. Things seemed so quiet—she was almost afraid to hope. Taking a breath to quell her excitement—a move that didn't work—Darvi knocked on the door. A man answered.

"Hello," he said kindly.

"Hello. I'm looking for Merry Scott. Does she live here?"

"Yes, she does. Come right in."

Darvi stepped inside when he held the door and squinted to adjust her eyes. The moment she could see, she realized her friend was standing not ten feet from her.

"Hello, Darvi," Merry welcomed with a huge smile.

"Merry," Darvi breathed, only now believing she had made it and moving forward to hug her friend.

The two women, one a soft strawberry blonde and the other a brilliant carrot top, hugged for a long time. Calder Scott, Merry's husband, stood off to one side, a wide grin on his face. The women were still hugging when Darvi heard someone call "Mama." She stepped away from her friend, her eyes huge.

"Merry?" she questioned softly.

Meredith Scott smiled the smile that first drew Darvi to her.

"Come on, Darvi. Come meet my husband and daughters."

Darvi was still mouthing the word "daughters" when Calder stepped forward.

"This is Calder," Merry began.

"Hello, Darvi," the tall man said as he held out his hand. "I've heard so much about you."

"It's so nice to meet you," Darvi replied sincerely. "I nearly panicked when I learned you'd moved away, but I found a way here."

"And these," Merry continued, "are our twins, Vivian and Pilar."

Darvi looked to where Merry pointed, through the doorway to the kitchen table, where two adorable, dark-haired moppets stared back.

"Oh, my" was all she could manage.

"Come, girls," Merry bade them. "Come and meet Miss Wingate."

"Please let them call me Darvi," that woman whispered as the girls scrambled from the chairs and ran to their mother.

"Here we go," Merry said in her quiet way. "Show your faces," she ordered the two who suddenly became shy and absorbed with their mother's skirt.

"Obey, girls," their father put in from the side, and the twins turned immediately.

"This is Vivian, and this is Pilar. Girls, this is my friend, Darvi. You may call her Aunt Darvi."

"Hello, Vivian. Hello, Pilar. It's so nice to meet you."

The girls giggled over this, and Darvi turned back to her friend.

"How old are they?"

"They were three last month."

Darvi shook her head. "So much time has passed."

"About four years," Merry confirmed. "They were born the first year we were married."

Darvi could hardly believe she was here. This friend was so special to her. Darvi didn't know if she'd ever told her that, but she would this time. This time she knew she could.

"Did you come alone, Darvi?" Calder suddenly asked.

"No," she turned to him, "but my escort seemed to think I would want a private reunion."

"Who is it, Darvi?" Merry asked.

"A friend of my uncle's. He wanted to wait by the creek."

Husband and wife exchanged a look before Calder turned away and said, "I'll just head out and invite him in to lunch."

Merry waited only until her husband was gone before sending the girls back to the table and ushering Darvi into the kitchen.

"Have a seat there, Darvi, and I'll get you a bowl of soup."

"Should I have gone out with Calder?"

"I don't think so," Merry said easily. "He'll just go out and introduce himself, I'm sure."

Merry said all of this while laying two extra place settings, making sure the bread was in reach, and then serving her friend a bowl of soup. It took a moment for her to see that Darvi was staring at her, a look of near desperation on her face.

"What is it, Darvi?" Merry asked gently, taking a chair close to her.

"I did it!" Darvi could wait no longer. "I asked Jesus Christ to save me from my sins. I wanted to pick the perfect time to tell you, but I just have to tell you now. I'm a believer, Merry, just like you."

Having prayed for this for years, Merry was surprised at her own reaction: one of tears. She tried to speak, but the words stuck in her throat. Silent tears trickled down her face, and when her little daughters saw them, their own tears began. This made the women laugh.

"Tell me everything!" Merry commanded when she finally had air again.

The words and sounds coming from the kitchen in the next minutes included an amazing blend of laughter and breathless sobs, none of which could be heard by Calder, who had finally spotted Dakota and was moving toward him. Calder was nearly to the rock the Ranger was sitting on before he realized that man had his shirt off and was trying to stop his side from bleeding.

"Hello," Calder called as Dakota glanced at him.

"Hello."

Finally at the boulder, Calder stopped and looked down on him. "It looks as though Darvi was something of a tyrant."

One corner of Dakota's mouth quirked. "She rode harder than I figured."

"Do you want me to have a look?"

Dakota took his eyes from the wound. "You a doctor?"

"Yes."

Dakota shrugged a little. "I saw a doctor in Austin. He gave me some powder."

"It wasn't Marcus Scott by any chance, was it?"

"As a matter of fact, it was."

"He's my uncle."

Dakota took a moment to compute this.

"I thought you were a Ranger."

Calder smiled. "That's my brother."

Dakota laughed a little.

"I'll get my bag," Calder said and started away.

Dakota was too weary to argue with him. He didn't think he needed any more mending, but he certainly felt worn.

Back at the house, Merry heard the door the moment it opened and went to meet their other guest. She was surprised to find her husband alone.

"He's hurt," Calder said by way of explanation.

Merry accepted this without question or comment. Darvi, on the other hand, followed Calder to the door on his way back out.

"Dakota's hurt?"

"Yes. I would guess a gunshot wound to his side."

Darvi's mouth opened. "He never said a word."

Calder's smile was full of amusement. "Somehow that doesn't surprise me."

Tempted as Darvi was to go with him, she thought she might be in the way. The blonde made herself stay put, but as soon as she saw him, Darvi would have a few questions for Dakota Rawlings.

❧ ❧ ❧

Dakota woke slowly, his body telling him he was rested and comfortable and that everything was all right. He remembered getting to the front porch and even going through the kitchen, but almost as soon as he'd lain on the bed he had been directed to, everything had begun to fade.

Now his eyes were opening, and for the first time since he left Desmond and Geneva's, he felt truly rested. Long days and nights, hard trails, and little comfort were a way of life to him, but having bullet wounds put it all in a whole new light.

"I found it a little surprising..." Dakota heard Darvi say and realized she was in the kitchen, right outside his door. For the first time he noticed the door wasn't shut.

"I never thought about people in the Bible quarreling or not loving each other, but Pastor Osman's sermon spoke to that very thing. I've been reading in Galatians ever since."

"Are you understanding it?" Merry asked.

"Some of it. May I ask you some questions?"

"Of course, Darvi. Why don't we get our Bibles and sit in the living room. The girls will be waking soon, and I can hear them better if I'm near the stairs."

Dakota heard their chairs move and lay in silence. It had been like listening to his own conversation with Marcus Scott. Darvi must have been in church on Sunday. Dakota glanced around to see if his saddlebags were in sight but didn't spot them. He had a sudden need to read his Bible.

With slow but comfortable movements he eased from the bed. A glance out the window told him where the privy was situated, and he thought if he moved quietly, he might be able to get out without disturbing Darvi and her friend. It occurred to him as he pulled on boots and found the back door that he hadn't even met the woman.

※-※-※

"I think I hear the girls," Merry said about 45 minutes later.

"Thank you for explaining some of this to me," Darvi said. "It makes sense to me now. I've sinned so many times since I believed. I'm not sure why I thought the people in the Bible would be different."

Merry smiled at her friend, still feeling rather amazed that she was even having this conversation. She had planned to go into town for some extra shopping after the twins awoke, but suddenly nothing else mattered. Darvi was here, and not just any Darvi, but a new sister in Christ.

"Mama?" A little voice floated down the stairway.

"Coming, Vivvy."

"How did you know that was Vivian?"

Merry shrugged. "I just know."

Darvi sat still in the living room after her friend walked up the stairs. She was still thinking about all the things Merry had explained and how much she had to learn when she heard a noise in the kitchen. With little forethought she stood to her feet and went that way.

Dakota, who had been reading at the table, had just put his Bible in the bedroom and returned to the kitchen when Darvi stepped into the room.

"I can't believe you did that!" Darvi attacked him without warning.

Dakota stared at her angry face, feeling rather dispassionate about her ire but thinking she looked rested and at home in these surroundings. Her yellow dress looked nice too.

"Did you hear me, Dakota?" she tried again.

"Yes, but I don't know what you're upset about."

Darvi's hands came to her waist. "You let me ride us as though there was no tomorrow and never once said you were hurt."

Dakota nodded with understanding. It took him a moment to figure out what she was referring to, but this made sense.

"I'm fine, Darvi."

Darvi looked irritated again, like a child who knew she was being patronized.

"That's why you were bleeding!" she snapped. "I know I always bleed when I'm fine."

Dakota tried not to smile at the sarcasm but couldn't help himself.

"Don't you laugh at me, Dakota Rawlings! I'm really upset about this." Her voice suddenly grew quiet; she wished she could learn to bite her tongue. "I was all het up to come here, and I didn't think about anyone but myself. I'm sorry."

Dakota couldn't help but respond to such repentance.

"I could have said something, Darvi, but I didn't. Thank you for your concern."

Darvi smiled a little at his forgiving tone. She regretted the way she'd talked to him but wasn't certain how to explain. At times she asked the Lord why He ever put up with her mouth.

All this was still rolling through Darvi's mind when she saw that she'd lost Dakota's attention. He was still standing in the same place, but his eyes were focused down and behind her; a smile was just starting across his lips.

Darvi knew what had his attention. Vivian and Pilar had come downstairs with their mother.

Four

"I'M MERRY SCOTT." THE DOCTOR'S WIFE was the first to speak and came forward to shake Dakota's hand. The girls stayed close beside her, but the shyness they had shown with Darvi was not to be found. Indeed, they seemed quite taken with this large, dark stranger.

"I'm Dakota Rawlings," Dakota said as he shook Merry's hand, catching the girls' interest but not looking directly at them. "I appreciate your hospitality. I'm sure I feel better for having come inside to lie down."

"Well, Darvi tells me you'll be taking her to Aurora to catch the train home, and you need to know that however long you're here, we expect you to use that room."

"Thank you," Dakota said, before his amused eyes swung to the strawberry blonde.

"Is that the plan? I'm taking you to Aurora?"

Darvi's mouth opened. "Didn't Uncle Marty tell you?"

"No. Maybe he thought you did."

"Oh, Dakota!" Darvi was horrified. "I had no idea. I mean, I just assumed you two had talked."

"It doesn't matter. Like I said, I have some free time right now."

"To rest up," Darvi said wryly, thinking she could cry. She had been so determined to get to Stillwater that nothing else had mattered. She now wondered whether her uncle knew of the situation.

"That was your uncle's plan," Dakota answered the unasked question, "but I don't think I'm going to be needing much rest."

"But you're not working right now?"

"No. My time is my own."

Sounding rather crushed, she said, "And I'm sure this is just how you had planned to spend it."

It was at that moment that the couple realized they were alone. When Merry and the girls slipped away, neither of them knew. Darvi moved toward the door that led to the backyard, obviously upset. Dakota followed.

"You need to listen to me, Darvi," Dakota said as soon as he followed her to the back porch. "You're upset for no reason."

"*No reason?*" Darvi began in outrage, but Dakota put his hand up, his face stern. Darvi subsided, something rather new for her, and waited for him to take a seat on the porch railing as she was in the only chair.

"I was hurt midsummer. Brace didn't want me back for six months. I came anyway. Since my escorting you puts me nearer my family's ranch, he said I should go there whenever we're done and check back with him in a month. The truth is, I don't feel a hundred percent, but neither am I dying. I'll probably be pacing at the ranch for three weeks before I'm supposed to report back in Austin. You may take as long as you like to get on that train in Aurora. My time is open. And unless you want me to wrestle a bear, I'm up for just about anything."

"But you were hurt some by how hard I wanted to ride," Darvi couldn't help but say.

"At any time I could have asked you to stop, Darvi, but I didn't. I have no one to blame but myself."

Darvi saw that he was right but still wanted to take responsibility. She looked away from Dakota's eyes and tried to work it out in her mind. When she looked back, he was still watching her. For some odd reason, her heart was wrung with compassion.

"How were you hurt, Dakota?"

"A gunfight. It wasn't that they outnumbered me; it was my miscalculation of where they were."

"You were shot?"

"Five times."

Darvi's hands came to her mouth.

"I'm fine," Dakota said gently. "I will tell you if I can't do something."

Darvi mentally promised to pinch herself if she cried, and it seemed to do the trick. Nodding swiftly and dropping both her hands and her eyes, she asked herself how God could stand all this weeping she did. Ever since she'd understood her own personal need for a Savior, she'd been bawling over the silliest things.

Not that Dakota's being shot is silly. I just wish I could control myself a little more.

"Are you all right?" Dakota asked. He hadn't taken his eyes from her since they'd sat down. Nevertheless, she did not look at him when she answered.

"I'm fine, Dakota, thank you. I'll just trust you to tell me if something's not right."

"All right," Dakota said as he stood. "And I'll wait for you to tell me when you're ready to go. Like I said, any time is fine."

He slipped back inside on Darvi's nod and found Merry and the girls in the kitchen. In the time he'd been gone, their fascination had melted away. They showed their faces long enough for an introduction but were terribly shy about looking at him. Dakota took pity on them and went into his bedroom and shut the door.

&-&-&-

"How do you feel?" Calder asked Dakota the moment he arrived home that evening and found him sitting alone in the living room.

"Better. Thank you."

Dakota had been sitting and looking out the large window to the woods behind the house. It was a very tranquil scene, and as the minutes ticked by, he felt himself growing more relaxed.

Calder sat down with him.

"Any more bleeding?"

"No. Thanks for helping me earlier. I think I needed rest more than anything else."

Calder smiled.

"What does that look mean?" Dakota asked, his voice a bit dry.

"Only that you sound like my brother."

"Was that a compliment or not?"

"Or not," the doctor replied, putting it plainly. "Most days, Chet has more guts than good sense."

Dakota let himself smile over this, a smile that grew quite wide when two little girls suddenly joined them.

"Papa!" they squealed in delight as the two scrambled for his lap.

They were hugged, kissed, tickled, and snuggled in turn before settling in to stare at Dakota in adorable splendor.

"Did you meet Mr. Rawlings?" their father asked.

Both dark heads bobbed up and down. Flyaway hair fell softly around their faces, and round cheeks glowed pink below sparkling eyes. They smiled easily, and their noses were so soft-looking and rounded that Dakota wanted to tweak them.

"How do I tell who's Pilar and who's Vivian?" Dakota asked as he studied their cookie-cutter images.

The two girls stared right back, and Dakota had to shrug.

Calder stepped in.

"Show him, Vivvy."

Vivian obediently pointed to her eye. Again Dakota studied her but still had to look to Calder questioningly.

"Vivvy has a tiny scar next to her eye," the older Scott explained. "Do you see it?"

"Oh, yes. How did that happen?"

"She had just learned to walk and waited until she was next to a rock to take her first serious tumble."

Dakota smiled at both girls and then looked to Vivian. "Did it hurt?" he asked, but Vivian only smiled at him.

Mercy, you two are cute! was all Dakota could think as he watched them. He didn't know how long he and Darvi would be in Stillwater, but he thought he could get very attached to these two girls. Though younger, they reminded him of Libby's sister, Laura.

"Dinner's ready," Merry announced from the edge of the room.

The men thanked her and stood.

Calder gave Merry a kiss, and one of the girls went into her arms.

"It smells good," Calder commented.

"Beef stew, biscuits, watermelon, and iced tea."

"Oh, my," Dakota said softly.

Merry turned to him, her eyes sparkling a little. "Don't you care for beef stew, Mr. Rawlings?"

"On the contrary, Mrs. Scott, quite suddenly I'm starving."

Having figured he would appreciate a home-cooked meal, Merry was very pleased. She was even more pleased when she saw that the girls were not going to stare at him all evening and then hide their faces when he looked their way. She was exhausted these days—she suspected she was pregnant—and in her mother's pride, she wanted Dakota and especially Darvi to see the twins at their best.

"All right, girls," Calder spoke after they had sat down. "Whose turn is it to pray tonight?"

"Vivvy's," Pilar was swift to say. "I was before."

Calder smiled at her wording and turned to Vivian.

"All right, Viv. Here we go. Dear Lord…"

"Dear Lor."

"Thank You for the food."

"For food."

"And all Mama's work."

"Mama."

"For friends."

This was met with silence.

"For friends," Calder repeated, his voice prompting.

Still it was quiet.

Calder finally had no choice but to open his eyes and look at his daughter. He found her staring around the table.

"Vivian, can you thank God for friends?"

"No."

"Why not?"

"Where's Beth?"

Understanding dawned. "Not *your* friends. Mama's and *my* friends. We have friends too."

The adults at the table had kept their eyes closed, but each had something over his or her mouth. Dakota's hand covered his upper lip, Darvi used her napkin, and Merry's apron helped her stem the laughter that lingered just under the surface.

"I'll go ahead and finish; you can close your eyes again," Calder stated.

Waiting until Vivian obeyed, the host went ahead with the prayer he had in mind, just barely holding his own laughter. No adults exchanged glances after Calder's amen, which was for the best. It would have been some time before anyone would have been able to eat.

🌿🌿🌿

"I didn't have a chance to tell you until now, but I'm so excited, Calder. She's been searching for so long. I knew Darvi's search had to end in Christ, but she didn't. I'm overwhelmed with God's grace and goodness."

"It's wonderful news," Calder said softly to his wife once they had retired for the evening. "Do you know how long she plans to stay?"

"No, but however long it is, it won't be long enough."

There was something quiet in his wife tonight, and for a moment Calder studied on what it might be. She was pleased about Darvi certainly, but not like he thought she would be.

"How was your day?" Merry asked, pulling her thoughts back to her husband.

Calder started to answer but stopped.

Merry looked at him. "Did something happen, Calder?"

"No," he went on smoothly, not wanting her to know he was distracted by her manner. He went ahead and told her about his office visits and one of the curtains nearly catching fire at the general store. They weren't many minutes outside of town, but enough that she would miss the daily happenings of town life.

"So it didn't actually light?"

"No, but the smoke was a nuisance, and it drew a crowd. Is there something you're not telling me?"

His detour in the subject was so abrupt Merry laughed.

"Where did that come from?"

"I was hoping to surprise a confession out of you."

"A confession over what?" Merry asked with just enough uncertainty that Calder's suspicions were confirmed.

"Out with it, Merry. I know something is on your mind."

"As a matter of fact, there is, but I don't want to tell you now because you're going to think I'm upset."

"Are you upset?"

"No."

"But something is wrong?"

"No, it is not."

Calder's brow lowered in thought.

"For a doctor, Calder, you can be a little slow."

It didn't take long from there.

"Are you certain?"

"Not absolutely, but fairly so."

"Why didn't you want to tell me?"

"Because I knew you'd ask for my symptoms, and I would tell you I'm tired, and you would say I'm the mother of twins, like you always do."

Calder laughed. "I'm sorry I'm so predictable, but you must admit that being tired would mean that nearly every woman in town was in a family way."

Merry smiled. "You're right, of course, but I think I can tell the difference."

Calder stood up from the foot of the bed and joined her on the side. He slipped his arms around her and held her close.

"I love it when you're expecting."

"Why is that?"

"Lots of reasons that I won't try to explain, but I do know I'm going to love this pregnancy more than the first."

"Why?"

"Because I've met the girls. I know how special this baby's going to be."

"So you believe me?"

Calder kissed her.

"Certainly. You know the signs in your own body better than I do."

"Thank you, Calder."

He didn't like being thanked for what he considered to be the job of a normal loving husband; that is, trusting his wife and caring for her.

"Did you really think I wouldn't believe you?"

Merry looked up at him. "I don't know. I just feel a little uncertain. I look into the girls' faces and I can't imagine loving another baby as I do them."

"Don't forget what your mother has been heard to say: Love multiplies; it doesn't divide."

Merry sighed a little, feeling more tired than ever. "I might have to experience that to believe it."

Calder didn't comment. He knew she would love this next baby. He knew her well enough to be at complete peace on the subject. But just then he had another thought that wasn't quite so restful. What if this birth was also twins? Calder was opening his mouth to ask Merry if she'd thought of that when he looked at her face. She was nearly asleep against him. He realized he was not going to fall asleep as swiftly, but not for anything would he mention the idea to Merry, at least not tonight.

❧ ❧ ❧

"Where is him?" Dakota heard one of the little girls ask before he actually spotted them.

"Where is *he?*" Calder corrected. "I think he's out back. Why do you ask?"

"I wanna see him."

Calder decided not to comment. He wouldn't mind seeing Dakota Rawlings either, but he didn't know quite how to go about it. As he and the girls walked from the back porch into the yard, Calder tried to determine why he was so drawn to the man. He knew there was something more to it than simply wanting to share Christ if he had the opportunity.

Maybe he reminds me of Chet was his last thought before Vivian spotted him.

"I see him! Hey!"

Dakota had been watching for them to come into view and now smiled as one of the twins came forward.

"How are you?" Dakota asked her.

"I'm Vivvy."

Dakota smiled. He didn't care that she'd gotten the question wrong. It was too much fun having her talk to him.

"If you were looking for peace and quiet, Dakota, you're in the wrong place."

Dakota smiled again. The huge tree stump, along with the shade thrown from a neighboring tree, was as inviting a place as Dakota had seen in a long time. He had read his Bible early that morning and was now trying to pray. He wasn't finding it as easy as he thought it would be, and that made him wonder if he might have missed something.

"Is this where the girls play?" he asked, glad for the distraction.

"Just about every day, and always 'house.'"

"Sounds like fun."

"How'd you sleep?" the doctor asked.

"Good."

"And the bleeding?"

Dakota smiled. "There's no getting around you guys, is there?"

"Not on your life. So tell me, are you still bleeding?"

"Yes, and I suppose you want to check it."

"Indeed I do, and if you don't mind an audience, I'll just look right now."

Dakota gently pulled the shirt from his waistband. Calder joined him on the stump, and the little girls moved in to watch as though it were an everyday occurrence.

"Are you sleeping on your other side?" Calder asked as he probed.

"As much as I can."

Calder looked up at him, his eyes thoughtful. "How many holes do you have?"

"Five."

Wondering how he could have missed this, Calder snorted in disgust and mumbled under his breath, "Might as well be your Uncle Chet sitting right there in front of you, girls."

"Are you hurted?"

"No," Dakota answered automatically, and to his surprise, Vivian turned to her father.

"Is he hurted?"

"Yep," Calder said mildly, a small smile on his mouth. "He just doesn't know it."

Dakota laughed a little and then winced.

"I need my bag," Calder announced and stood. "Stay put, girls."

Dakota watched him walk away before looking down at the twins. They seemed content to stare up at him, and Dakota wished he could think of something to say. He just decided to ask them if they were excited to start school someday, but he wasn't fast enough.

"I have to go," Pilar said out of the blue, her little brow furrowed as she stared up at him.

"Okay," Dakota said slowly, thinking that her father had said to stay put.

"Me too," Vivian chimed in, and Dakota watched as they walked around him and the stump but didn't go to the house. He stared after them, so he knew the exact moment they stopped and waved for him to come. Too curious not to, Dakota followed. His mouth stretched into a smile when he saw the little girls head to the privy. He had no idea why his presence was needed until they approached the building, stood still, and looked up at him. The handle was over their heads.

"Do you need me to get the door?"

Little heads bobbed in unison, and once he had the door open, they stepped inside. Wondering how he'd come to be standing there, Dakota shut the door and waited. In time he heard this:

"Look, Vivvy, a flower."

"Where?"

"Here."

"Where?"

"Here."

"Oh!"

Dakota's shoulders shook with silent laughter, but he didn't comment.

"I'm done" soon came from the privy, and not long after, the door was pushed open a bit. Dakota reached to hold it wide while the girls filed out. They came and stood side by side and looked up at him. For some reason, Dakota was speechless. He felt rescued when he saw that both of Pilar's little boots were unbuttoned.

"Here, let me get these for you."

Dakota hunkered down to do the job. Although he was not able to get all the buttons, he managed the top few. When he looked up, they were both staring at his face.

"What's your name?" Vivian asked.

"Dakota."

"Koda?"

"That's close enough," Dakota said, smiling into their eyes and thinking once again, *Mercy, you two are cute!*

The slamming of the back door brought his attention around. The threesome looked to see the doctor approaching, bag in hand.

"I guess we could do this inside," Calder commented as he followed Dakota back to the stump.

Dakota didn't answer. The yard was beautiful, full of wildflowers and tall grasses. It was a child's heaven all right, and Dakota knew why the girls played out here every day.

"Where is Darvi this morning?" Dakota thought to ask, taking his mind from the foul-smelling bottle Calder had just uncorked. Just before the painful liquid touched down, Dakota wondered if it would burn.

"She and Merry went to town. Thursdays are my mornings off. I keep the girls, and Merry gets out for half the day." This said, Calder looked into Dakota's face. He knew the stuff he was using not only smelled bad but had a tendency to sting. Dakota's face was utterly impassive, but Calder was not fooled. The big man was in pain and keeping his mouth shut in order to hide it. But Calder was in for a surprise.

"That burns," Dakota said quietly. "If I'd known you were going to treat me like this, I'd have gone to town with the ladies."

Calder was still chuckling over the comment when the girls declared they were hungry. All four went inside to find something to eat.

Five

"LOOK AT THIS FABRIC, MERRY. THE GIRLS would look wonderful in this dark pink."

Merry looked doubtful. "It would be great for trim, Darvi, but the twins need a dark background or they never look clean."

Darvi nodded but couldn't honestly say she understood. As a child she was not allowed to get dirty until she came for her annual summer visit to Austin. Her family had a yard in St. Louis, but it was all very trimmed and proper. She could pick flowers, but her fingers were not to touch the dirt. For a moment Darvi wondered how she had survived.

"What are you thinking about?" Merry asked, interrupting her thoughts.

"Just now I was asking myself how my mother and uncle could be so different and still have the same parents."

Merry suddenly looked intense and said, "You've never talked much about your mother. How is she different from Marty Bracewell?"

Darvi looked pained. "It would take less time to tell you how they're the same." She shook her head a little. "My mother must have known Uncle Marty let me run wild during those visits. I learned to ride and shoot. I came back with a tan, scratched up my arms and legs, and probably had a little dirt behind my ears, but she never said a word.

She just plopped me into the tub, proclaiming that travel made one 'so dusty,' and put me back into my routine."

"And from then on you were expected to be a little lady once again," Merry guessed.

Darvi smiled wryly. "That about sums it up. I would sit in my proper little dress and shoes and long to be back climbing trees with you. Merry!" Darvi exclaimed with a sudden thought. "Will there be trees in heaven?"

"I'm not sure. I have a memory of reading something in Scripture about that, but I couldn't tell you where."

Darvi's eyes sparkled with delight. "I love all these things I've yet to learn."

Merry's eyes widened with surprise. "Most people feel just the opposite, Darv. They want to know it all right now and are frustrated that they don't."

Darvi gave a little sigh. "I was so smug, Merry—so settled in my own world and sure I knew who I was and where I was going. No matter how much I don't know right now, I do know one thing: I'll keep searching and being in wonder, but I won't ever forget that God's Son died for me, and someday I'll live forever with Him."

"I have all I can do not to hug you and burst into tears all over again."

Darvi smiled. "I don't mind. I'd probably join you, but I have a better idea. Let me take you to lunch."

"Lunch? Is it that late?"

"No, but we forgot to eat breakfast, and I'm hungry."

Merry, feeling she were walking on a cloud, tucked her arm into Darvi's and said, "I'll lead the way."

❧ ❧ ❧

"Did I mention how I met your uncle?" Dakota asked between bites of the fried egg, bacon, baked bread, and hot coffee that Calder had prepared.

"No, I don't think you did."

"I first met him when I went to his office about the wound in my side, but then I visited this church and he was there with his family. They invited me to lunch."

As Dakota was hoping, Calder took immediate interest. "What did you think of the church?"

"I liked it. I didn't have a Bible at the time, so it was somewhat hard to follow along, but I've thought a lot about what both the pastor and your uncle said."

"So you discussed the sermon with Marc?"

Dakota answered by way of explaining what the sermon had been about and why it had been confusing. To his relief, Calder seemed to understand completely.

"I've had some of those same questions. Were you settled with Marc's answers, or do you still have questions?"

"I have questions, but not about the sermon," Dakota said, realizing as he did so that he was not very comfortable admitting this.

"About what?"

Dakota answered with his eyes on his plate. "Prayer."

Calder could see that he would need to go easy. He simply said, "If I can help, I'd be glad to."

"Thank you."

The men went on eating, Calder almost absentmindedly assisting the girls before asking Dakota a general question. The men talked easily about their jobs, neither showing outward appearances of stress.

When do I let things ride, and when do I push a little? It was a question Calder wrestled with all through the conversation. The meal ended, and Dakota even helped him clean the kitchen, but the subject of Dakota's questions on prayer did not come up again.

❦ ❦ ❦

How do I really know You hear me when I pray? Dakota asked the Lord not long after the meal. *I know what Slater and Desmond have said, and at first I felt that You heard me, but right now I'm not so sure.*

Dakota stood at the window in his room, barely keeping himself from pacing. Things had not gone as he had hoped. He had wanted to ask Calder where this doubt was coming from and where the answer could be found, but Calder had the girls to handle, and Dakota also knew the women would be back at any time, since the doctor had only half the day at home.

"I can't believe You would save me like You did and then hide from me," Dakota now whispered toward the glass, his heart aching to be heard and to know he wasn't alone. "If You're listening, God, I need some answers. I need to know that this is real." Tears clogged Dakota's throat, and he didn't try to keep praying, not even in his heart. He didn't believe it was right to throw a challenge at God's feet, but he couldn't think of anything else to do or say. If only he knew where to look in the Bible for answers.

A noise coming from the kitchen beyond his closed door drew his attention. It sounded as though the women were back. The trained gentleman in him immediately sensed they might need help unloading the wagon. Glad to leave his tortured thoughts behind, Dakota went to investigate.

❧❧❧

Dakota couldn't have said where Thursday went, but Friday arrived in a flurry of activity. He'd been up and dressed only a short time when he heard Darvi's and Merry's voices in the kitchen. The little girls chimed in from time to time, but the moving of chairs and other activity made it sound as if spring cleaning had arrived on September 1. Dakota stepped out to find just that. All the curtains were off the windows, and Darvi was elbow-deep in a sudsy tub, a tub of rinse water at her side.

"Good morning," Merry greeted him, setting a plate of food on the table. "How about some breakfast?"

"Thank you," Dakota replied, trying not to stare at the chaos around him.

"Sorry about the mess. I made the mistake of saying that I never got to my spring cleaning. Now Darvi's on a mission."

Dakota sat down to a high stack of griddle cakes, bacon, and hot coffee, a smile on his face.

"Trust me when I tell you that this is a feast, and washing or no washing, this beats where I usually eat."

"Where do you usually eat?" Darvi asked in genuine interest.

"On the trail. The first three things the Rangers want to know is whether you can ride, shoot, and cook."

"It's Koda!" one of the twins suddenly declared from the doorway, charging in to climb onto the chair next to his.

"All right, let me see," Dakota ordered before looking at her eye. "Ah, no scar. This must be Pilar."

That little girl smiled at him in pleasure and then settled in to watch him eat. Dakota talked to her some, but she would have occasional bouts of shyness and not answer. The scene changed entirely when Vivian showed up. The second twin looked surprised to be left out of the pleasure of watching Dakota, and with a little frown at her sister, Vivian pushed into the chair next to her in order to glue her eyes on their guest.

"What are you two doing?" their mother finally turned from the dishes she was washing to ask.

"Watching Koda."

This stopped Merry entirely. "What did you say, Pilar?"

The little girl had no idea what she was referring to, so she just looked at her. Merry tried Dakota.

"What did she call you?"

"Koda."

Merry's mouth dropped open in an unfeminine way, her head shaking in bewilderment.

"It doesn't matter," Dakota assured her. "I don't mind in the least."

"Girls," she began anyway, "I want you to call Mr. Rawlings by his name."

Their little heads bobbed just before Vivian turned to speak to him.

"Koda?"

"Yes, Vivian."

Merry's mouth was opening to scold her when Darvi's laughter rang out.

"Darvi! Do not laugh at this."

"I can't help it! They're so sincere."

Merry saw that she was right and gave up. It was not the way she wanted the girls to address adults, but she decided against fighting this particular battle.

Having finished his breakfast, Dakota suddenly stood and spoke. "Here, Darvi, let me get that."

"Oh, thank you."

Dakota took the heavy basket of wet curtains from her hands, thanked Merry for breakfast, and followed Darvi outside. He half-expected the girls to follow but soon found himself alone with Darvi at the clothesline. She plucked fabric from the basket, pegging the curtains carefully in the sun, Dakota moving with her.

"Dakota?" she said softly after a few minutes.

"Yeah?"

"Did you mean it when you said your time is your own right now?"

"Yes, I did."

Darvi looked at him before going back to work.

"Is it going to interfere with any of your plans if we stay until Monday?"

"Not in the least."

"Do you mean that?" Darvi turned to him with such hope on her face that Dakota was amazed.

"Certainly. We can stay longer if you like."

"I would like to," she said as she went back to the clothes basket, "but I think company can get old very fast.

I don't want to wear out my welcome, but I do want to stay through the weekend. It's rather important to me."

"That's fine. Do you mind my asking why you want to stay?"

Darvi hesitated. This was so new to her, and she was sure if he asked her any difficult questions, she would make a complete mess of things. However, the man beside her was waiting. Seeing no help for it, she admitted, "I want to go to church with Calder and Merry."

Darvi had all she could do to keep her mouth shut when Dakota said, "I'll join you if you don't mind."

Dakota saw the surprise in her eyes, but the twins came looking for them just then and neither one had time to say another word. Less than an hour later Dakota left for town. Darvi didn't wait five minutes before telling Merry what he had said.

꽃-꽃-꽃

Calder knotted his tie on Sunday morning, not quite able to grasp the last few days. He couldn't think of the last time he'd been so busy. Merry and the girls were having the time of their lives with their guests, but Calder had delivered four babies, wrapped broken bones, patched split heads, and all this among his other duties. He was starting to think the people of Stillwater were on some type of mission, one that would let them visit their doctor on a regular basis. Calder thought he would be ill as well if they kept it up, and all of this knowing that Darvi and Dakota were leaving the next day.

Dakota had even come into town and stopped at Calder's office, but he'd been with a patient and had two more waiting. The big Ranger had not looked put out, but Calder had been frustrated by it all.

There was a time when I begged You for a successful practice, Lord, and now I'm complaining. Please help me to enjoy the time I have with these folks and leave the rest to You.

"Papa?" a little voice called from outside the door.

"Come in."

Calder listened to his daughter try before he stepped over and opened the door.

"Mama says eat."

"Okay, Viv. I'll be right down."

Vivian waited for him, and when they both gained the kitchen, Calder was pleased to see that neither Darvi nor Dakota had come in yet. He didn't want to miss any more time with them. In less than five minutes everyone was gathered, and they sat down as a group. Calder prayed, and to his amazement, Dakota had a question as soon as he was finished.

"Do you ever worry that God isn't hearing you, Calder?"

"I haven't for a long time, but I used to."

"What changed for you?"

"Something my father said. He asked me if God's Word was true or not. It forced me to evaluate what I believe, and the truth is, I believe every word of the Bible. With that in mind, I looked at the different people who were devoted to prayer, including Jesus Christ. I know I can follow their lead."

"Where did you find those examples in the Bible?"

"I have some verses written in the front of my Bible that might help. Would you like me to copy them for you?"

"I would, thank you."

"Have you spent much time reading the Bible, Mr. Rawlings?" Merry asked.

"Just recently I have. I'm afraid that not all of it makes sense to me."

"I don't think anyone would claim to understand all of it," Merry added with a smile. "If he did, I'm not sure I would believe him."

Darvi was careful not to look at Merry, but she was nearly falling into her plate to listen to this exchange. Realizing she was staring at Dakota, she forced herself to eat.

From there the time simply sped away. Everyone was barely finished when Merry said they were running late, and before Darvi knew it, she was sitting in church, the Scott family to the left of her and Dakota on their other side.

Some of the songs were familiar, but the sermon was something she'd never heard before or even considered. The pastor told them, with verses to support it, that God had not only saved man, but saved him with a plan. God had good works for His children to do, and His will was evident on every page of the Bible.

Darvi was still thinking about the sermon when she walked absentmindedly out the church door. She had told Merry she wanted a moment alone at the wagon. She was nearly half a block down the boardwalk when a male voice stopped her.

"Well, hello."

Pulled from her musings, Darvi turned to find two men leaning against the side of a building, both dressed in denim, clean shirts, hats, and boots. There was nothing disreputable about them; indeed, they were clean-shaven and well pressed, but Darvi thought it rude to address her without an introduction. Her chin went into the air, but they only smiled, pushed away from the wall, and started to move toward her.

"Been to church, have you?"

"You, sir," she began, but stopped before starting the set-down she was ready to give him, not certain her old tactics were a good idea.

"Sir?" The man who was fairer-haired spoke again. "Did you call me sir? Oh, I like that."

"And I'd like it if you'd move on and leave the lady alone."

Neither man looked particularly guilty or intimidated by the large, dark man who appeared behind the woman, his entire face visible above her head, but neither did they want to tangle with him. Pretty as the woman was, the dark, intense eyes of the man who shadowed her were a little more than they bargained for.

Watching them walk away, Darvi stood very still. She could tell she was shaking a little and wasn't up to facing Dakota. He didn't know this. Only a moment passed before he stepped around and faced her. Darvi made herself look up.

"Are you all right?"

"I think so," she said with more bravado than she felt.

"What did they want?"

"I don't know."

"But they wouldn't move on when you told them to."

"I didn't tell them to move on."

Dakota's brows rose on this. "Why is that?"

Darvi's face filled with frustration before she answered. "I don't know! I'm a different person now, Dakota, and I don't think I'm supposed to talk to people that way."

Dakota's eyes narrowed, his own temper rising.

"Let me get this straight. You didn't want to hurt their feelings?"

Darvi scowled at him but didn't answer. Seeing the upset and confusion in her eyes, Dakota softened. He spoke quietly, his voice compassionate.

"Unless I miss my guess, Darvi, you and I have had a recent change in our lives."

The strawberry blonde nodded.

"If yours is anything like mine, right now you don't know which way is up."

"That about explains it. It's been wonderful," she was swift to add, "but I'm so unsure about so many things."

Dakota saw that Calder was headed their way. He gave him a quick wave and turned Darvi back toward the church. As he hoped, Calder only waved back and turned himself, giving them a moment alone.

"No matter what changes have occurred, Darvi, God wants us to keep using our heads. I refuse to believe that there's some verse in Scripture that says once you accept Christ, you have to let men accost you."

"No, I don't suppose it does say that, but my tongue's been getting me into trouble for a long time."

"Nevertheless, you know what appropriate attention is and what it is not. If you wanted those men out of your face, you had every right to tell them."

"But I was angry, and I didn't want to blast them with my temper."

"That's wise of you, but you can still tell someone, quite firmly, I might add, that you don't wish to speak to him."

Darvi stopped and looked up at him.

"I'm not going to argue with you, but I'm going to have to think on that."

"That's fair enough," Dakota agreed. "What did you think of the sermon?"

Darvi sighed. "Wow."

"I know what you mean."

"I just never thought about God having a plan for us. Did you?"

"Not personally, no. My parents taught my brothers and me to believe there was a God, but it's only recently that I considered the fact that God has thoughts of me or that He would want a relationship with me. It's a little more than I can take sometimes."

Darvi was still framing a reply when Calder pulled up with the wagon. The whole family was already on board, and the girls tried to climb onto both of them the moment they were seated. Darvi ended up holding the Bibles, and Dakota took both girls on his lap.

"Koda?"

"Yes?"

But that was all Pilar wanted to say. She laid her head against him, and Dakota held her close. Vivian spent the whole ride looking up into his face but didn't care to talk either. The girls gave him such a longing for Laura Peterson, his brother's young sister-in-law, that Dakota determined to visit Slater right away. He was thinking about how he could do this when Darvi shifted beside him, and he was reminded of his present job. Working not to let his emotions take over but not quite making it, Dakota's thoughts were very determined.

I'll get Darvi off safely, and then I'll make my way home. I'll visit Cash for a while and then go see Slater and Liberty. If Brace doesn't want me back by then, I'll go back to the ranch for good!

❧ ❧ ❧

"Are you going to be all right?" Dakota asked Darvi once they had left the house. She hadn't cried when they had said goodbye, but her face was so set that Dakota knew she was in agony. The fact that she didn't answer him also told him she was just hanging on.

Not in a hurry this time, they rode easily. Dakota was very rested, and Darvi had not wanted to leave. Neither did she want to talk, at least not for some miles. Indeed, it was midmorning—they were long out of Stillwater—before she broke the silence.

"Weren't those little girls cute?" she asked quietly.

"Oh, yes," Dakota replied with a smile. "I fell in love the first moment I saw them."

"They liked you too."

"I hope so."

"Merry told me," Darvi assured him. "She said Vivian and Pilar are usually more comfortable with women. I guess their father owns their hearts, but with you they made an exception."

Dakota smiled. "They weren't very vocal, but they sure liked to look at me."

Darvi smiled as well and turned to stare at him.

"What?" Dakota wished to know.

"I'm just trying to see you through their eyes."

Dakota good-naturedly shook his head. "Well, tell me when you figure it out."

With that the two were content to ride in silence for a time. Darvi looked completely at ease, like a child who's well taken care of, and that must have been because she was well looked after. Dakota was constantly on the alert. He was mentally thinking about the roads that would take them to Aurora and also where they could lunch, as well as finding a suitable place to set up camp before dark.

Dakota had stocked up on provisions, so he wasn't worried, but when the sun was right over their heads, he decided to mention to her that they were not going to make any sort of town that night.

Upon this announcement, Darvi pulled her mount to a stop.

"We're not going back through Blake where we stayed before?"

"Not if we're headed to Aurora so you can catch the train. Blake would be out of the way."

Her hat shaded her face quite nicely, but she still put her hand up to the brim and looked around them.

"Where will we spend the night?"

"There's an oak grove about five hours from here. It's off the road, but there's a large stand of trees, and the stream there is deep and fast flowing. I think we'll be in good shape if we can make that."

"Then we'll be in Aurora tomorrow night?"

"Probably not, but if you want to ride hard, we can try."

Darvi thanked him for the information and heeled her horse back into motion; indeed, she even picked up the pace some. At the same time, her mind gave her heart a short lecture.

You had to see Merry. You couldn't live another day until you saw Merry. Would you have been quite so eager, Darvi, if you had known you were going to be sleeping on the ground? Darvi rode on without even trying to answer.

Six

"Is this the place?"

Busy scouting the area, Dakota didn't answer, but Darvi knew it had to be. He had taken them off the main road about 30 minutes back, and the trees were just as he had described. Darvi could also hear the rippling sound of water over rocks.

"Okay, Darvi," Dakota spoke as he came back toward her on foot, "Come on this way around the trees. We'll set up camp for the night and have some dinner."

Darvi did as she was directed, knowing that hotel room or not, it was going to be good to get out of the saddle. Once again she was reminded of how her determination to see Merry had clouded all else. They had certainly ridden harder *to* Stillwater, but she didn't remember feeling sore. Now as she dismounted, she barely stifled a groan.

"You weren't sore on the way to Scotts," Dakota commented from behind her.

Darvi turned to see him watching her.

"How did you know I was sore?"

A slow smile stretched across the Ranger's face.

"I just watched you get off that horse."

Darvi tried to look stern but ended up laughing a little. At least she could do that. What she couldn't do was rub the parts of her anatomy that ached with stiffness and fatigue.

"Why don't you walk down by the water? I'll take care of your horse."

Darvi looked as grateful as she felt before thanking Dakota and unfastening her satchel from Finley's saddle.

"I think I'll freshen up a bit."

"All right. Keep your eyes open and stay within ear-shot."

Thinking he sounded just like Uncle Marty, she went on her way, moving gingerly as sensation returned to her limbs. Pain or no pain, it wasn't long before she noticed what a lovely setting it was. The day was still plenty warm, but just the sound and sight of the water seemed to cool her, and finding a large rock right at the edge was like an answer to prayer. Darvi sat on it, slipped off her boots and stockings, and placed her feet in the water. The action seemed to cool all of her. Had it been dark, she'd have gotten all the way in, but for the moment this did the trick.

Her satchel came next. She reached for the bag and brought out a large handkerchief, one she'd borrowed from her father. After soaking it, she bathed her face and neck. In very short order she felt like herself again.

"Are you all right?" she heard Dakota call.

"Yes, thank you, I am. Do you need some help?"

"No, I'm fine, thanks."

"I have my feet in the water already."

Darvi heard the laughter in Dakota's voice when he called back, "Sounds great. I'll probably join you in a minute."

Darvi smiled in contentment, all misgivings about camping slowly dying away. She decided as she sat there that she wanted a fresh pair of stockings. Her hands were back in her bag when she heard the rattle. She stopped moving, even though she could feel the outline of her gun beneath some of her garments. Her eyes shifting frantically, she finally spotted it. A small rattlesnake was coiled on the ground about a foot away from the rock. As Darvi watched, it uncoiled a bit and started to move away from her, but

Darvi still brought out her gun. She realized her mistake too late. Sensing her movement, the snake recoiled to face her, the rattles sounding off again.

"I don't think I can do this," she whispered even as she held the gun at arm's length, her finger ready to pull the trigger. Her mind raced through the things she'd heard about snakes, such as their ability to jump the length of their bodies. She wanted to gauge the distance but was afraid to take her eyes from the reptile.

"Darvi, you all right?" Dakota chose that moment to check on her.

The snake still watched her, his tail now silent.

"Darvi?"

"Dakota," she managed in a small voice. Then louder. "Dakota."

"Darvi, are you—" Dakota was saying as he came into view, his brow lowering as he watched her hold something black out in front of her with both hands. He moved closer and saw that it was a stocking draped over a gun. Why it took him so long to see what had her frozen in place, he didn't know, but moving in swiftly, his gun coming clean from his holster as he walked, he fired one shot before the snake jolted with the impact and lay still.

Her eyes still huge, Darvi kept her gun trained on the dead serpent even as she watched Dakota approach.

Dakota was compassionate when he saw the fear in her face, but he still smiled and plucked at the black stocking.

"Does the gun work without this?"

Darvi slowly lowered the weapon. "I was afraid to shoot. I thought I would miss such a small target."

"That still would have scared him away."

"But then I would have wondered all night where he was." Her eyes flickered toward the snake. "Now I'll know."

Dakota then saw that she trembled a little.

"You were very brave."

"I don't feel brave. I feel like calling for my mother."

Dakota bent and put his arm around her shoulders and gave her a squeeze.

"Thanks, Dakota."

"You're welcome. I'll stomp about some and make sure he has no family." As Dakota started his search, he kept speaking. "Tell me something, Darvi, does trouble just naturally follow you around?"

"What does that mean?" she asked, working discretely to put her stockings on.

"Oh, first you follow a complete stranger down the streets of Austin, who just happens to be me, and then you have two men following you in Stillwater, and now you attract a snake. It just causes a man to wonder."

Stockings and shoes in place, Darvi turned to set him straight. "I'll have you know, Dakota Rawlings, I can take care of myself very nicely."

Dakota didn't even glance her way. "It's beginning to make sense why Brace didn't want you coming on your own."

"You're all the same," she muttered, checking around the rock before climbing down. She gathered her things, gun still in hand, and moved back in the direction from which she had come. What she saw stopped her. Darvi didn't know how Dakota had accomplished it so swiftly, but he had set up a very orderly camp. A glance to the right showed that he had tethered the horses near food and water and already had a fire coaxed along, with two bedrolls opposite each other. Darvi knew she was in good hands, but she hadn't expected this. Dakota had told them he could cook. Darvi didn't know why she hadn't figured on the rest.

He lives his life on the trail. What did you expect?

"I think we're reptile-free for the moment," Dakota proclaimed as he joined her. "I hope you like your coffee strong. I don't know any other way to make it."

"I do like it strong, but believe me when I tell you that I'll eat and drink whatever you give me."

"Hungry, are you?"

"Well, not starved, but as usual, I've acted without thinking. It never occurred to me that we wouldn't be in a town tonight. If I was on my own, I'd be going hungry."

As though she'd just proved his point, Dakota smiled. Catching it, Darvi's chin came up.

"I would have done fine on my own," she told him firmly. "I would have come up with something to eat."

Fearing he would only get himself in trouble, Dakota didn't comment. Not fully understanding the female brain, however, he still found more than he bargained for.

"Do you doubt it?" Darvi demanded, not willing to let the matter drop.

Dakota looked at her.

"Actually, I don't. Plucky as you are, you would probably do fine, but don't ask me to condone your being out here on your own, Darvi. I won't do that."

Darvi wisely shut her mouth. She hadn't expected as much as she got, and she determined to let it drop before she pushed Dakota into saying something she didn't want to hear. *She* believed she could do fine, and that was all that really mattered to her.

❧ ❧ ❧

The meal was very good. Merry had sent some baked goods with Dakota, and that man had a good supply of trail food. He turned dried meat into beef and gravy over rice, a biscuit on the side. They ate cookies with their last cups of coffee.

Darvi volunteered to wash dishes, and she was at the stream doing this when Dakota realized they had company. Two men approached on one horse, a small, hard-ridden beast. Their eyes watched him but were more interested in the horses nearby.

"Hello," the man on the front called.

Dakota didn't like his smile but still said, "Good evening."

"Nice horses," the second man spoke as they dismounted.

Dakota saw no reason to comment. He hoped they would move on without a confrontation, and almost at the same moment, he heard the clank of pots and knew that Darvi was returning.

"Not now, Darvi," he said under his breath, but there was no way she heard. Indeed, completely unaware of the danger, she entered the campsite talking.

"I don't know if I got this one pot clean. It was very stubborn. I hope you aren't too—"

Dakota didn't even look at her, which meant he saw every bit of interest on the visitors' faces. He decided to confront the situation head on.

"The horses aren't for sale."

The men both snickered before the first one said, "We ain't got no money anyhow."

"Well, that only leaves you one option, gentlemen," Dakota went on amiably, "and it's only fair to warn you that I'll shoot you before I let you take our horses."

They seemed to weigh this up for a time, looking at each other and then back to Dakota, who partially blocked their view of Darvi.

"She your wife?" number two asked.

"The lady is not your business," he said flatly, his hand not moving to his gun, but his whole body shifting in a no-nonsense way. "And since we're camped here for the night, I think it might be best if you head on your way."

Hesitating only for a moment, the men climbed back onto the weary animal and continued down the road. Both Darvi and Dakota watched them for some time. Darvi's imagination had them doubling back, so she kept her eyes on them for as long as she could. When she finally glanced up at Dakota, it was to find him watching her.

"I suppose you're going to say that was all my fault?" she asked calmly.

"No, I wasn't going to say that, but it would help if you didn't look so good."

Knowing she was not at her best, Darvi nearly laughed. "What do you suggest?"

Seeing the amusement in her eyes, Dakota barely kept from smiling. "Well, you could blacken a few teeth and maybe dye your hair a mud brown."

"I'll think on it," Darvi assured him before adding, "it's your size and color, by the way."

Dakota blinked.

"What's my size and color?"

"The reason the twins stare at you, and also the reason those men in Stillwater and the men today left without an argument. Depending on who they are, people either find you a great comfort or completely intimidating." This said, she turned to put the pots down and then to sit down on her bedroll, reaching for her satchel as soon as she was settled.

For a moment it was on Dakota's mind to ask which way Darvi found him, but he thought he knew the answer. She'd half-hidden behind him while he talked with the men. Somehow he didn't think she was intimidated by him in the least.

※-※-※

Dakota did not get into his bedroll when darkness fell and Darvi climbed into hers. There was still a small flicker of fire left, and he wanted to go back to Calder's letter, which was filled with Scriptures. He started to read the letter again, thankful that Calder had written out some of the verses.

Dear Dakota,

I want to start by thanking you for asking me about this subject. It's easy to do things by habit and not conviction. It was very good for me to be reminded why prayer is so important.

Colossians 4:12 says: "Epaphras, who is one of you, a servant of Christ, salutes you, always laboring fervently for you in prayers, that ye may stand perfect and complete in all the will of God." Epaphras is devoted to prayer.

Colossians 1:9 says: "For this cause we also, since the day we heard it, do not cease to pray for you, and to desire that ye might be filled with the knowledge of his will in all wisdom and spiritual understanding." This is Paul speaking here. Note the way he says he didn't cease; he was another person devoted to prayer. James 5 says that Elijah was such a warrior in prayer that God held the rain back for more than three years.

And then to my favorite, Jesus Himself—God's own Son— was willing to give up sleep to meet His Father to pray. Mark 1:35: "In the morning, rising up a great while before day, he went out, and departed into a solitary place, and there prayed." I don't know about you, Dakota, but I don't think Christ would give this kind of example to us if His Father wasn't listening.

As Dakota finished reading the letter, he saw that Calder had included many other verses for him to look up, as well as telling him that he would pray for understanding in the matter. He closed with God's blessing and an invitation to visit anytime.

Dakota sat for a while longer and thought about his own faith. It had been so clear to him that he was lost and that God had found him, but somewhere in the mix he'd gotten the impression that his first-time faith was all he would need.

I've got to trust You all day, every day. I see that now. Not just to save me, but that You're listening and that You care. That was never clear to me before now, but this is what Desmond was talking about when he said to match my feelings against Your Word. If they don't hold up, then I can't hold on to them.

Thank You for saving me, Lord God. I'm still amazed at this second chance, and even this second chance to understand how You work.

His heart still prayerful, Dakota went back to his Bible to look up the other verses from Calder, asking God to help him understand the truths. The flickering light made it a challenge at times, but Dakota read until he could see no more. With the last dying flames behind him, he checked on the horses, which he had moved closer to camp, and finally settled in for the night. Darvi had stopped moving around, and Dakota assumed she had fallen asleep. He knew she would be sore in the morning and that riding Finley all day was not going to help, but he saw no help for it. Dakota found himself praying for her, and somewhere along the line he dropped off to sleep. It didn't last long, though, as Darvi suddenly gasped and woke.

"Dakota?"

"Right here," came his deep voice comfortingly through the darkness.

"Did they come and take the horses?" She sounded panicked.

"No. I checked on them right before I settled in."

He heard her sigh.

"I thought my dream was real," she admitted. "I'm sorry I woke you."

"It's all right."

It was silent for a moment.

"You don't sound as though you were asleep."

"I don't sleep very soundly when I'm on the trail."

Again silence covered them, and again Darvi was the one to break it.

"Dakota?"

"Yeah?"

"I don't want to intrude, but will you tell me how it happened for you?"

"My salvation?"

"Yes. I mean, if you want to."

"It's not a very long story. You knew I'd been shot and I told you it was bad, but I don't know if I told you that while I was in that gunfight, I thought I might die. When I realized I hadn't, I knew it was time to face what my brothers had been telling me."

"How many brothers do you have?"

"Two."

"And they both believe?"

"Yes. I thought that preachers used hell as a scare tactic to get people to church, but when I was faced with dying, I realized I wasn't ready. If hell was a real place, I was in trouble. If Slater and Cash had been telling me the truth, I knew I was lost.

"After I got hurt, I stayed with another Ranger. My brothers came to see me there, and I asked them to help me understand salvation. That's about the size of it."

"Had you been searching for a long time?"

"Running was more like it. I just didn't want to accept the fact that I sin. I'm around a lot of very desperate people, and somehow I thought I was better. I didn't like being lumped into the sinner category."

"Thank you for telling me," Darvi said softly. Dakota thought he heard tears in her voice.

"Are you all right?"

"Yes," she said, but it was on a sniff.

"How did it happen for you?"

"I won't be able to tell you without crying. It's all I've done lately."

"Well, don't let tears stop you."

"It's a long story," she replied, tears even thicker in her voice.

"I'm not going anywhere."

Dakota heard her blow her nose and cough a little. He wanted to tell her they didn't have to talk, but thinking she might fall back to sleep, he kept silent. A few minutes passed and she began.

"I don't know if you know this, Dakota, but I'm from St. Louis. And not just any part of St. Louis. I grew up in one of the nicer homes in one of the better sections of town. My family has always lived in style. In fact, I can't remember not having just about anything I wanted. We were very self-sufficient, my whole family, and because of that, I just never gave God a thought. We didn't pray at meals or go to church; we just took care of ourselves.

"But there was a woman in town, a pastor's wife, and she and my mother got to know each other through the St. Louis Ladies' Guild. I was just a little girl when I heard my mother tell Mrs. Beacher—that was her name—that she didn't believe anyone lived for eternity, not in heaven or hell. My mother believes that our life on earth is the end. You live and then you die. When Mrs. Beacher pressed her, my mother said that we live on through our descendants, and almost to prove that point, my mother has pictures of our ancestors all over the house. The hallways are lined with their paintings and photographs. So is the library and the large parlor."

Darvi fell silent for a moment.

"I grew up so smug and sure, Dakota. I didn't have a care in the world—at least not until I visited Austin in the summers and played with Merry Scott, who was then Merry Voight. She had the audacity to tell me she knew there was a heaven, and to top it off, she said she was going there."

Dakota smiled as he listened.

"I could have strangled her. I thought it was the most foolish thing, but she wasn't teasing me or acting proud. She had a deep joy about this fact, a joy I had never experienced over anything. Most of the summer I would play my heart out with her, not letting myself think too deeply, but when I went home I was miserable. Not only did I want to be back running free in a way I never could at home, but then I had time to think about what she said, and every summer I knew tremendous fear that she might be right." She sighed a little and continued quietly.

"This went on for more years than I care to think about. I eventually stopped visiting in the summer. My interests changed, and boys were noticing me. I even became engaged to be married, and then the unthinkable happened. It was just this spring. The house was abuzz with plans for a June wedding. My mother was showing the caterer through the house, and he asked about the largest portrait in the hall. Later I tried to tell myself that she was busy and distracted, but I couldn't quite convince my heart. My mother, who was going to live on through her children and grandchildren, couldn't remember Great Uncle Jenkins' name. She looked very forlorn for a moment but then passed it off with a laugh.

"Later, when I was alone, I walked through and looked at all the portraits in the house. I couldn't tell you the names of half of them. I asked myself how, if I didn't know these people and my mother was already forgetting their names, could they still be living?

"The fact that they were all very dead and always would be was like a blow to me. I walked around in a painful cloud the rest of the day, and the next morning I canceled a date with my fiancée and went to see Mrs. Beacher." Darvi sighed again, this time sounding very tired. "I understood now all the things that Merry had said to me during those hot summers in Austin, and as soon as Mrs. Beacher explained, I knew in an instant that my sin had put Christ on the cross and that I was lost without Him. I'd never known such peace, but it only lasted until I arrived home. I can't begin to tell you the mess I made of things.

"The weeks that followed were like something out of a nightmare. My parents were deeply hurt over what I was telling them. Then Mrs. Beacher, who was meeting with me each week for Bible study, asked me if my intended was a believer. I had to tell her no."

Tears were coming now, and Darvi didn't try to stop them.

"I can't tell you what it did to all of us to have me break off my engagement with Brandon. He was so hurt, and I was feeling lost and confused. My mother said it was just a stage and that I would get over it. She went right on with the wedding plans until I left for a few days to get her attention. I didn't know what else to do. And all the time Brandon was coming around, telling me he'd love me anyway, but I knew it wasn't right. I finally wrote Uncle Marty and asked if I could come. He wired me right away and said yes. I was so exhausted by the time I arrived that I ended up ill. I know my mother must have written to him, but he never said a word to me.

"In all the hoopla, I'd completely forgotten about Merry. After spending days in bed, I woke up one morning and knew I had to see her. But we had never kept in touch by mail, and I didn't know she'd moved. That's why I followed you down the street, and that's why you're stuck with me right now."

"I don't feel I'm stuck with you, Darvi, and I don't want to hear you say that again."

"All right." She sounded very contrite, and Dakota wished he could see her. He had written his parents about his conversion and received a rather surprised letter from his mother, but it was nothing like what Darvi had experienced. In fact, although admitting that she didn't understand, his mother told him that she and his father would support him in whatever he wanted to do. It had always been that way with his parents, and Dakota was just now seeing how good he'd had it. His parents' lack of faith in Christ still concerned him, but there was no anxiety as he prayed for them every day and tried to prepare his heart for the next time he saw them.

A sniff broke into Dakota's thoughts.

"Thank you for telling me, Darvi. I'll pray for you."

"Thank you. Please pray that I'll figure a way to get out of this mess I've landed myself in."

"I can't pray that, Darvi, because I don't see it that way."

"What do you mean?"

"I mean, you can't marry a man who doesn't share your faith and commitment to Christ. I'm sorry that your family has taken it so hard, but they're going to have to get used to your decision."

Darvi was so shocked she was speechless. This worried Dakota.

"Am I out of line, Darvi?"

"No, I'm just surprised that I haven't seen that before. I've got to let my mother work this out. I can't worry about her response to Christ or my decision."

"I agree with you. My parents do not share my faith in Christ, and I'm thankful they don't give me a hard time. Nevertheless, I can be tempted to worry about their eternity and choices when God says worry is a sin."

Again Darvi sighed, but not because she was overwhelmed. She knew worry was a sin, but she hadn't seen that this was what she was doing.

"Thank you, Dakota," Darvi said for the last time. "You've helped me a lot."

"You're welcome," Dakota responded, feeling very inadequate. There was so much he didn't know, and for a moment he had doubted his own words to her. He finally fell back to sleep—they both did—each one praying for greater understanding and wisdom in this new life, a life they wouldn't trade for anything, but one so foreign they might have been living in another world.

Seven

Aurora, Texas

JARED SILK'S EYES NARROWED IN ANGER as he read the newspaper column. After all this time he should have been used to it, but he knew if Annabelle Hewett had been in the room just then, he would have been tempted to strike her.

He read it yet again:

> What does Aurora's newest bank have going this time? How about loan rates that are not only too good to be true, they're impossible to believe! One can't help but wonder how owner Jared Silk can afford clothing that clearly didn't come from a catalog. We'll all be waiting with great anticipation at the town's fall festival. Will Silk's face be as red as his new cravat?
>
> A. Hewett

Had Annabelle been in the room right then, she would have seen just how red the banker's face could get. Jared was so furious he nearly barked at the person who knocked on his office door. Remembering just in time that the bank's doors were already open, he tempered his response to a terse reply and told the men to enter. Even though he'd sent for them, seeing them did nothing for his mood.

"Have you read this?" he asked one of his personal assistants.

"Yes," Seth Redding answered calmly, taking a chair as though he had all day.

"I'm sick of it! I want it stopped. Do you hear me?"

"What exactly are we supposed to do?" the other man, Eliot McDermott, asked. "She's free to write whatever she chooses, and we know from the last little job that busting up the newspaper office won't stop it."

"Shut your mouth!" Jared hissed at him as he rose to shut the door, even knowing the hall and stairway were empty.

The men, half-brothers who could have had respectable jobs, watched their boss secure the door and stalk to the window. From the second-story view, he stared down on the street, his frame tense with helpless frustration.

"What she writes is all true, Jared," Eliot added. "I don't know why you fight it."

"I don't pay you to think," Jared now said coldly, never taking his eyes from the window. The statement wasn't true, but the banker was too angry to see reason.

The brothers exchanged a look. At times like these they were tempted to ask themselves why they put up with him, but the answer was never far from their minds: the money.

"I think I'd like to talk with Annabelle Hewett," Jared said.

Seth came to his feet, and Eliot's stance became tense.

"Now, Jared," Seth began, "you can't go snatching that lady off the streets. She's too well known."

Jared finally turned to the men, his face filled with a calm they had learned to dread.

"You're right; I can't do it. But you can and you will. I don't care how you handle it. I don't even care if you hire someone else, but I want you to offer a personal invitation to Miss Hewett."

"An invitation to what?"

"Why, to my home for dinner. We'll have a nice meal and talk awhile. I'm sure I can convince her that she's quite mistaken."

The men didn't bother to hide their displeasure, but Jared was not swayed.

"Just let me know what day I'm to expect her. And boys, keep it neat. I have a reputation to uphold in this town."

Knowing they had no one to blame but themselves, the brothers filed out. They didn't linger at the bank but headed right onto the street and over to the saloon to discuss the idea. They had a plan in very little time, but later, Seth returned to the bank only to find that Jared had come up with a plan of his own. Nevertheless, this job was going to cost the banker a little more than usual.

❧ ❧ ❧

"You don't have to stay," Darvi proclaimed to Dakota for the third time.

"So you've said." His reply was as calm as always, and Darvi gave up.

They had made excellent time getting to Aurora, and during their travels Darvi was surprised to find that Dakota's home was very near. He could be there in a matter of hours. Darvi saw no reason for him to stay the night just to put her on the train. However, he was not about to leave. Darvi was glad for the company but felt she'd been trouble enough.

"So where do you want to spend the night?"

"I've got to get my trunk from the train station, and then I'll check into the Belmont."

"Why don't I get the trunk?" Dakota started to suggest, but Darvi was already shaking her head.

"I appreciate the offer, Dakota, but I need my clothing as soon as I check in, and I'll be able to find the trunk in no time, since I know what it looks like."

"Sounds fair enough. By the way, what are we doing with Finley?"

"I'm to leave him at Garth's Livery, or some name like that. My uncle has plans to get him back. I didn't ask where it was, but I don't think it will be too hard to find."

"Have you stayed in Aurora before?"

"No, I haven't."

"How do you know about the Belmont?"

"Uncle Marty. He lectured me for a full 24 hours before I left." Darvi's voice went monotone before she went on, "What to watch for, where to go, do everything Dakota says, don't look at strange men, don't leave your room after dark, get your trunk from the station, leave the horse with Garth, and I can't remember what else."

Dakota had a good laugh over this litany but thought it sounded like Brace. He was also changing his mind about Darvi being on her own. He would never leave her to fend for herself, but she was very quick to catch on to things and as plucky as he'd first expected.

The train station was a bustling place, and it took some doing to track down the bags and trunks that were being held. Darvi had to give her name and a description of her small trunk, and then the man was gone for what seemed to be ages trying to find it. Because her name was not on the outside, he made her open the top and show her name under the lid. The fact that she had the key should have spoken volumes.

Finally satisfied, the man released the trunk to her care. Dakota hefted it onto Eli's back. It wasn't the ideal mode of transportation, but if they asked the station to deliver it, there was no telling when the heavy piece would arrive. There was a lad of 12 or 13 who stayed close to the hotel lobby and was willing to carry it to Darvi's room when she checked in. Dakota followed in their wake, his own room key in hand.

"Thank you," Darvi told the young man, slipping a coin to him.

"Thank you," he returned politely and went on his way.

"Are you on this floor?" Darvi asked Dakota.

Dakota looked at his key. "I think so, but I must be a few doors down."

"I know it's getting on in the day, Dakota, but can you give me time to clean up before we eat?"

"I was going to ask you the same thing. There's no way I'm going to enjoy my dinner until I've ordered a bath."

Darvi smiled at his understanding.

"I'll come back here in about an hour. How does that work?"

"Wonderful. I'll see you then."

Saddlebags in hand, Dakota went to find his room, not knowing that an hour was optimistic. Nevertheless, the two travelers finally sat down in the hotel dining room, both ready for a hot meal and the comfort of eating indoors.

"Dakota," Darvi asked over coffee, their order having just been taken, "how did you become a Ranger?"

Dakota smiled. "I caught the bug when I was about 13. We'd had some trouble with cattle rustling, and the Rangers came in to help. I'd never seen such tough, capable men. I was in awe of every one of them. From that time forward I dreamed of having my own sturdy mount, side arm, rope, and Bowie knife. I had access to all those things on the ranch, but they weren't mine. At the time I had no concept of the responsibility, but even when I understood the position, I still longed to work hard and uphold the law in Texas."

Dakota stopped for a moment before admitting, "It was all I ever wanted until my brother Slater came to Christ. Cash and my grandmother already believed, but I never thought Slater would. The change in him was uncanny, and then he left the Rangers to settle in one town. I was ready to string him up, but he stood up to me and told me his decision was made. The change in his life got me to thinking that I might have missed something.

"I don't know if I thought of it when you were telling your story, Darvi, but Slater did what you need to do.

Although everyone in the Rangers was telling him he didn't need to quit, he knew he couldn't stay on the trail. He stood up to me and to Brace, and I know God has blessed him for it."

It was on Darvi's mind to ask Dakota if he would stay with the Rangers now, but for some reason she held back. His salvation was as new as hers. Maybe he hadn't thought that far. Then again, she knew nothing of Slater. Maybe their situations were nothing alike.

"So are you ready to go home and face your family?"

"I think I am. I'm trying not to think of conversations in my head. I've done that in the past, and it never works. The person never says what I think he's going to, and so everything I've rehearsed is a waste of time."

Dakota was impressed. It was so easy to do just that. He'd done it many times himself.

"Well, you can go knowing that I will pray for you."

"Thank you. And I'll be praying for you. I never thought about anyone being able to have an influence on Uncle Marty. Maybe your life will touch his."

"I hope so. I care for him a lot."

Darvi found herself wanting to cry and hoped their food would come soon. Quite hungry, she suddenly realized a wave of homesickness was washing over her. The combination of hunger, her uncle, and a need to go home rained down on her with such intensity that she almost gasped.

Dakota stayed very quiet. They had talked for hours the day before, and Darvi had apologized for her tears on two occasions. Both times Dakota told her it was all right. He hoped that if he remained quiet now, she would not feel the need. It helped to have his stomach growl, and for Darvi to hear it.

"I think they've forgotten us," she said, trying not to sniff.

"I think you might be right. I'm going to have to make myself chew. Right now I think I could swallow things whole."

Neither one felt compelled to talk after that. Their food arrived about ten minutes later, and that was all they needed. By the time they finished, the days on the road were catching up. With little more than a plan to meet for breakfast, they bid each other goodnight.

ॐ·ॐ·ॐ

Darvi stood on the train station platform in a navy blue suit, her satchel open as she secured her ticket inside. Closing the top, she looked up at Dakota who stood in front of her.

"All set?" he asked.

"I think so."

"You look very nice in that suit, by the way."

Darvi looked up at him innocently and asked, "You don't think I should blacken a few front teeth?"

Dakota put his arms up in surrender.

"I'm not going to live that one down, am I?"

"Oh, I don't know about that," Darvi said playfully. "If you happen to see a certain uncle of mine and perhaps mention to him that I was a perfect angel on this trip, I might see my way clear to forget what you said."

Dakota laughed again.

"I'll do it."

Darvi smiled up at him. "Thanks for everything, Dakota. I can't tell you how good it was to see Merry and then hear of your revival as well."

"I like that," Dakota decided. "My revival. That just about sums it up."

Darvi didn't want to get teary again, so she said nothing. Not one who liked waiting for the train whistle to blow, she said goodbye right then. Dakota gave her a great hug, one that Darvi gladly returned, and then stood and watched her get on board. He searched the windows and waved when he spotted her, but as soon as she looked down at her lap, he turned away. It was going to be wonderful to get home, but he hated to see Darvi go. He walked back toward the hotel and livery, his heart a mix of emotions.

Halfway to the hotel, Dakota stopped in midstride. He didn't know why he hadn't thought of it sooner, but he could keep in contact with Darvi. The whistle had already blown, but he knew if he hurried he could get her address.

He arrived back in plenty of time, but she was not at the window. Thinking she might have moved, he quickly searched along the cars, surprised not to see her. When the train began to pull away, he comforted himself with the fact that he could get her address from Brace. Dakota turned again toward the hotel but froze before he'd walked five steps.

Moving along between two men was a woman: strawberry blonde and wearing a navy suit. Dakota wondered if he was seeing things even as his feet began to propel him in that direction. He wasn't overly concerned. After all, why would anyone take Darvi from the train?

His own teasing about trouble following her now came to mind. With no definite plan, he picked up the pace just as they entered a crowded area of downtown Aurora.

❧❧❧

Darvi could not believe this was happening. Where the men had come from she couldn't say; she had looked up and there they were, one of them already taking the satchel from her side. Any protest she had died in her throat upon seeing the knife. The man hadn't pulled it from its sheath, but he'd made sure she saw it before their eyes met. For this reason, Darvi instantly obeyed his order to accompany them from the train.

She now walked between them, much faster than she would have on her own, the town passing rather swiftly. She nearly lost her footing at one point. Starting to gasp, she felt something hard press against her side. That these men meant business was more than clear.

Darvi was working to keep her head when they suddenly turned down an alley. They were at the side and then the back of a building almost before she could think. Almost. Deciding that she wasn't going to comply any longer, Darvi began to pull on the hand holding her upper arm, just as she opened her mouth to scream. She didn't see the fist that came down on the top of her head, so when blackness crowded in she had no idea why.

༈ ༈ ༈

Dakota had spotted them again and even knew what alley they turned down, but to his amazement, there was no one in sight. He couldn't even find three distinctive sets of footprints in the gravel. Sure that he'd misjudged, he tried the next alley down but could see that it was too far.

"I know this is where they went," he said under his breath as he continued to study the buildings. "I just don't know for sure that it was Darvi."

Dakota had a look around that brought him to a door in the back, but it was locked. Not a man given to flights of fancy, he wondered what to do next. Finding out if Darvi had actually left on that train was nearly impossible, but that would have settled his mind. He tried to assess whether or not he had actually seen anything amiss. The woman did not look upset or forced, but she certainly had Darvi's coloring.

Dakota was at a loss. He'd planned to send word to Brace that he'd gotten Darvi off safely, but right now he could not even do that. For the time being he found a bench in front of the general store and sat down to think.

※-※-※

"*You knocked her out?*" Eliot asked in outrage.

"She started to struggle," the taller of the two abductors said, defending himself, but a look from Eliot quieted him.

"When do we get paid?" the other tried, but he shut up when Seth's eyes grew as black as his brother's.

Neither man dared to comment when Eliot opened the door, his message clear. As soon as they were gone, Eliot and Seth stared down at Darvi and then at each other.

"How hard do you think he hit her?" Seth asked.

Eliot lifted one of Darvi's eyelids and shook his head. "She's out cold."

"Here, let me move her to the davenport. She's going to topple out of that chair."

Seth lifted her easily, amazed at how light she felt, his heart pumping with very real fear that they had hurt the influential Annabelle Hewett. But something else happened inside of him when he laid Darvi back against a pillow, her face so pale that he was startled. Trying not to hear his own heart pounding, Seth placed his fingers alongside her neck. He picked up a steady beat and hoped it was only a matter of time until she woke.

"She's prettier than her picture," Seth commented as he stood to full height, looking down at their guest. Eliot came over to look, his gaze somewhat dispassionate.

"Things must be better for her. Even knocked out, she looks better than the last time I saw her."

"I don't know."

"We could throw a little water in her face," Eliot joked, but Seth frowned. For some reason the idea repelled him. He knew she could be vicious with her words, but knocked out cold, Annabelle Hewett looked rather young and vulnerable.

"I'm going to get something to eat," Eliot proclaimed, heading toward the kitchen of the apartment that Jared kept in town. Its rear exit to the alley had come in handy many times over.

"I'll join you," Seth added, his eyes on Darvi until Eliot called again.

"You'd better bring that bag of hers so we can check it out. You never know what a lady like that might be packing."

❧ ❧ ❧

Darvi woke in confusion. Before she even opened her eyes, she tried to think why the top of her head felt bruised. Her memory returned with a jolt, but she continued to keep her eyes closed. She didn't know where she was, but it might be to her advantage to let whoever had taken her think she was sleeping.

"She's coming out of it," she heard a soft male voice say. She finally gave up and opened her eyes. She did not find the men from the train. These men were tall, well dressed, and good looking. Darvi thought they might have rescued her and began to sit up.

"Where am I?" she asked.

"Don't you know, Miss Hewett?"

Darvi nearly looked behind her. "Were you talking to me?"

Both men smiled, thinking she was very good.

"We're glad you stopped to see Mr. Silk," Seth now went on smoothly. "Unfortunately you've missed him. He *would* like to see you, however. In fact he's asked us to extend a dinner invitation to his home at your earliest convenience."

"Who is Mr. Silk?"

Eliot looked cynical, but Seth began to ask himself just how hard she'd been hit.

"So when can we set a date?" Eliot pressed on.

"A date for what?" Darvi asked, beginning to wonder if she had really awakened.

"Miss Hewett..." Seth began patiently.

"Who is Miss Hewett?" Darvi demanded.

The men's faces grew hard, and Darvi came to her feet, albeit awkwardly.

"Where am I?" she tried again.

The men just stared at her.

Darvi walked to one of the room's windows and looked out. She knew it was still Aurora, but she couldn't quite picture where. She'd been tired the night before and eager to get on the train that morning. Was it that morning?

"Is it still Wednesday?"

"Yes."

"Do you have the time?"

"Miss Hewett," Eliot tried this time.

"Stop calling me that."

"All right, Annabelle, why do you wish to know the time?"

"That's enough!" Darvi's voice cracked with enough force to surprise even herself. She stared at them, eyes furious, her hands coming out to make her point.

"I don't know what's going on here, but you will stop calling me that name. My name is Darvi Wingate. I was on the train this morning bound for St. Louis when two men threatened me with a knife and removed me from my seat. I want some answers, and I want them now."

"I should have known she was going to make this hard," Eliot said to Seth.

"Yeah, I suppose you're right. Let's give her some time to think."

The men filed from the room then, and Darvi was completely confused. Her attention strayed around the small living area as she searched for answers, so she was startled when one of the men returned.

Seth handed Darvi her satchel.

"I thought you might want this."

Darvi took the bag.

"The gun is out," he added, holding her eyes for long moments before exiting once again.

I have to think, Darvi told herself, trying to ignore the headache. With that her eyes caught sight of the door. Bag in hand, she went to it and found it open. Hating to leave her gun and thinking she might be dreaming after all, she began to walk out onto a wooden landing that led to a tall flight of stairs. There was a door at the bottom. She was just closing the apartment door when she heard, "Did you lock that door?"

Darvi didn't even bother to catch the latch. Knowing she'd been found out, she lifted the front of her skirt and flew down the stairs as fast as she could move. She didn't make it halfway before an arm caught her around the waist. Darvi froze, waiting for him to let go, but he didn't. Not seeing any other way, she began to scream and struggle. A sound had barely escaped her when a hand was put over her mouth. The voice at her ear was quiet, almost gentle, but the words were no less serious.

"The last thing I want to do is hurt you, but I can't have you escaping or screaming." Saying this, Seth shifted her so she could see his face. The terror in her eyes nearly got to him, but he still said, "Understood?"

Darvi nodded and stayed quiet when he slowly removed his hand.

"Now, back up to the apartment you go. We have to come to some type of agreement before you leave."

"What agreement?"

"Well, it's like we said. Mr. Silk wants you to come to dinner, as you missed seeing him today."

Back in the apartment, Darvi turned to see him put her satchel on the floor while the other man locked the door.

"I don't know who Mr. Silk is, and I didn't come here on my own. I don't know how much plainer I can make it."

The men said nothing. The one nearest the door pocketed the key, and the one who had caught her on the stairs only looked at her. A moment later they exited the room again.

Eight

"Excuse me," Dakota interrupted the man at the ticket window.

"Yes, sir, what can I do for you?"

"I was just wondering if there's any chance you remember a woman buying a ticket this morning? She wore a navy suit and had reddish blonde hair."

The man nodded. "I remember her. Headed to St. Louis."

"Yes, she's the one. Do you happen to know whether she was on the train when it left?"

The man looked thoughtful. "Well, I assume she was. She didn't come back to say she missed the train. They always do that when it happens."

Dakota debated how to ask the next question delicately. "Did you by any chance happen to see her leave the station area?"

"I didn't see her go, but then I can't see as much as the men out front. You might want to check with them."

"Thank you."

Dakota stepped away from the window fighting the frustration rising within him. He'd already talked to the men who worked along the tracks. They hadn't seen anyone leaving who matched Darvi's description and told him to check with the man at the ticket window.

I don't think I can do anything else, Lord. Is it a lack of trust to wonder if she's all right? If that wasn't Darvi, then why haven't I seen another woman like her in town today? But Dakota's questions went unanswered. He honestly didn't know what to do. His money, including the funds that Brace had given him, was down to nothing. If he stayed in town, it would have to be outside tonight. He was more than willing to do this if there was a need, but if this was nothing more than a case of mistaken identity... On the other hand, if Darvi needed him, Dakota would never leave her.

Deciding to stay in town one more night and keep his eyes open, Dakota went in search of a cheap meal. He hadn't eaten since breakfast, and it was now way past noon. He had to assume if he didn't have answers by morning, he would have to leave well enough alone.

🌿🌿🌿

"I need to let Cassy know I won't be home tonight," Eliot said of his girlfriend.

"Maybe Nate's in town. He could tell her," Seth replied, speaking of Cassy's son.

"I'll head out and check." Eliot stood. "How is she doing?"

"The last time I looked she was reading her Bible."

The men shared a smile, and Eliot slowly shook his head. "She's good. I'll give her that."

"That she is, but I must tell you, the lady fascinates me."

"You've seen her column in the paper, big brother. Don't forget she has claws."

Eliot left to the sound of the other man's laughter. Seth went back to his paper. He had only just returned to his reading when Darvi came to the door.

"May I please leave now?"

Setting the paper aside, Seth shook his head. "We have to come to an agreement," he said, keeping his voice gentle.

"You're going to have dinner with Mr. Silk, and you're even going to tell your readers about it, both before and after. You've had some pretty ugly things to say about him over the last year, and it's time to do some repair work."

Looking as devastated as she felt, Darvi turned away. Not giving her more than a few moments alone, Seth followed her. He found her sitting and looking toward the window, but since it was growing dark outside, he knew she could see little.

For a time, Seth cursed Jared Silk's very existence. None of this was going the way they had planned. Nevertheless, Seth knew he had a job to do.

"I'm sorry you won't cooperate, Miss Hewett, but if you'll just work with us, you can go home."

"Please don't call me that."

The lantern was not turned very high, but it did illumine the side of Darvi's face, catching the smooth skin on her cheek, the adorable shape of her turned-up nose, and that incredible mouth. Seth felt his heart turn over with tenderness for her and wanted to shake his head at this interest. His boss would be enraged if he knew. Annabelle Hewett was the enemy, and he would do well to remember that!

"Now listen," he spoke harshly, coming close to Darvi and towering over her as her head whipped around. "I've got better things to do than sit around here and wait for you to admit the truth. You can knock off this act and come clean. You know what I want, and I'm not going to wait forever."

Nearly growling with frustration when the light would not give him a clear view of her eyes, he turned it higher. The tears, fear, and confusion he saw were almost his undoing, but he made himself go on, albeit in a quieter tone. Reaching for an old newspaper, Seth sat next to Darvi and searched until he had found her column.

"Look at this. You say right here that Jared Silk is a con artist, but do you have any proof? You stir up a lot of trouble for one of the town's more popular businessmen. Mr. Silk just wants to know what you have against him. He believes if he could speak with you, you would see that you have him all wrong."

Darvi looked at the paper, telling herself she was not going to cry or panic. She tried to lick her lips, but her mouth was alarmingly dry.

"I didn't write this. I don't know how else to tell you. I'm not Annabelle Hewett. And if your plan is to starve me until I say that I am, then you're going to have a corpse on your hands."

Seth stopped dead in his tracks. This was not supposed to have taken all day. They hadn't given Darvi a thing to eat or drink. He was saved from falling all over himself when he heard the door open. He met his brother when he was no more than a foot inside, the smell of food enveloping him.

"*We forgot to feed her!*" Seth whispered in panic.

"I remembered that when I was out," Eliot whispered back. "I've brought some dinner from the hotel."

Seth straightened his tie and jacket and even smoothed his hair. Chin raised and determined to be all business, he returned to the living room.

"We have some dinner for you now. Come on through to the kitchen and eat."

Hoping he was not playing games with her, Darvi went ahead when he motioned for her to precede him. The room was not overly large, but she was directed to take one of the four chairs around the kitchen table. The smell of food assailed her; her mouth ran with saliva so suddenly she had to swallow several times. She'd been praying all day for strength, but if they planned to make her sit here and not eat, they might have a hysterical woman on their hands.

"Here you go." Eliot set a plate in front of her, some silverware on the side. A glass of water came next, but Darvi just sat, her hands clenched in her lap. The men had food of their own, but she was afraid to trust this situation.

Trying not to look at her, Seth started on his food. Eliot couldn't. He watched her sit there for a few seconds and then spoke up.

"You can eat."

"I don't have to do something first?"

"No."

Eliot's reply was very quiet. He had just gotten a taste of what his brother had seen. He made himself look down at his plate, but he couldn't miss the way she picked up her water, her eyes closing in relief as she drank. Drinking often, she began to work her way through the food. The rice was wonderful, but the chicken looked so good that she soon had a piece in her hand. She was just starting to feel normal when she glanced up to see that someone had filled her water glass again. Pausing only to wipe her hands, she reached for it. Not until that point did she realize the men were watching her.

For some reason, color filled her face as she slowly set down her glass. To her surprise, the men rose. They set their plates on the side counter and turned to her.

"When you're finished, come back to the living room so we can talk."

This order came from Eliot, and Darvi only nodded before they went on their way. She finished slowly, managing to eat every bite. It was during this time that her brain went back to work. She knew that the living room was out the door and to the left, but the one man had not exited that way. He'd come from the other side.

Working not to scrape her chair on the floor at all, Darvi stood up, wiping her face and hands as she went. She didn't move her plate and did everything she could to keep her feet silent. Determined not to look toward the living room, she planned to hit the doorway and head right, hopefully out the first door she came to. And it worked, right up to the moment she had her hand on the knob. It was then she noticed the large hand that had appeared just over her head. It was holding the door shut.

Darvi turned in disgust to find Seth looking down on her. Having gained back some of her old pluck, she lifted her chin into the air.

"I almost made it," she told him before slipping past and heading to the living room.

Seth was glad she couldn't see him, giving him time to wipe the smile from his face.

"Please sit down," Eliot instructed her right away, his tone firm.

Darvi complied.

"I've got a sample of the articles I want you to write. You'll put one in tomorrow's paper, and the other one will go in the day after you dine with Jared."

He tried to hand the papers to Darvi, but she wouldn't take them. Eliot let his head fall back, frustration written all over him. He didn't want to strike the woman he thought to be Annabelle; he just wanted to release her back into the alley and be done with it.

"I don't write for the newspaper," Darvi tried again. "If you want to take me down there and ask them yourself, that's fine. Maybe then you'll see I'm telling the truth."

This was getting ridiculous. Jared's scheme had seemed a little far-fetched when he'd plotted it for them, but now this attempt to execute it was just plain foolishness.

"May I leave?"

The men looked at her.

"No," Seth spoke up, trying not to be led by his heart. "I still think we can work something out."

"But it's dark out; I have to go."

"Where do you have to go?"

Darvi didn't answer. She just knew she needed to get out of there.

"Did you find Nate?" Seth asked of Eliot.

"Yes."

Seth stood.

"If you'll come with me, Miss Hewett, I'll get you settled for the night."

Darvi could not believe her ears. She could see these men did not mean her physical harm and that they truly had mistaken her for someone else, but that didn't make the whole episode any less frightening. For the dozenth time that day, Darvi was forced to push Dakota's face from her mind. He would have taken such good care of her if he were here, but he wasn't, and she had to accept that.

Following the man who picked up her satchel, Darvi left the room behind him. They went down the hallway and past the kitchen to a small bedroom. There was very little in the room. He set her satchel on the small bed.

"The window is nailed shut, but even if you do figure a way to open it, it's a two-story drop. If you need something, I'll be across the hall or in the living room."

Seth said all this while forcing himself not to look at her. He headed to the door and almost made it but looked back even as he had his hand on the knob. It was a mistake. Darvi stood looking around the room, that expression of a lost, forlorn child back on her face. Seth couldn't get out of there fast enough. He nearly ran to the living room and threw himself onto the davenport.

"Something doesn't add up, Eliot, and I don't mean maybe. If that woman is Annabelle Hewett, she's the greatest actress who ever lived."

"I was thinking the same thing. It has crossed my mind that she's playing us for the biggest fools alive, but it's getting harder to buy."

The men sat in silence until Eliot had another thought.

"Could it be a relative, even her daughter or younger sister?"

Seth shook his head. "She's never heard of Annabelle Hewett. She can't be faking that."

"I thought for a moment that she was going to tell us someone was waiting for her or that she had someplace to be, but then she stopped."

"I thought the same thing. It even looked like she wanted to make something up and couldn't think of it fast enough."

Eliot stood with a groan. "Take the first shift. I'm tired."

"All right. I didn't lock her door, so check the front again. I've got the key."

"All right. Call me before you nod off."

"Will do."

Seth was left alone with his thoughts, and they weren't happy ones. He had no idea what to do next. Not tired in the least, he determined to sit on the sofa until he had that woman figured out.

※ ※ ※

Darvi sat on the edge of the bed, her arms wrapped around her middle, wishing she hadn't eaten all the food. Her stomach was so upset from fear that she thought she might be ill. She had sat alone in the living room most of the day, even nodding off at times. She hadn't liked going to the kitchen; the living room seemed safer. This whole ordeal was wearing on her.

I'm so confused right now, Lord. I don't think they mean to harm me, but I want to be let out. I'm not afraid to go back to the train station and try again, but these men have me at their mercy.

Just thinking of the word mercy reminded Darvi of God's great mercy to her. She still did not have answers but was greatly calmed as she prayed. She poured her heart out to the Lord and asked Him to comfort her and provide wisdom. She didn't feel at all tired, but when Seth checked on her some two hours later, he found her sleeping in her clothes, curled up not far from the edge of the bed.

☙☙☙

Dakota didn't leave Aurora without some misgivings, but on the whole he knew a great peace. He hadn't seen his brother, a man he dearly loved, in a long time.

He asked God to bless Darvi, trusting she was still on her way home and knowing she would face her family soon. Outside of town, Dakota picked up the pace. He would be in Kinkade tonight and home for the first time in ages.

☙☙☙

Eliot came back to the apartment, breakfast in hand. Seth had just finished shaving, and as Eliot passed Darvi's room, he saw that the door was open and she was still sleeping. Apparently Seth had covered her with a blanket. The younger man's hands shook just a little as he set the plates down, but he wasn't given much time to compose himself. Seth came into the room just a moment later. One look at Eliot's face told him something was wrong.

"What's the matter?"

"I just saw Annabelle Hewett heading into the newspaper office."

"You're sure?"

"Positive."

Seth couldn't hold his smile.

"Do not be smiling about this, Seth. What about Jared?"

"Jared or not, Eliot, this is the best news I've ever heard."

Eliot stared at his older brother. They'd been through so much together. Seth was as levelheaded a man as he'd ever met. Why now? Why her? Eliot couldn't think of worse timing. He was on the verge of telling his brother just that when a small cry came from the other room. Both men moved across the hall to investigate. They found Darvi on the floor looking very sleepy and bewildered.

"Did you fall out of bed?" Seth asked as he came forward.

Darvi, who had just awakened from a horrible nightmare about these men, tried to scoot away from him, but her legs caught in the blanket. Seeing her fear, Seth halted.

"When you're ready," he said quietly, "we have some breakfast for you."

"I'm not hungry."

Seth only nodded and cleared out of the room, shutting the door behind him.

"Let me handle this," he told Eliot as he moved to the outer door. "Don't tell her what we know. I'll go take care of things with Jared and come back here."

"What are you going to do with her?"

Seth didn't even hesitate. "Take her home."

"To the ranch?"

"Yes."

Eliot was given no time to comment. Seth slipped out the door, and the remaining brother locked it in his wake.

❧ ❧ ❧

"What do you mean the plan won't work?" Jared demanded, having already closed his office door.

"Just that. We tried and it failed."

"Tried? How?"

Looking much more composed than he felt, Seth met Jared's eyes.

"We had a woman picked up who bears a striking resemblance to Annabelle Hewett. She tried to tell us she wasn't Hewett, but we didn't believe her. Then Eliot spotted Hewett in town this morning. We still have this other woman at the apartment."

Jared's look became shrewd.

"That's perfect. Now that you know exactly who Annabelle is, you can still pick her up and get her to agree to my terms."

"No."

"What do you mean, no?"

"Just what I said. The whole idea is crazy. Do you know how many people would miss Annabelle Hewett? I thought of that before, but not until we had this woman who doesn't even live in Aurora did I see that this won't work with anyone as well known as Hewett."

"But I want her stopped!"

"Be that as it may," Seth responded in a voice that had gone cold, "you'll have to find another way to do it."

Seth stood, and Jared wisely backed off. It had taken years to find men to work for him who had the sophistication that Seth Redding and Eliot McDermott displayed. He paid them well, but they were worth every dime. And over the years he'd learned some things. He knew when he could push and when he'd gone too far. The men did have their limits.

"What will you do with this woman?"

Seth shrugged as though he didn't care. "Take her to the ranch for now."

"What's her name?" Jared asked before thinking, then swiftly held up his hand to stop the question. "I don't want to know any more. Just handle it."

Seth started toward the door.

"I'll let you know when you're needed again."

"All right. We'll be in the apartment until after dark."

Jared only waved in his direction, his mind already working on the next plan. Never once did the banker's brilliant mind remind his heart that he could have used his intelligence to gather wealth honestly. This was the way he'd always done things. A different approach had never occurred to him.

❧ ❧ ❧

Darvi rubbed at her hip. She had finally climbed from the floor, but she felt stiff and sore, and her hip ached. She must have landed directly on it. She rubbed the back of her neck, glanced around the room, and noticed the steam. Moving to the pitcher and basin, she saw that someone had brought her hot wash water, soap, and towels. A wash sounded good, but to do it right, she would have to unbutton her dress and loosen her clothing. The thought alone sounded wonderful.

Darvi moved toward the room's only chair, a thin piece of furniture but her only choice. She carried it across the floor and tried to jam the back under the doorknob. She no more had it settled when someone knocked.

"Are you all right?" Eliot called from without.

"Don't you try to open that door. I've put a chair there."

"Why did you do that?"

"Because I want some privacy."

There was silence and then, "If I hear glass breaking, I'll bust the door down."

Darvi didn't answer.

"Do you hear me?"

"I hear you."

Darvi wanted to hear him walk away, but when he didn't, she still went to the basin. Hearing the splash, Eliot's suspicions about her trying to escape eased, and he went back to the kitchen to check on the two breakfasts he had set on top of the stove. He could see the food was drying out, but he thought it still looked edible.

In the room, Darvi took as much off as she dared and began to scrub with a vengeance. It occurred to her for the first time that her surroundings were impeccable, but her own fear had naturally caused her to perspire. Bathing was a definite help to her spirits.

I'm going to get out of here today, Lord, she proclaimed as she started to rinse off. *I don't know how just yet, but I'm not going to sit around here again and try to convince these men.*

They can take me back to the train station, or I'm going to cause such a ruckus that I'll bring the whole town down on their heads.

Darvi hoped she could actually manage all this once she was faced with it. It was easy to be tough behind closed doors.

"You told Dakota you would do just fine on your own," she whispered to her reflection in the small mirror even as tears filled her eyes. "Oh, Dakota, I hope I didn't lie to you."

Nine

Darvi exited her bedroom about an hour after she fell out of bed. She didn't have a confirmed plan in her mind, but she was going to keep her eyes and ears open. She found one of the men in the living room, his jacket off, his feet on the table. She was grudgingly impressed when he stood and reached for his jacket. It made the whole situation all the more curious.

"What exactly do you do for a living, Mr.—"

"McDermott," he supplied. "I'm a personal assistant to Jared Silk."

Darvi nodded. She had been too stunned yesterday to act. Today she was going to learn who this Jared Silk was and why Annabelle Hewett wrote about him.

"Would you like some breakfast now?"

"No, thank you. I don't suppose it would do any good to ask you to let me leave."

"I'm afraid not."

"In that case, may I share some of your paper?"

"Indeed. Please help yourself."

"Thank you."

Darvi was scanning the pages just a moment later, but Eliot was a little slower to go back to his reading. Since she was reading attentively, he was able to study her undetected. Something had happened since the day before. She was not the least bit afraid of him right now, and he again experienced some of the fascination his brother was feeling.

Completely unaware of his scrutiny, Darvi could not believe what she was reading as she went through nearly every newspaper in the two piles that sat on the floor of the living room. Not all of Annabelle Hewett's articles were about Jared Silk, but when his name was mentioned, the woman was nothing short of scathing. A chill went down Darvi's spine. Jared Silk must hate this woman, and these men thought they had her in captivity.

At the same time...

Darvi's mind worked fast. She wondered if this might not be her way out. Clearly the men believed she was a reporter. Darvi wasn't sure if there was ever a right time to lie to someone, but at the moment she was tempted. Hearing the door open and watching the man in the room get up, Darvi kept studying the newspapers and working on the plan that was budding in her mind.

$$\text{-3--3--3-}$$

"Where have you been?" Eliot asked when he met Seth at the door.

"I had some things to pick up, and then I went ahead and bought lunch."

Eliot shook his head. "She never ate any of the breakfast. What did Jared say?"

"He wanted us to grab Hewett this time, and I said no."

"That sounds a little too easy."

"Not really. He pushed me, and I pushed back. He backed down and said he'd send for us when he needed us."

This Eliot could believe. Jared slid along on the edge of the law, but he never crossed Seth. Seth could find work too easily, and they both knew it.

"How has she been?" the smitten brother asked.

"She's reading through the newspapers. She's not afraid like yesterday. I swear she has something up her sleeve."

Seth looked thoughtful. "My bet is she's pretty harmless, but she did have a gun in her bag. We'll just keep on as we're doing, and hopefully I won't have to gag her before we leave here tonight."

"Seth, are you sure about this?"

"Very sure."

"This kind of thing can bring a whole lot of trouble."

Seth studied his brother's pensive face before glancing toward the doorway as if he hoped to see Darvi.

"Just go along with me, Eliot. I can't explain it, I just know what I have to do."

The men's eyes met before Seth put a hand on his brother's shoulder. A moment later he went to the living room.

"Lunch is ready."

Darvi looked up to see the other man addressing her. She set the paper aside, and much as she had done the night before, preceded him to the kitchen. Mr. McDermott was already there, the food ready and waiting. Darvi was nowhere near as starved, but she was hungry. She didn't know where they picked up the food they brought in, but the beef and vegetables on her plate were very tasty. She didn't rush. She was still asking herself if lying to the men who had her abducted was wrong when she went ahead and plunged in.

"I would like to look at those sample letters now," she said quietly, watching their faces.

The men had all they could do not to look stunned.

"You would?" Eliot questioned.

"Yes."

Eliot and Seth were careful not to look at each other as Eliot came slowly to his feet, went to the other room, and returned with the pages. Darvi took them from his hand.

Eliot, watching his brother watch Darvi, had to smile. Seth was doing everything in his power not to show it, but his heart was nearly in his eyes as he gazed at this woman, understanding exactly what she was up to.

"And if I write this for the paper," Darvi clarified, "you'll let me go?"

The men hesitated.

"Isn't that what you said?"

"There's been a slight change in plans," Seth began. "I'd have to run it past Mr. Silk."

Darvi tried not to show how far her heart sank. She had not expected this, but she was going to keep trying.

"Can you do that now? Can you check with him today?"

Seth appeared to consider this. "I think I can do that. If you're finished eating, why don't you let us talk it over and get back to you."

Darvi desperately wanted to know what he meant by a change in plans but thought she should take what she could get for the time being. Trying not to appear as uncertain as she felt, she rose from the table and left the room.

Both men remained very quiet, so they had no trouble hearing Darvi check the door in the living room. They knew it was locked. Next they heard more rattling of newspapers. Seth leaned back in his chair, a full-blown smile on his face.

"Now tell me, Eliot, had I met her under any other circumstances, would you like her more?"

"I like her now, Seth, and it's very easy to see why you're taken with her."

There was so much to add to this, but Eliot did not waste his breath. His brother was lost on this woman.

Eliot stayed where he was even after Seth went to the other room and had a few words with Darvi, obviously telling her he was headed to see Jared. Eliot even heard her thank him, her voice sweet and grateful. Not sure she should be left alone for too long, Eliot did a quick cleanup job in the kitchen and went back to reading newspapers with Darvi in the living room as soon as Seth exited the apartment.

❧-❧-❧

Kinkade, Texas

Cash Rawlings dusted off his jeans as he walked through the back hall of the ranch house, his ears picking up the sound of a deep male voice. His cook, Katy Sims, laughed like a girl, and suddenly Cash knew exactly who was in the kitchen.

Sitting on the counter as though he'd been there all his life, Dakota looked up when Cash entered, a huge smile covering his face.

"It's about time you got in. I've been sitting here for at least ten minutes."

The brothers met in the middle of the room, unashamedly embracing each other for long moments.

"How are you?" Cash asked, still holding the younger man by the arms.

"Good, I think. Ready for a bath and a hot meal."

"We can do both. Right, Katy?"

"As if you have to ask!" she said in her indomitable way. Cash only smiled.

"Come on," Cash invited Dakota. "Come into the den. I've got to show you something."

From the kitchen the men moved across a sprawling living room graced by a huge stone fireplace and into Cash's personal office. The oldest of the Rawlings brothers led Dakota to a framed portrait, turning to see his reaction.

"When did this arrive?"

"Just last week."

The men gazed at the beautiful picture of their parents, Charles Sr. and Virginia Rawlings. Neither parent smiled, but both had warm expressions. Dakota's eyes lingered on his mother's. Cash had been blessed with her eyes—warm and welcoming. Dakota's gaze next went to his father. It was like looking at himself in 20 more years.

"They look great," Dakota declared.

"That they do. Mother wrote that she was sending it, but I didn't know what to expect. The ornate frame and bowed glass are such a surprise. It's more elegant than ranch life, but I'll take it anyway."

"Now if Mother were here right now, she'd say it was time you had a woman's touch around here."

"She'd say the same thing to you."

"Have you been to see them lately?"

"No. I'm thinking of going just before Grandma's visit."

"How is she?"

The men fell into easy dialog about everything from their grandmother to the increasing number of cattle Cash had on the ranch. At one point Katy called that the water was hot for bathing, and Cash encouraged Dakota to go first.

"Do I smell that bad?"

Cash smiled, his eyes not bothering to disguise the love he felt.

"It's so good to have you home."

"I'm glad you feel that way. I'll probably stay for a while."

"Good. How's the new life going?"

Dakota sighed. "I have so many questions."

The men would have started on those questions right then, but Katy came from the dining area with orders.

"Cash! Are you going to let this boy bathe?"

"Go, Dak, before she has a fit."

Katy had been with the family since the men *were* boys, so the look they exchanged was a familiar one. They did as they were told. Cash followed Dakota into the large bathing chamber off the kitchen at the rear of the house so they could keep talking. Katy grumbled under her breath that they acted just like kids, but that didn't stop her from standing outside the door, listening for a moment to their nonstop talk and grinning from ear to ear.

❧ ❧ ❧

Darvi had everything she could do not to wring her hands and pace. All her brave thoughts melted as she sat and thought about the meaning of "a change in plans." Several times she had asked Mr. McDermott what could be keeping the man he called Seth, but he seemed as uninformed as she.

Another glance at the window told her darkness was crowding in. It was inconceivable to her that she had spent two whole days in this apartment, no one knowing where she was. She had not communicated a firm arrival date to her parents, and Dakota thought she was on her way home. The thought caused panic to claw at her throat. The men hadn't been threatening to her; they just wouldn't let her go. Working desperately not to crumble but to keep her voice strong, Darvi stood.

"I have to go now. It's been too long. He's not coming back, and I can't stay here anymore."

Eliot came to his feet, mentally begging Seth to return before he had to gag this woman to keep her quiet.

"I think it won't be long now."

She wasn't going to hear that again. Darvi looked toward the window, anger taking over.

"It's getting dark outside! I've probably missed my train again. Now you must let me out of here."

This said, she strode to the window and started to open it. Eliot could not stand the thought of hurting her, so he simply tried to take her by the arm.

"Don't touch me! I'm going to scream until someone comes."

"Is there a problem?" Seth's voice sounded at the edge of the room.

Darvi turned swiftly from the window, her eyes hot with betrayal.

"What kind of people are you?" she spat. "Now I want out of here, and I won't hear another excuse. Do you hear me?"

"Yes, I do hear you," Seth replied quietly, thinking a day had never been so long. It obviously had been for her as well, but certainly for another reason.

"Get your bag ready."

Darvi was surprised but went immediately to do as he bid. In less than a minute she was standing in the hallway, ready to go.

"May I take this for you?" Seth offered.

"No, thank you," Darvi said without looking at him, and Seth wondered how much ground he might have lost by staying away so long.

"Let's go," Seth said quietly and surprised Darvi again by taking her back through the living room. She remembered the stairs well, but it was getting dark and she had to take hold of the railing. A wagon was waiting in the alley, but Darvi didn't move toward it.

"Thank you," she said stiffly, thinking this entire ordeal had been a nightmare and asking God to let it be over.

"Climb in; we'll give you a ride."

"No, thank you," Darvi stated plainly. It was already quite dark, but she decided to take her chances alone. She didn't get five feet before a large arm dropped around her shoulders and steered her toward the wagon.

"What are you doing?"

"I can't let you go to the train station," Seth said, hoping she was not going to scream.

"Please, don't do this," Darvi entreated him. "Please, let me go."

"I can't," he whispered, and with that swung her up into his arms, stepped on the wheel, and sat down with her in the back of the wagon. Eliot immediately put the team into motion, and Darvi screamed. Wanting very much to put his mouth over hers, Seth had to be satisfied with his hand, only to get it bitten. At the same time Darvi's other hand clawed at his face, and it took some doing to subdue her. Unfortunately, that freed her mouth for another scream.

Eliot was cutting through alleys and behind businesses as fast as he dared, but he feared that if she sounded off again, they were going to get nabbed. He cringed at the thought of the explaining they would have to do. Some of the police force were on Jared's payroll, but no one would turn a blind eye to their abducting a woman.

Still hearing scuffling in the back, Eliot could see that they'd almost made it. Another half mile and they'd be far enough out of town that he could move the horses a little faster and not cause suspicion. From there, they would head to the ranch, some five miles out. At that point she could scream all she wanted to; no one who could do anything would hear her.

Darvi couldn't fight anymore. Seth held her very effectively, and biting his hand only lasted a few moments each time. She lay panting beside him, noticing for the first time that he wasn't trying to take advantage of her. Nevertheless, she didn't like it. She tried to speak, which caused him to ask. "Are you going to scream?"

Darvi shook her head no.

Seth let go.

"Where are we going?" Darvi pushed the words past a raw throat.

"To my home."

"Why?"

"Because we are."

Darvi tried to see him in the dark.

"Didn't Mr. Silk want to see me?"

"I didn't even ask him."

Darvi sighed. What in the world was going on?

As though he'd heard her, Seth answered. "We'll get you to the ranch, and Cassy will settle you in. Tomorrow I'll try to explain it."

"Who's Cassy?"

"Eliot's girl."

Darvi was silent for a moment.

"I'd like to sit up now."

Seth was swift to help her. He'd had her pinned to the floor of the wagon, her wrists held in one of his hands. He now put a hand to her back and helped her sit up.

"Do you want to sit on the seat with Eliot?"

"No, thank you," she said before curling into a ball, wondering if she should try to jump for it. She glanced around at the blackness and knew it would be a mistake. She'd be terribly lost out here, and they would be hunting her, not to mention the fact that the team was moving fast now. Darvi thought she might injure herself if she tried it. She placed her forehead against her upraised knees and asked God to help her think.

❧ ❧ ❧

Darvi was surprised at what she could see of the house. Without permission Seth lifted her from the rear of the wagon and set her on the ground. The front door opened and the light spilled out, telling her the satchel was in Seth's hand.

"Come on in," a woman's voice called. "I've got dinner on."

Darvi entered a large, low-ceilinged room that was as well scrubbed as the apartment had been. To Darvi's amazement, a number of people were inside, almost all men. All but the woman sat eating a meal around a huge kitchen table. They turned to look her way, but a comment from the woman, something Darvi didn't quite catch, sent them back to their plates.

"I put her in with Nate and Lindy," Cassy said after Eliot kissed her.

"Do you want some dinner?" Seth asked from beside her, but Darvi didn't answer. When she felt a hand on her back propelling her forward, she obeyed.

They crossed the big room and entered a short hallway. Two doors sat across from each other.

"You're in here," Seth whispered, his voice low, "with Nate and Lindy."

"Who are Nate and Lindy?"

"Cassy's children. They're already asleep, but you won't wake them. I'll get the lamp for you."

She was doing it again, and Seth had to harden his heart. The light caught the vulnerable look in her eyes; confusion and fear were plainly evident.

"No one will hurt you here," he said, keeping his voice low, not because of the children, but because of his runaway emotions. "Keep the light burning all night if you want. Sleep as late as you like. If you need something, Cassy and Eliot's room is right across from you. My room is back out through the big room and down a bit. Just call out if you need us, but don't try to run away. We're a long way from town."

Darvi could only stare at him.

That wasn't good enough for Seth. Speaking firmly, he asked, "Did you hear me?"

Darvi nodded.

"All right. Get some sleep now."

Saying this, the tall man exited and shut the door. When he got back out to the big room, the men were finishing up and heading back to the bunkhouse. Seeing him come, Cassy put a plateful of food down in his spot and watched him sit down.

"Is she all right?"

"I think so."

Cassy looked at him for a moment. "What makes you think she'll still be here in the morning?"

"Because right now she's too afraid to run. Before she's here two days, she'll figure something out, but right now her spunk is gone."

Cassy sat down and took a long drink of her coffee. She was a beautiful woman, smart and kind and head-over-heels where Seth's brother was concerned. She ran a successful cattle ranch, and for the most part, life was good. She'd been hoping for years that Seth would find a woman to love, but not like this, not one he had to capture. What she saw as equal amounts of good and bad in the brothers still amazed her. The good she saw in Seth made her want better for him than this.

"I can't say as I like her," Cassy admitted.

"Come on, Cass." This came from Eliot. "Give it a chance."

"He's supposed to find someone who loves him in return!" Cassy shot back at Eliot, both talking as though Seth wasn't there.

"It doesn't always work that way."

"Give it time." This came from the man in question, his voice calm and confident. "If she stays long enough, she'll love us."

"I hope that's true," Cassy said, "but if she doesn't like kids, you can haul her back to the train station or wherever she came from."

"I wouldn't expect anything else, Cassy."

Much of the tension left the table at that moment. These three had lived together and been friends for a long time. It was natural that Cassy didn't want another woman coming in to upset that balance.

"I'm turning in," Seth said, finishing his food and standing up. "Thanks for dinner."

"Are you going to keep watch?" Eliot wished to know.

"I don't think so. I'll be up early, and I somehow doubt she'll be gone. If she is, I'll deal with it then. Maybe you could just check on her when you retire, Cassy. I would, but if she's still awake, it might make it even harder for her."

"I'll do it. What's her name again?"

"Darvi. Darvi Wingate." The name was said softly, a gentle smile on Seth's mouth.

"Why now? Why her?" Cassy asked of Eliot after Seth went to his room.

"I've been asking myself the same questions."

"So what are we going to do?"

Eliot shrugged a little. "Just wait and see."

Ten

DARVI'S LIDS OPENED, AND SHE STARED at the log wall in front of her face. She frowned in confusion before closing her eyes in remembrance. Tempted to pinch herself, she knew it was useless. This was no dream, and it was time she faced that.

Rolling to her back, she spotted a window above her bed, sat up, and looked out. Bright sunshine filled the sky, and she could tell it was going to be another hot day. Just as suddenly as she remembered the last few days, she recalled having roommates. Before undressing last night, she'd taken the lamp close to the room's full bed and seen two sleeping children. She now looked that way, wondering if they were still abed.

What she saw made her blink. Sitting on the edge of the bed, dressed and ready to go for the day, was a little girl. She stared right back at Darvi, her expression open and curious.

"Hello," Darvi tried.

The little girl continued to stare.

"What's your name?"

"She can't talk," a little boy said from around the door he'd just opened a bit. "But her name's Lindy."

"Thank you," Darvi told him before turning back to the little girl. "Hello, Lindy."

She gave a little wave and smiled as the boy entered the room and sat beside her.

"I'm Nate," he supplied, his face just as open and friendly as his sister's.

"Well, Nate and Lindy, I'm Darvi. It's nice to meet you."

The words were no more than out of her mouth when someone knocked. Seth stuck his head around the door. Modest as her gown was, Darvi still reached for a bathrobe that wasn't there. She had to content herself with pulling the covers a little higher.

"Come on you two. Give Darvi some privacy."

"What did you call me?" Darvi asked as the children scrambled out.

"Darvi," he admitted, his eyes watchful.

"How long have you known?"

"Since before you fell off the bed yesterday morning." Darvi's eyes lit with flame.

"We can talk about it," Seth reassured her.

"Oh, no," Darvi countered, her voice tight. "*We* are not going to talk about anything. I'm not saying a word. *You* have a lot of explaining to do."

Seth only nodded. "Whenever you're ready."

Darvi got up the moment he shut the door. Certain she was finally going to get on that train, she dressed yet again in her navy suit, trying to ignore some of the creases, and from years of solid habit, made her bed. After packing her bag, Darvi went out to do battle. This was all before finding the large room almost empty. The woman they referred to as Cassy stood at the stove. As soon as she spotted Darvi, she took a plate from the oven.

"I have some breakfast for you," she spoke as she moved to put it on the table.

It was on the tip of Darvi's tongue to refuse, but then she saw it was dished up and ready.

"Thank you," Darvi only replied and sat down, thanking the woman again when she was served a steaming mug of coffee. Trying to calm her now-racing heart, Darvi bowed her head and thanked God for the food. She might never see this woman again, but she wanted her impression to be a favorable one.

"Darvi, is it?" Cassy asked when her guest's head came up.

"Yes, and you're Cassy?"

That woman nodded.

"I met your children. I hope I didn't disturb them."

"Not at all. There is a spare room, but it's right across from Seth's. He felt you would feel safer in with the children. You can move if you like."

"I appreciate the offer, but I won't be needing either room another night."

Cassy only nodded, knowing it would not help Seth's cause for her to comment.

"May I ask you where Mr. McDermott is, or, um, Seth? I don't know his last name."

"Redding. Seth Redding. Eliot had to run into town, and Seth is around somewhere. I know he wants to talk with you."

The eggs and steak on Darvi's plate were delicious, and so was the thick slice of bread, but it was somewhat lost on her. She spent the entire meal searching the door and windows for any sign of Mr. Redding. He didn't appear until after she was finished. As soon as Darvi saw him come in, she went for her bag. Back in the large room, the handle in her grasp, she spoke.

"You may explain to me when you return me to town."

"I'm not returning you to town, but we can go for a walk and I'll tell you what happened."

Darvi could have stomped her foot with frustration, but as with everything else in this situation, she was helpless. She set her bag back against one wall and followed Seth outside. He walked them toward the distant woods, his stride shortened to match Darvi's. Not that she was very close to him. She walked a few steps behind and some ten feet away. Seth glanced over at her stormy face and knew he would just have to begin.

"Eliot—he's my half brother—and I work for Jared Silk; he's a banker. He's not all that honest, but he pays us well, and we're good at what we do." He glanced to see if she was listening, but she looked away when their eyes met. "Jared's sick of Annabelle Hewett's column. If the truth be told, she's often right about him, but he wants her stopped. He came up with the plan to talk to her, and our job was to convince her to have dinner with him.

"The men we sent grabbed you because you look like her, and also because she's always headed somewhere. Her job takes her all over town, so it wasn't surprising they found you at the train station. We thought we had Annabelle until Eliot saw her heading into the news office early yesterday morning. By that time, it was too late."

"What was too late?"

"I had already decided that I liked you."

Darvi stopped and gawked at the man. She could hardly believe her ears.

"It's not forever, Darvi, at least your being forced to stay here isn't forever, but I'm just so sure that if you stay for a while, you'll come to care for us."

Darvi was stunned. This tall, confident, good-looking man was staring at her with his heart in his eyes. Darvi's head was spinning. She shifted her gaze to the wide open land and the trees beyond. Even from here she could hear the low sound of the cattle and understood how they made their living.

"Mr. Redding."

"Please call me Seth."

Darvi put her hand up. "All right. Seth. Let me get this straight. You work for a man who wanted a woman abducted and threatened, but the wrong woman was taken. Now that you've met me, and even realizing I'm not Annabelle Hewett, you want me to share your life?"

"I was hoping you weren't Hewett, since working for Jared would have made that relationship impossible. Much as I hated for you to be afraid, I was very pleased to learn you weren't her."

Darvi thought about the way she'd been treated in the last 48 hours. Not once had the men given the impression that she was going to be physically harmed. They had been downright gentlemen, but it didn't make what they had done less wrong.

"I get the impression that you're a very nice man, Seth. Your family," Darvi almost stumbled over the word, knowing Eliot was living with his girlfriend and her children, "seems very nice too. So how is it that you believe you can spot a woman, desire her, and take her?"

"I know it's outrageous, but I'm sure if I let you leave, I'll never see you again."

"That's right, you won't!"

Seth put his hands out as though he'd made his point.

Darvi could not believe this. Things simply didn't happen like this these days. This was 1882. This was civilization. A man simply did not come in, pick out the female he wanted, and carry her off into the night!

"You have to take me back to town," Darvi persisted, working to keep her voice even. "You have to return me so I can catch my train home. Have you thought about what my family might be feeling when I don't show up? You can't keep me, no matter how you feel. I am a person with rights and feelings, and I want to leave."

"To my head it sounds very logical, Darvi, but my heart's just not convinced."

Darvi threw up her hands in frustration and turned back toward the house, muttering all the way. She hit the door so angry she completely forgot that she wanted to make a favorable impression on Cassy.

"Do you know," she nearly shouted when she got inside, "that he plans to keep me?"

"He said as much," Cassy admitted, turning from the stove top and wiping her hands on her checkered apron.

"And do you condone this, or are you going to help me get out of here?"

"I can't help you leave, if that's what you're asking me. I wish Seth had done this another way, but I still won't interfere."

"Then you're a part of it."

Cassy shrugged. "I guess I am."

Darvi looked as stunned as she felt.

"He's a big boy, Darvi. I don't try to tell him what to do. I'm sure you can appreciate that."

As a matter of fact, Darvi could. She knew she must not take this out on anyone but Seth. In fact, she somehow sensed that not even Eliot was involved.

"We got ten!" Nate shouted as he and Lindy came through the front door. "Ten eggs!"

"Good job. Did anyone get pecked?"

The children proudly displayed their small hands.

"Hi, Darvi," Nate said when he spotted her. Lindy waved her greeting, but Darvi offered only a limp smile in return.

"Okay, you two," Cassy chimed in. "Get your slates. We've got some arithmetic to work on."

Cassy put the eggs to one side and came to stand near Darvi, her voice low.

"Is this your traveling suit?"

"Yes."

"It doesn't look like you're going to be getting on the train today. I've got some dresses if you want to change."

"I have two more dresses with me, but I thank you."

"Let me know if you need anything," Cassy said as she moved to her children.

A way out was Darvi's only thought, but she kept this to herself.

❧ ❧ ❧

But we all, with open faces beholding as in a glass the glory of the Lord, are changed into the same image from glory to glory, even as by the Spirit of the Lord. Therefore, seeing we have this ministry, as we have received mercy, we faint not, but have renounced the hidden things of dishonesty, not walking in craftiness, nor handling the word of God deceitfully, but by manifestation of the truth commending ourselves to every man's conscience in the sight of God. But if our gospel be hidden it is hidden to them that are lost. In whom the god of this world hath blinded the minds of them who believe not, lest the light of the glorious gospel of Christ, who is the image of God, should shine upon them.

Darvi read the verses from 2 Corinthians 3 and 4 a second and third time before sitting back thoughtfully.

She would not have chosen to be in this place, but she knew from other passages that God was in control. It was hard to imagine a reason for this, but she understood now that if others couldn't see the gospel—the good news of Christ—in her, they might remain lost. Darvi read the verses again.

But does that mean I just sit here? Or do I do something to get back to town? Darvi had no answer and kept on praying. *Lord, I need You to show me a way out of this. I will never love Seth Redding because he doesn't love You, but those verses say I'm to care about the souls of these people. Part of my heart still can't believe this has happened, but I know that You have Your eye on me.*

Darvi spent a little more time in prayer and in reading her Bible before changing into an everyday dress and going back out to the big room. Cassy and the children were still working at the table. They looked up when she came in.

"Are you any good with spelling?" Cassy asked.

"Pretty good. It all depends."

Cassy raised the book when Darvi approached.

"Is there a rule I can tell the kids about adding *ed* or *ing* to a word?"

"What words do you have for examples?"

"Well, "study" for one. Stud*ied* puts an *i* in, and study*ing* leaves the *y* in place."

"Oh." Darvi was sympathetic. "That is a hard one."

While the women pored over this, the children's noses pressed close as they listened, Seth came back. He had not wanted to rush Darvi, knowing she would need time to see that, unconventional though his approach may be, he wanted only to take care of her. He thought it might be easier if he made himself scarce for a time, but it had then occurred to him that she might be giving Cassy a hard time. He knew he couldn't allow that. Seeing her working at the table with some of the people he loved most in the world did his heart a world of good.

Not waiting to be invited, Seth joined them. Lindy went right for his lap, and when Cassy had the kids go back to their spelling words, she stayed right where she was. It was not lost on Seth, however, that Darvi never spoke to him or even looked at him. This surprised him—she didn't seem to be that type of person—but considering all the circumstances, he thought she might not have seen herself as having any other recourse.

He was relieved when Cassy had something else for the kids to do and called them away. Seth spoke quietly before Darvi could get away.

"Darvi, please don't tell me you're going to spend every day not looking at me or talking to me."

Darvi finally looked him in the eye, her own gaze regretful. "I have no desire to be mean or rude to you, and I appreciate your not hurting me or threatening me, but you need to know that if I could leave here, I would. You need to understand that I'm hoping you'll come to your senses and return me to town. I'm praying for that very thing."

Seth looked thoughtful, even as he reminded himself he was going to have to be patient.

"At least I know where I stand," he finally said. "And since you're so sure of your feelings, you can't object to my trying to change them."

He wasn't listening. Darvi shook her head to clear the confusing mix of emotions.

"I'm not the woman for you, Seth, and the sooner you face that, the easier all this will be."

"Now, there you're wrong. You are the woman for me. I know you are, and given time, you'll know it too."

Darvi looked into his eyes. He was completely serious. She had been close to only one other man in love, and that had been Brandon. Seth's eyes looked the same: tender and warm, full of eagerness to please, with just enough male interest to remind Darvi that he was a man. She stood up.

"Darvi, please don't go."

She paused, making herself meet his eyes.

"I'm not running from you. I just need to get out for a little while—for your sake, I might add, not mine."

"You're sure?"

She only nodded and started away.

"Darvi?"

She turned one last time.

"You look beautiful in that yellow dress."

Darvi didn't try to hold back her sigh, but she still said, "Thank you, Seth."

※ ※ ※

Even though Darvi was trusting the Lord to get her out of the mess she was in, she still set her mind to planning. She spent her first afternoon with the children, who showed her every inch of the barn. Darvi saw the chickens, the milk cow, several horses, a goat, and even two pigs. She also took note of the doors, where the saddles and tack were stored, and the access to the haymow. Her mind was working out how she could use all of this when she heard

Cassy say she was taking the wagon to town first thing in the morning.

The children were already in bed, and the big room was full of ranch hands. As Darvi was eating, a plan was forming, one that she saw no harm in trying. She had told Seth she didn't want to stay there, and she meant it.

"Excuse me—" a male voice finally got through to her. Darvi looked up to see one of the hands addressing her.

"Do you still write for the paper?"

Darvi shook her head. "You've confused me with someone else. I've never written for the paper."

The man, who was very well mannered—they all were—went back to his plate. Darvi did the same, but she could feel both Seth and Eliot's eyes on her. Choosing to ignore them and wishing the children hadn't gone to bed so early, Darvi finished her meal feeling very alone. It was a relief to see Cassy starting the dishes. Darvi left the table to offer her help.

"Why don't I wash?" she suggested, knowing the dryer had to know where to put things away.

"All right. Did you have enough to eat?"

"Yes, thank you, it was delicious." Darvi glanced at the half-dozen ranch hands still eating. "Did they come in for breakfast and lunch and I miss them?"

Cassy laughed. "No. My cook has been with me for years, but he's getting on. He wanted to retire, so I made a deal with him. If he would do the breakfast and the noon meals in the bunkhouse or on the range, I'd do supper for everyone, including him. He didn't even hesitate. He knew supper was the hardest meal of the day."

Darvi nodded, knowing what she meant. The platters that held the meat and side dishes were huge, not to mention the dozens of plates, bowls, and cups, along with all the flatware. Trying not to think of how her hands were going to feel when she was done, Darvi started in. She was impressed when she heard the men thanking Cassy on their way out, and even more so when both Seth and Eliot offered to help.

"I think for tonight we have it under control," she said kindly, "but don't forget us in the future."

The brothers also thanked her and went on their way. Unknown to Darvi, Cassy did this on purpose. She wanted to talk to the newest houseguest alone.

"Are you all right?" she started by asking.

"Yes," Darvi answered, but she didn't elaborate.

Cassy tried not to rush her feelings, but she couldn't help it. Only a few minutes had passed before she said, "I hope you know how much Seth wants this to work."

"I probably don't fully understand it, but then no one seems to understand my position either."

"What makes you say that?"

Darvi turned to look at her.

"Was this originally your ranch or Eliot's?"

"It was mine."

"So you brought Eliot here and held him until he fell in love with you?"

Cassy had the good grace to drop her eyes in shame, but it didn't last for long. The longing she was seeing in Seth's eyes was killing her. The other men had all they could do not to gawk at Darvi tonight, even though some of them had steady girls, but their eyes weren't filled with love the way Seth's were. Cassy knew how little they could promise. Seth could hand Darvi the world on a platter, and probably would.

"I guess I wish you'd give him a chance. I know it's just been a few days, but if you got to know him, you might feel differently."

"I already know some things I wish I didn't know."

"Like what?"

"I have no desire to show disrespect to you or the people you love, Cassy, but I'm horrified by what Seth and Eliot do for a living, and I'm sure I don't know the half of it."

"Talk to Seth. Your affection might mean that much to him."

"That's just it, Cassy, if I bring this up to him, he's going to think that if he changes, I'll love him. That's not going to happen."

Cassy's face clouded with anger. "What are the men like where you come from, Miss Wingate, that Seth Redding is not good enough?"

Darvi knew she should have held her tongue, but they had gone this far and she was going to finish it. She turned from the wash water and faced the other woman.

"Just a few months back I realized I was a sinner and needed to have a personal relationship with God. Because of God's Son, I'm a different person. I didn't have to do this; it was my free choice. But now that it's done, I'm working to live my life in a way that's pleasing to God, and one of those ways is not marrying a man who does not share my faith. The Bible is very specific about that.

"If Seth were to know Christ someday, that would be great, but he can't do that just to win me. He's got to do that for his own soul's sake. It's a matter between him and God. If I still sound to you as if I think I'm too good, I'm sorry, but God as my witness, my only desire is to do what I know to be right."

Cassy was stunned. Of all the things she expected to hear, this was not it. She had not an argument left in her head. She was not a religious woman, but she had high respect for anyone who was. Cassy dried a pot and watched Darvi's profile. She had to say something so Darvi would not think her upset. Absolutely nothing came to mind, but the dishes were almost done and she *couldn't* let it end like this.

"Thank you for telling me, Darvi."

Darvi turned in relief. She had remembered too late that this woman hadn't even bothered to marry the man she loved. Darvi had been wishing the tongue right out of her mouth. Cassy's words were an olive branch she was not going to turn down.

"I think we're about set here, Cassy. Is there anything else I can do?"

"No, thank you, Darvi. I think you've earned the right to put your feet up for the evening."

The women didn't exchange any more words, but both left the wash area with the small comfort that the strange relationship they found themselves in was still intact.

Eleven

"ARE YOU ALL RIGHT?" ELIOT ASKED CASSY when he retired that night.

"Um hm" was her only answer as she rocked in the chair. She was ready for bed but not there yet. For dozens of reasons Eliot knew her answer was not the end of it, but he was tired and just wanted to sleep, so he found himself somewhat cross with her.

"If you don't want to talk about it, Cass, that's fine, but don't say you're all right when you're not!"

Cassy didn't answer. She stayed in the chair even after Eliot climbed into bed, her heart pained and uncertain. She hadn't felt this way in a long time, not since after her husband had died and left her with a baby and a toddler and a ranch to run on her own. Those were black days, and she didn't want to go back there again, but some of the old feelings were returning.

"Cassy," Eliot said softly now, not able to sleep with her upset. "What is it?"

"She has strong religious beliefs."

"Darvi?"

"Yes. It's more than just being taken against her will; it goes against her belief in God. That really bothers me."

"Has she told Seth?"

"She won't do that," Cassy stated and went on to explain Darvi's reasons.

For a time the couple was silent.

"It's gotten me to thinking about the days after Chad died, about God and the way I was raised." Cassy turned to look at him for the first time. "I was raised to know better than to live with a man I wasn't married to."

Eliot was out of the bed in a flash, over to her chair and turning it so he could see her face in the light. With his hands tenderly holding her face, he whispered the words in his heart.

"I'm the one who's been asking you to marry me for five years, Cassandra. I can't promise I won't die, but I'm the one who's always wanted marriage. You'll get no argument out of me."

"Oh, Eliot. I don't know what I've been waiting for, but I think it must be time."

He leaned down and kissed her very softly.

"I also need to tell you, though," he knew he had to add, "this has nothing to do with God. I'm not sure there is a God. I think the only heaven we'll ever know is right here—good or bad—this is it. The only thing I know for sure is that I love you."

Cassy nodded. Her own beliefs were not that far distant from his. Her grandfather had been a preacher, but her own father had wanted nothing to do with God. He was moral to a fault over issues like drinking, wife beating, adultery, and fornication, but God was never mentioned. In truth, Cassy didn't know exactly what she believed. She only knew right now that she was tired. She finally climbed into bed, comforted by Eliot's presence beside her but wondering what it would be like to have the peace that Darvi Wingate seemed to own.

Darvi knew she would not be able to hold her breath, so she didn't even try, but by reciting her family's names very slowly, she was able to keep her breathing shallow. As she hoped, Cassy checked on the sleeping children before she left, not realizing Darvi was under the covers in her clothes and ready to make a run for the barn the moment the woman exited the room. She had done this and was now under the blanket behind the seat, barely able to hold her wits about her as she felt the team pull the wagon from the barn.

I'm going to make it! I'm really going to make it! Darvi had all she could do not to shout with delight. She'd been forced to leave her bag behind, but she would remedy that when she got to town and made a little call to the sheriff's office. She didn't have malicious thoughts toward these people, but what had happened to her could not be allowed without repercussions.

If she remembered correctly, she had spotted the law office when she and Dakota were trying to find the livery. She thought it might…

Darvi's thoughts were cut short, and her whole body jumped when the report of a rifle shattered the silence. She heard Cassy mutter, "What in the world?" and then felt the wagon slow and halt as a fast horse galloped up and stopped as well. Darvi's heart sank.

"I think you have a passenger."

It was Seth's voice.

"You're kidding" came from Cassy just before the blanket was tugged on and Seth came into Darvi's view.

"I'm going to town with Cassy." Darvi stated the obvious.

"No, you're not," Seth replied firmly, his hand already out to help her. Darvi ignored it. She climbed awkwardly from the wagon, none too pleased about being caught.

"Seth," Cassy began the moment Darvi stepped down, "I don't know if this is a good idea. She doesn't want to stay."

"There hasn't been enough time, Cass. You can't expect—" Seth stopped because Darvi was headed for the horse. It had no saddle, but she didn't care. He caught her around the waist and hauled her back to the wagon with him.

"I'll see you when you get back," he told Cassy, but she was far from pleased. She watched Darvi struggle in his arms but knew there was nothing she could do.

Clicking to the team, she set the wagon in motion just as Darvi landed a strong backward kick against Seth's shin. He grunted in very real pain but didn't let go until he had the horse's reins securely in his hand. That little move got him glared at, but he couldn't find it in his heart to be angry. He had brought this on.

"Do you want a ride?" he volunteered, even as the creak and rumble of the wagon faded in their ears.

Darvi didn't answer. She was too disappointed with her foiled plan. She thought that getting as far as she had meant she would actually make it.

I'm giving up, Lord. I thought it was a great idea, but we're just too isolated out here. At times I think I'm going to lose my mind. I'm trying to trust, but right now I just want to scream and run from here as fast as I can.

Darvi was so intent on her praying that she stumbled into a hole. Seth's hand was right there to catch her. She hadn't realized he was so close.

"How's your leg?" she asked, eyes ahead as she walked swiftly back.

"It hurts."

Darvi had all she could do not to smile, but she knew that would have been wrong. Was it wrong to kick the man who was holding her? That one she couldn't answer.

Returning to the house and going straight to her room, Darvi tried not to start planning again.

❧ ❧ ❧

Kinkade, Texas

"This church family is wonderful," Dakota said sincerely as he and Cash rode home together from an all-church Saturday afternoon picnic.

"I certainly think so. I mean, we're not without our problems, but God has greatly blessed in this place."

"Is Grandma's church like this?"

"Very much so, just smaller. Her pastor is a younger man with a young family. We've had some great talks, and he's very grounded in the Word and eager for his congregation to grow. Grandma adores him, and he never stops telling her what an encouragement she is."

Dakota was silent for a moment, the clop of the horses' hooves the only sound.

"Do you ever think about our situation, Cash?" the younger man asked thoughtfully. "I mean, the way God reached down for you and Gram, and now Slater and me? Sometimes it's almost more than I can take in."

Cash couldn't speak. He too was amazed at what God had done, but as always, his heart went to his parents.

I know You want their salvation more than I do, Father. Please help Dak and me to be the examples we need to be. Help my folks to find You before it's too late.

"I was just praying for the folks," Dakota said.

"So was I."

From there, the men rode home in silence.

Aurora

Darvi was tired of sitting in her room with no place to read but her bed. She had only her Bible with her, but she wasn't going to sit in this bedroom anymore. She didn't think Cassy was back—somehow she thought that woman might be leaning toward her side—but she was still going to go out to one of the chairs by the fireplace to read. To her relief, she found the room empty. Taking a comfortable chair, she welcomed the opportunity to look around.

It was an interesting layout. Only two rooms led off of the main room, and from what Cassy had said, they were both hallways to bedrooms. The big room held everything else: kitchen area, dining area, and living room furniture set up around the fireplace. There were windows on two sides. The kitchen table was long and wide with a variety of mismatched chairs. The two davenports and three rocking chairs were well worn but clean looking.

Darvi settled back with her Bible and turned a little to catch the light from the window. She had covered only two chapters when Eliot, Seth, Nate, and Lindy came in. Lindy came right to her, her eyes intent on Darvi's Bible. Darvi smiled and watched her touch the book and then pat her little chest.

"Do you have a Bible?"

She shook her head no and patted the Bible and her chest again.

"Do you want me to read to you?" Darvi wasn't long in catching on.

Her little head bobbed again, this time in excitement.

"I would be happy to read to you, Lindy, but you need to ask Mr. McDermott first."

The men couldn't help but overhear the conversation. After the events of that morning, Seth was keeping his distance, but Eliot came right over.

"Do you mind if I read the Bible to Lindy?"

The man looked completely untroubled. "Not at all." Even his voice was unconcerned. "It's just stories."

Eliot was on his way back across the room when Darvi asked Lindy a question.

"Do you have another book I might read to you, Lindy?"

The little girl frowned in confusion.

"I want to read to you, Lindy," Darvi clarified, "but I don't think these are just stories."

Eliot came back.

"Darvi, Cassy won't mind if you read the Bible to Lindy."

Aware that every eye in the room was on her, she still said, "But if I have to tell her this is just another storybook, *I* mind very much."

"Run and get a book from your room, Lindy."

When the little girl scampered away, Eliot met Darvi's eyes.

"So you think the Bible is from God?"

"Yes, I do," Darvi answered, glad that he understood what she was saying.

"I can't speak for Cassy on that, so if you don't mind reading something else..." Eliot let the sentence hang, as Darvi was already nodding.

"Not at all."

That was all the more time Lindy needed to come back with a thick book of nursery rhymes, stories, and poems. Darvi saw nothing wrong with the book, but it was something of a letdown for her. She sincerely hoped to read to Lindy from the Bible one day but invited the little girl into her lap and read from the story Lindy opened to. It was a familiar one from Darvi's childhood, and she had to fight the homesickness that welled up inside of her.

She wasn't usually prone to missing home so much, but she had been primed and ready to go back, even if there was a battle, and now having been cheated out of that, her heart yearned for home more than it ever had before. For a time she read without thought, her mind on how she and her parents had parted. She knew things would never be completely settled unless they came to Christ, but she also thought it was right to have as little tension as possible between them.

Not aware of the little girl's drooping lids, Darvi read through the entire story before she noticed that Lindy's head had fallen to the side. She set the book down, but because they were both comfortable, Darvi kept rocking and holding her. It was a bit warm to be cuddling, but the amazement of how kind and sweet these children were to her, a virtual stranger, wrung Darvi's heart. While they were sitting quietly, Seth joined them.

"Do you want me to take her?" he offered.

"She's fine, thank you." Both adults whispered.

Seth worked to keep the emotions from his face, but seeing Darvi with a child was doing wild things to his heart.

"Tell me, Seth, why aren't the children in school in town?"

"Nate was," Seth explained, "but when it was Lindy's turn to go, the teacher didn't believe that she couldn't talk. He believed she *wouldn't* talk. He hit her until she bruised and even bled. When Cassy learned of it, she nearly went after him with the shotgun but realized that it was violence that had gotten Lindy hurt. Instead, she never took either child back, determined to teach them on her own for all their school years if she had to."

Darvi could have cried. It was so sad and painful to think of someone hitting this mute little girl.

"Has she ever talked?" Darvi asked the question that suddenly came to mind.

"Yes, but when she wasn't yet three, she watched a bull gore her father to death. She hasn't uttered a word since."

Darvi couldn't take any more. She didn't want to care for these people. She didn't want to get attached to this place. She wasn't supposed to be here, not really.

Making herself speak normally, she closed the conversation.

"Thank you for telling me." With that Darvi laid her head back and closed her eyes. She didn't hear whether Seth left; she didn't care if he did, but she had to be finished hearing about this family.

I'm so totally off balance right now, Lord, I don't know what I'm doing. What is my place here? How do I deal with my captors? Lindy and Nate are innocent of what Seth has done and what their mother and Eliot are a part of. Help me to never take my frustration out on them, but I do ask You to take me from this place. I don't want to be here.

Darvi thought she might cry and made herself stop thinking such thoughts. She was very warm and uncomfortable and felt sweat starting to break out where Lindy lay against her. It was with nothing but relief that she heard a wagon approach. Lindy heard it too.

Perking up as if to say, "It's Mama!" she was off Darvi's lap in a flash.

Darvi stayed where she was, fanning herself slightly with her hand. Even Seth had gone to meet the wagon, and somewhere in the commotion she heard Cassy through an open window saying something about the next day being Sunday.

Where had the days gone?

Praying for renewed strength to make it through, Darvi put her Bible back on her bed. Not seeing any other help for it, she went out to join the family.

☙ ☙ ☙

"Oh, Darvi." Cassy spoke her name the moment she came from her room Sunday morning. "Do you have a moment?"

"Yes," Darvi said, noting absently that no one else was around.

"The men have gone into town and taken Nate along," Cassy volunteered, answering the unspoken question.

Determining not to start planning an escape and working hard not to think about how much she wanted to be in church, Darvi accompanied Cassy to her bedroom. Lindy was already there, sitting on the bed with a book. Cassy walked to the wardrobe, pulled a dress out, and hung it outside the door. This done, she stepped back.

"What do you think?"

"It's beautiful," Darvi said sincerely of the lavender gown with the long sleeves and high neck. It wasn't overly done with frills, but the bodice, neck, and cuffs were all trimmed in dark purple lace and strips of satin. The effect was very attractive, and it wasn't hard to imagine Cassy, with her blonde hair and blue eyes, looking very lovely.

"It's my wedding dress."

Darvi turned to look at her.

"You're getting married?"

"Yes, and it's all because of you."

Darvi didn't know what to say. She had questions but was afraid of the answers. What had she said or done to compel Cassy to get married? And what did Eliot think?

Watching her search for words, Cassy thought she might be more comfortable if Lindy left the room. Using gentle words, Cassy asked her daughter to take the book into the other room for a few minutes.

"I've shocked you," Cassy said when they were alone.

"You have, yes. I can't imagine what you mean."

Cassy became rather fascinated with her fingers and nails.

"I put it to Eliot this way: I was raised better than to be living with a man who wasn't my husband. Your convictions about God reminded me of that fact."

"And Eliot's not angry with me?"

"No. He's been asking me to marry him for five years, and I wouldn't. It's stupid on my part. I already buried one husband and somehow thought it wouldn't hurt as much to lose Eliot if we weren't married, so I didn't want to take any vows. It's ridiculous, I know. I can see that now."

Darvi was stunned. Cassy had not wanted to be married, but Eliot had. Where Darvi came from, catching a handsome husband was all young women could talk about; the men, on the other hand, until they were smitten, seemed to dread the very thought.

"Congratulations, Cassy," Darvi said suddenly, realizing she was being watched carefully. "When is the day?"

Cassy smiled. "We haven't gotten that far. I just happened to spot this dress yesterday, so I went ahead and bought it. Eliot likes it a lot, but we haven't really made further plans. But the kids are thrilled," she added swiftly, "and Seth hugged me and said it was about time."

This was not St. Louis. And never was Darvi more reminded of that. Women who took up residence with men without bothering to marry them were a shame and a disgrace in the community. Darvi didn't think she was too sheltered, but she couldn't honestly think of one woman who would admit to being intimate with a man outside of the bonds of matrimony. Texas wasn't as settled as Missouri certainly, but right and wrong were still right and wrong.

"Well, I'm happy for both of you, Cassy. I really am."

Cassy forced herself to say only a quiet thank you. She knew for a fact that Eliot was going to try to talk some sense into Seth, but knowing how stubborn the oldest brother could be, Cassy did not want to get Darvi's hopes up.

To distract herself, she offered breakfast and hot coffee to the other woman, not to mention she always cooked a slab of beef on Sunday afternoons, and time was awasting.

※ ※ ※

"Do I look all right to you?" Seth suddenly asked Eliot.

Eliot frowned at him. "You look like you always do. Why, are you feeling sick?"

"No."

Seth's answer was short and he broke eye contact with Eliot, but Eliot was not done. He'd been hoping all morning for a lead-in of some type.

"Why did you ask?"

"I don't know. I was just wondering if maybe she finds me repulsive or something."

"They don't think like we do, Seth. When are you going to see that?"

The other man didn't answer. Eliot tried again.

"You can't expect to hold her body and have her heart follow."

Seth's eyes closed. The words about holding Darvi were a little too much for him right now. He had been tempted so many times just to grab her and kiss her until she knew she was loved, but her eyes held him at bay. She was not a woman to be trifled with, and he didn't want to do anything now that might mess up his chances later, not to mention the fact that he could still feel where she kicked him in the shin.

"I just need to give her some more time," Seth repeated in honest belief. "I can already see that Cass and the kids care for her. Her heart is tender and sweet. She'll come to love us. She'll come to love me. She won't be able to help herself."

Eliot knew the door was closed. He didn't agree, and he knew Cassy hated it this way, but this was not his call.

Five minutes later the men left the dining room of the hotel. Jared had scheduled a meeting.

❧ ❧ ❧

Darvi had told herself not to plan. She had scolded and carried on in her heart, but that hadn't stopped her feet from taking her toward the barn. She had helped Cassy with some things in the house for a time, even going to get eggs from the barn and vegetables from the garden with the children, but now her mind was on escape, and she was not going to be stopped. If only she could get out right after everyone went to bed for the night. She knew she couldn't hide in the bunkhouse—that could be disastrous—and if she hid in the barn, that would be the first place they would look. Then she thought of the outhouse. Would anyone ever think to look behind it? Darvi surreptitiously moved around the outside of the barn now to have a look, rounded a corner, and ran smack into Eliot.

Not bothering to hide her frustration, she crossed her arms over her chest and looked very stern.

"I thought you were in town."

"I was, but I dispensed with my business and I'm back."

She watched Eliot smile at her and knew he'd figured her out.

"Will you please talk to him?" she entreated quietly. "Will you please tell your brother he can't do this?"

"It won't do any good, Darvi. He loves you."

"He can't love me." Frustration rose in her voice. "He doesn't even know me."

Eliot shrugged. "Sometimes it works like that. I set eyes on Cass five years ago, and I've never gotten over it."

It was one of the most romantic things Darvi had ever heard, but it wasn't right—not here, not now.

"Why me?" was all she could think to say.

Again Eliot smiled. "Maybe if he had seen you on the street and not met you like he did, you would feel differently. He's not going to let you go, Darvi, so you might try to figure out if there's something about him you can love."

"Eliot, it doesn't work that way. Surely you can see that?"

"I can, yes, but then no one is trying to take Cass and the kids away from me. I know I wouldn't be so reasonable then."

Darvi could see that no amount of words would sway him. They stared at each other for a few moments before Eliot, still dressed up for town, moved and held out an arm for her to lead the way. Darvi wanted to argue that she didn't want to go back inside just yet, but mentally her mind was growing strong. She'd let them think she was going along with everything they asked, but if she ever got a chance to leave, she'd be gone before anyone could take another breath.

Twelve

Kinkade

"I THINK I'LL HEAD OUT TOMORROW AND visit Gram," Dakota said after dinner on Monday night.

"Okay," Cash agreed quietly, setting his paper aside.

Dakota was not looking at him, which gave the older brother a chance to study him. Something was wrong. He didn't know what. Indeed, he couldn't imagine what was troubling him, but Dakota was clearly tense. Cash had never been anything but direct in the past and saw no reason to change now.

"Out with it, Dak," he ordered.

That man looked up and frowned.

"Out with what?"

"That's just it; I don't know. But something is wrong. I can tell."

Dakota looked at him. It didn't take long to admit, at least to himself, that something was on his mind.

"You're going to think I'm crazy."

"I already do."

Having Cash tease him was all he needed. In the next few minutes he offered a rundown on his time with Darvi and ended it by explaining what happened after he put her on the train.

"So you never saw this woman's face?"

"No, and if I think about it long enough I go around in circles. It hasn't been that many days, but I just wish there was some way to get word about whether she arrived safely." Dakota stopped and stared at his brother. "Will I trust more when I've been at this longer, Cash? I want to leave it in God's hands, but if anything should happen to Darvi, it would be all my fault."

"How do you figure?"

"I was responsible to get her home."

"No, you weren't. You just told me you had to get her on the train in Aurora. If you hadn't had it in your heart to keep in touch with her and gone back for an address, you wouldn't know a thing. None of what you've described is your worry. I can see why you're concerned, but you did your job."

Dakota honestly couldn't argue with him there.

"Did you see anyone else in town who you could have mistaken her for?"

Dakota shook his head. "Not in the brief time I looked around, but it's a good-sized city. It's hard to know just how far to track."

Cash could see his point, and it was unsettling.

"Have you sent word to Brace?"

"You mean asking if he's heard from Darvi?"

"Right."

"No, I didn't want him to think anything was wrong when I had no proof. I guess I could ask without voicing any of my doubts."

"Why don't you do that? It's a normal enough question."

Dakota thanked Cash for the advice and decided to stop at the telegraph office on his way to his grandmother's the next day. He asked for a section of the newspaper and both men settled in to read.

☙ ☙ ☙

Dakota felt better having talked to Cash and went to bed with a light heart. He didn't figure on what would happen in the morning. Cash was in his room before he even finished dressing.

"I'm not a man given to foolish notions," he said without greeting his brother. "You would agree with that, wouldn't you, Dak?"

"Absolutely."

"So what I'm about to say to you might seem strange."

"Okay."

"Go back to Aurora and check again for Darvi."

Dakota stopped all movement.

"Do you mean it, Cash? You really think I should go?"

"Yes, I do. I can tell you want to, and I ache at the thought that Darvi might be in trouble. I don't want you to head off on a wild goose chase, but the truth of the matter is she could have been taken from the train. If you don't find her, we'll have to wait until you get word from Brace as to whether or not she arrived. If she does need you, you'll be there all the sooner."

Dakota was thoughtful. His brother was certainly not given to impulsive or rash behavior. It had been on Dakota's heart off and on that Darvi might need him, but he had felt so helpless. Having Cash be so practical about checking back in Aurora was all the permission he needed.

"I'll start right after breakfast."

"All right. I'll make sure Katy has provisions for you. Do you have any money?"

"Yes, I went by the bank yesterday."

Dakota had been enjoying his time with Cash very much, and he loved working the ranch, but the incident with Darvi and the train had left him doubting himself. He thought it had been God's way of testing him to see if he was truly trusting, and it might have been, but it was with a light heart that he headed back the way he had come. He asked God for wisdom and strength but also found himself talking to the woman herself.

If you need me, Darvi, I'm on my way.

֍ ֍ ֍

Aurora

"What is it?" Darvi asked Seth without taking the box he held out to her. They were alone by the trees to the west where Seth had found Darvi walking.

"Just take it," he urged.

"Not until you tell me what it is."

"It's a gift for you."

Darvi's hands went behind her back.

"You've got to stop bringing me gifts, Seth. This is not going to work."

"Just take it."

Darvi eyed him and the box.

"I'll take the box and look in it, but that doesn't mean I'm accepting this gift."

His eyes were warm with amusement, and Darvi almost wished that he would grow angry.

He wasn't constantly around, but since Sunday, if he was anywhere in the vicinity, he was courting her. He had brought her flowers, both from town and along the roadside. A book of poems arrived one day, and a comb for her hair the next. Gifts would come to the ranch even when he hadn't gone to town but Eliot had. This told Darvi that Seth was planning ahead.

Darvi had started to mark the days in her Bible as they passed. She had been on Cassy's outlying ranch for eight days, and each day she had to work at trusting God to bring this nightmare to an end.

"Take it, Darvi," he urged one last time, and Darvi did so.

She opened the box and peeked inside. What she saw made her eyes huge before she nearly threw the gift at him and tried to run. She didn't get far. His arms came around her, and for the first time he attempted to hold her close. Darvi tried to get away, but there was no possibility of overpowering him. When Darvi saw escape wasn't going to work, she planted her palms against his chest and held herself away from him as much as she could. When she looked up, he spoke.

"The ring isn't for now," he panted slightly, "but it's to show you that I'm serious about us."

Darvi started to shake her head.

"Don't say no. Give us a chance. I know we could have a wonderful life together, and the ring is to prove that to you. You say the word, and we'll be married. That's how strongly I feel about you."

Darvi could only stare at him. What in the world was she to do?

When she froze, Seth's head started to descend.

"Don't!" Darvi commanded with some force, and he stopped with several inches still separating them.

Seth studied her features very slowly, his eyes warming noticeably.

"That upside-down mouth of yours is going to drive me crazy."

Darvi's chin came up. "Let me go."

Seth did so, although very slowly, his eyes never leaving her face.

"I'll never marry you," Darvi said quietly, "and if that's what you're waiting for, then you can release me now."

Their eyes met for long seconds, and for the first time Darvi saw a flicker of something other than patience. To her surprise, it didn't frighten her.

"Keep your hands to yourself, Mr. Redding," she added in low fury, "or I won't be responsible for my actions."

Still meeting his eyes to tell him she meant business, she took several more seconds before turning and walking back to the house. She wasn't a dozen feet along when she heard him behind her, but he did not attempt to catch up to her or to engage her in conversation, all of which was fine with Darvi. She had nothing else to say to the man.

❧❧❧

"She doesn't want him," Cassy whispered in frustration. "Why can't he see that?"

Eliot didn't answer. Cassy had just taken her hair down, and he was rather preoccupied with the way it looked. He leaned over the bed to kiss the side of her neck, but she turned and glared at him.

Seeing it, Eliot shook his head in longsuffering.

"Let me get this straight. You're mad at Seth, so you're going to take it out on me."

Cassy frowned. That was exactly what she'd been about to do. Now feeling upset with herself, she turned back away from him. Eliot didn't want to talk about Seth and Darvi right now, but he made himself join her on the edge of the bed and even took her hand when they sat side by side.

"What is it you want me to do?"

"That's just it—I don't know. I know they're both unhappy, and I feel so helpless. It would be great if she could stay. She's so sweet with the kids and willingly helps out, but this isn't where she belongs, and as much as I want Seth's happiness, I can't agree with what he's doing to Darvi."

Cassy turned her head to look at him. "If someone took Lindy and wouldn't let her go, I'd be out of my mind with worry. Seth has got to see that he's doing the same thing to Darvi's family."

Eliot didn't like this comparison at all. Lindy was like his own child, and this analogy hit a little too close to home for him.

"I'll talk to him again."

Cassy did not look grateful.

"I'd better warn you, Eliot McDermott," she threatened. "If I get a chance to help Darvi get out of here, I'm going to do it."

Eliot put gentle arms around her, but the voice at her ear was very firm.

"You will do no such thing."

"Do *not* tell me what to do!"

She suddenly wanted nothing to do with him, but Eliot did not let her pull away. In fact, he slipped an arm under her knees and deposited her on his lap. Cassy's eyes were filled with betrayal as she looked at him, and Eliot almost wished she would struggle some. He smoothed the hair from her face, his hands gentle and his heart filled with love.

"I'm sorry that Darvi is caught in the middle of this and that you're hurting over it too, but I'm not going to betray my brother, and if you think about it, you don't want to either."

Cassy's eyes filled with tears.

"It's a lousy excuse, but Darvi is not in any danger here. Seth's intentions toward her are honorable. I do think he's going to see pretty soon that she's not going to change her mind, but taking her from him is not the answer. He's got to come to it on his own."

Cassy still wanted to be angry, but Eliot was right.

"Cassandra..." Eliot's voice came softly to her ear.

Cassy looked at him.

"What day are you going to become my wife?"

Feeling almost shy, she fiddled with the apron she still had on and refused to look at him.

"I don't know."

"You have the dress, which means we're halfway there. I'm not going to let you get away from me now."

Cassy looked up with a smile. She loved him so much.

"You name the day," she was able to say, knowing it was time.

"October 30."

"Oh!" Cassy had not been prepared for such a definite answer. "When is that?"

"Two weeks from this Saturday."

A measure of panic clawed at her throat, but she wasn't able to talk about it as Eliot was lifting her and setting her on her feet. He then bent, kissed her brow, and started toward the door.

"Where are you going?"

"To the spare room."

It took a moment for Cassy to catch on, and when she did, her eyes softened with emotion.

"I love you," she said.

Eliot smiled. "And I love you, Cassy girl. I wouldn't be heading out this door for any other reason."

Cassy let him leave, but her heart was ready to burst. She couldn't possibly explain what had just happened to Darvi but wanted once again to thank her. Had it not been for Darvi, Cassy might not have seen the misguided direction of her entire life. She was convinced that she would have gone on for years living in sin with Eliot and not thinking about the right thing to do.

She got ready for bed very slowly, missing Eliot's presence already but knowing it was for the best.

Seth is the same kind of man, Cassy thought as she settled under the covers. *His and Eliot's jobs are not always the best, but they're good men who know how to love.* Completely forgetting Darvi's beliefs, her heart was quiet for a moment before wishing: *If only Darvi had met him some other way.*

※ ※ ※

"My name is Dakota Rawlings," Dakota said to Aurora's sheriff. "I'm a Texas Ranger."

The other man stuck his hand out to shake Dakota's.

"Joe Laverty. What can I do for you?"

"Actually, I just wanted to let you know I'm going to be in town for a few days, maybe longer. I've lost track of someone, and I think this person might be in your town."

"Who is it?"

"I'm not at liberty to say right now, but I wanted you to know that I plan to stay out of the way and do my job as quietly as possible."

The sheriff, who had respect for most Rangers, thought Dakota seemed genuine. He was a curious man and didn't like not knowing exactly what was going on, but since the Ranger had stated his willingness to stay out of the way, he knew he'd have to let it go.

"Well, if we can be of any help from this office, be sure to let me know."

"Thank you, sir."

"Where will you be staying?"

"I'll probably camp outside of town. I noticed you have a bathhouse and a number of eating establishments." Dakota smiled a little. "It looks as though I'll be able to stay clean and fed."

When Dakota turned on the charm, it could be very effective, and it worked now. Sheriff Laverty smiled reluctantly and only waved when Dakota moved to the door and went on his way.

He'd arrived the day before, not late in the day by any means, but late enough to put off a visit to the local constabulary. The day was fresh, the visit to the sheriff was taken care of, and now Dakota was headed out into the streets of Aurora to see what he could find. He sensed that it was a well-settled town with what appeared to be many successful businesses, and as a rule the folks seemed friendly.

Not wishing to draw any undue attention to himself, Dakota had arrived in clothing a little less suited to his work than usual and having already let his beard go a few days. It didn't take him long to look scruffy, and that was just what he wanted. Eli was at one of the liveries, and Dakota now prepared to move about on foot and have a closer look around Aurora. Not knowing exactly what he was looking for made things a bit tricky, but he was certain that if something was amiss in this town, he would spot it.

A horrible feeling of dread came over him as he thought about how easy it would be to take a woman and disappear with her, but Dakota forced himself away from those thoughts. It would only disturb his concentration and hinder his goal. He didn't know when or where he would find answers, but look he would.

It occurred to him very suddenly that he could wire Brace and Darvi's family from Aurora and ask after her, but he hesitated. If she'd made an appearance, he could return to his life. If she hadn't... Deciding to give it at least a few more days, Dakota began his tour.

🌸🌸🌸

Cassy was nearly pacing before Darvi emerged from her room the next morning. The strawberry blonde had been very quiet at dinner the night before and retired to her room the moment she was able. Cassy had not witnessed the exchange with Seth, but she knew from watching both people that something had gone on. She and Eliot were to be married in only two and a half weeks, but Cassy was not waiting to tell Darvi that. She just wanted to make sure she was all right.

Breakfast was long over, cleanup was done, the men had headed into town, the hands were out with the stock, and the children sat reading books. There were dozens of things Cassy could do, but she wanted to see Darvi first. All of Eliot's talk was not doing her any good at the moment. His telling her that they couldn't take Darvi from Seth and that deep in her heart she wouldn't really want that was sounding very hollow in her ears right now. If she didn't want to, then why did she wish she could load Darvi into the wagon and take her to the train? She and the children could give her a nice send-off.

Cassy was beginning to get quite worked up over this idea when the bedroom door opened. She turned to see Darvi enter, her mouth set.

"Where is Seth?" she wasted no time in asking.

"He and Eliot went into town."

Darvi's shoulders slumped. She had been ready to do battle with the man, and now he was gone.

Just the sight of Darvi turned all of Cassy's intentions to dust. It wasn't that she hadn't seen Darvi in the pale blue dress in the past, but today her cheeks were blooming with color and her eyes sparkled. And it wasn't just that. Darvi was one of the sweetest women the ranch owner had ever known.

Cassy had never been in such a quandary. It was so easy to see why Seth loved Darvi, and for that reason, Cassy could not interfere. She found her heart reasoning that Seth might be correct: Maybe Darvi would come to love him and wish to stay.

"I don't suppose there's anything I can do," Cassy finally voiced, knowing that she could, but wouldn't.

"Not unless you're willing to take me back to town," Darvi said, not bothering to read the other woman's expression or to wait for an answer. She headed out the door then, around the house, and toward the barn.

As yet, Cassy had never hindered her from looking around. Knowing that both brothers were gone left her free to look a little. She told herself she wasn't exactly planning, but if something just happened to jump out at her, she'd be foolish not to give it notice.

Once inside the dark reaches of the barn, she looked out at the house. The bedroom window above her bed appeared to be some four feet off the ground. She had tested the window just that morning and been surprised to find that Seth had not nailed it shut. There was nothing to step on when she climbed out, so it would be a bit of a drop, but neither was there a prickly bush to fall into.

"Darvi!" Cassy called from near the house.

Darvi waited a moment and emerged into the sunlight. "Yes?"

"Would you like something to eat?"

"Is it near noon?"

"No, but the children are hungry, and you didn't get breakfast."

Darvi waved. "Thank you. I'll be right in."

Still feeling as though she might have one person on her side, Darvi was pleased to see that Cassy didn't hesitate but turned around and went directly back inside. Darvi followed at a snail's pace, taking note of the layout of her window at close range. She had no idea if the information would ever be useful, but somehow she felt better for being prepared.

❧ ❧ ❧

Sitting down in the hotel to treat himself to a hot meal for lunch on his third day in town, Dakota ate slowly and gave himself plenty of time to think. He was not discouraged, but he was starting to wonder a bit. Were things in this town just a little too neat, or was he getting overly suspicious with his line of work and Darvi's disappearance? Was the law doing its job in Aurora?

Two days had passed, two full days of watching, waiting, and making subtle inquiries, and still he had no leads as to what might have happened to Darvi. He'd all but stalked the alley where he thought she might have been taken, but there was nothing of even the slightest interest going on.

He learned that at least five stills were set up in full operation, quietly attended but working nevertheless. He found two homes where men came and went at all hours of the night, but the saloons appeared only to have some dancing and lots of cards and drinking.

What he'd seen of the law in action had been impressive. He had watched an officer haul a man off for spending a little too much time outside the home of Mrs. Gillham, who gave piano lessons to the town's young ladies. Several drunks had made trips to the jail, and when one of the general stores had a customer who refused to pay, the law answered in great haste.

"What can I get you?" a friendly woman in a clean apron asked as she appeared at his table.

"How about the special?"

"With or without gravy?"

"With gravy, please, and coffee."

"For one?" she asked with more than a little show of interest.

Dakota smiled. "Yes, thank you."

She was smiling in return, her eyes inviting, causing the Ranger to shake his head as she walked away. He hadn't shaved in days.

Maybe she likes scruffy, half-started beards, he speculated even as his stomach growled. Glancing around to see if she was bringing his coffee, Dakota froze.

He forced himself to look down at the tablecloth before shifting his gaze again. He could hardly believe what his eyes were telling him. His coffee was delivered, but he took little notice. He didn't even pick up the mug. All he could do was ask himself why he had thought he needed to come back to Aurora.

Thirteen

I CAN'T BELIEVE THIS, LORD. I HAVEN'T BEEN ABLE to get Darvi from my mind. I told Cash all about it and made him concerned, and here...

Dakota stopped and tried to slow his racing thoughts before glancing over at another table in the hotel restaurant. Sitting with two male escorts was a woman of striking appearance. She was also a near twin to Darvi Wingate. Dakota had all he could do to keep his teeth in his mouth.

Was this the woman I saw that day? Had the incident at the train all been completely innocent?

Dakota made himself take a few deep breaths. He didn't want to overreact, but that was taking some effort. By sheer force of will, he kept himself from dashing to the other table and demanding from the woman her whereabouts the day he put Darvi on the train.

"Here you go." The waitress had returned, placing a steaming plate of food in front of him, the edges nearly running over with a huge cut of beef and a heap of mashed potatoes, both covered with a dark gravy, which also ran into a mound of cooked greens.

"Thank you," Dakota said quietly, too distracted to miss her disappointment at not gaining more eye contact.

The Ranger ate slowly. After the initial shock wore off, he noticed that by using a large oblong mirror right across from his table, he had an almost perfect view of the woman and two men.

Already planning to wire Cash about his mistake and then head home in the morning, Dakota ate in a leisurely fashion, his heart calming some even as he glanced in the mirror from time to time. He was nearly through with his meal when he noticed something else. A man, fine in dress and manners, sat a few tables away from the strawberry blonde, a newspaper propped in front of him. Even though the man never lowered the paper from reading level, neither did he look at it. With remarkable consistency, he kept his eyes on the woman's table. No one sat at the tables in between, and the woman's table was against a wall. There could be no other person holding his interest. And if that hadn't been enough to convince the Ranger, he eventually watched the woman and two gentlemen exit, just 15 seconds before the lone man got up to follow.

Dakota left a coin on the table to cover both meal and tip and did a little following of his own. He still planned to wire Cash and tell him he had it all wrong, but he didn't think he'd say he was headed home, at least not yet.

❧❧❧

"Why didn't you go to town today?" Darvi asked in frustration.

"I wasn't needed," Seth told her calmly, completely ignoring everything she'd said that morning.

Arms crossed tightly, Darvi tapped her foot impatiently and nearly shooed him as she would the dog. The children were helping their mother bake a cake, and to get out of the house and away from Seth's watchful eyes, Darvi had volunteered to get the eggs. It hadn't made any difference. Seth tagged along right behind her, even though she had let him have a good piece of her mind that morning over her captivity.

"I don't need help getting eggs, Seth," Darvi said as she turned her back and walked away from him.

"You never know," he replied, bringing up the rear with this assurance. "Some of those hens can be pretty feisty."

Darvi didn't answer, but Seth didn't care—he much preferred her to be like this. When she got all quiet and sad, he had to make himself continue with his plan. When she was fiery and told him what for, he knew he'd never let her go.

He was still shaking his head about how he'd found her. Never in his life had he imagined such a woman existed. Never had he known such a mix of fire and uncertainty. He knew he would love her for the rest of his life.

"And why don't you just tell me," Darvi suddenly spun and demanded, "just what is it you do for this Jared Silk?"

Seth shrugged. "Whatever he needs."

"Like what?"

"Oh, a little of this and a little of that."

Her arms crossed again. "I hope you know that was ridiculously vague."

"Was it?"

Darvi's eyes narrowed. "It's rude to answer a question with a question."

Seth stopped just short of saying, "Is it?"

"Go ahead and ask me about my work," Seth encouraged her. "I'll try to answer."

This took Darvi by surprise. She didn't want to get close to this man. Her chin rising, she laid it on the line.

"No matter how you answer me, it's not going to stop my wanting to leave."

"I understand that. Go ahead and ask."

"Is he a banker?"

"Yes."

"Why would a banker want you to take a woman from the train unless he's hiding something? What gives either one of you the right to do such a thing?"

Knowing she wouldn't like the answer, Seth hesitated. Jared's view—as well as his own—was that a man did what he had to do. Seth knew he didn't look the part of a criminal, and rarely did he use the word to describe himself, but deep in his heart Seth Redding knew what he was. He also knew that wherever Darvi Wingate was from, she did not socialize with people who considered themselves above the law. Not having Jared here to defend himself, Seth let him take the heat.

"Jared feels that sometimes we do what we have to do. It's not too much more complicated than that."

"Not complicated?" Darvi said in disbelief, her mouth open. "You step in and turn people's worlds upside down, and I'm supposed to see that as simple?"

Seth had nothing to say. He hadn't expected her to respond like that and knew anything he might tell her just now was only going to push her further away. He was glad when she turned again for the barn. He hadn't liked the little shake of her head, the one that said she was offended by his actions, but at least he didn't have to explain himself anymore.

Quite suddenly he found himself wishing he had let her gather eggs on her own.

$$\text{3-3-3}$$

It didn't take long to see that the redheaded woman was well known and liked in Aurora. Dakota kept his distance behind both the woman, who now walked alone, and the man who followed her from the hotel, but he still thought he caught a name now and again.

Ann Bell. Dakota was certain he had heard right. He had stopped in front of the bank—looking for all the world as though he was window shopping—and was quite sure this was what people were calling her. Neither she nor the man stopped near the bank, but Dakota had caught up a little too swiftly. He took his time fixing his boot, hoping no one was onto him, and in less than a minute was on the move again.

His work paid off. The woman went into the newspaper office, and the man took up a position to watch everything that went on behind the large front window of the building. Dakota could see that even a rear exit would be detected. Dakota decided to go for his horse. The woman was distinct enough that he'd be able to describe her to the sheriff and get some answers, but the man was another story. If the man sat all afternoon and watched the news office, Dakota would regret retrieving Eli, but if he made a big move, Dakota wanted his horse.

Knowing that the man could be long gone before he returned, Dakota nevertheless fetched Eli, tied him in the alley, and went back to stalking the stalker. As Dakota watched him, he felt a grudging admiration. The man was cool, very cool. When a lady passed, be she 15 or 50, he raised his hat and gave a polite bow. He didn't appear to be observing anyone, but he keenly noted any activity involving the door of the news office.

Dakota was beginning to think that the life of a detective was a curse. His restless limbs were begging to move when the man consulted his pocket watch and walked down the street. Dakota left Eli where he was and moved just enough to watch the man enter the Aurora Bank. Dakota wondered how long he could take the inactivity. He knew very well that the man could leave out the back somewhere and he would never be the wiser. Heavily exhaling with relief, Dakota noticed the man had reappeared and was headed into the very livery where Dakota had boarded his horse. Dakota moved again, this time to mount up and be ready. Again, his patience paid off.

Coming from the livery on a fine animal—a city horse, as Rangers thought of them—the man rode south down the main street of town. He was not a short man, and his horse was of a size that made it easy to track. Dakota was careful to look disinterested as the man hit the edge of town and kept right on moving. He never picked up the pace but rode easily, his attitude that of a man without a care in the world.

Down the road some five miles, Dakota watched the rider calmly turn down a well-worn side road. Dakota kept his eyes forward and allowed Eli to plod along, but only until a group of trees hid him from view, whereupon he doubled back through the woods, working to gauge just where the man might be headed.

Long before he was close enough to see anything, Dakota heard cattle. Only a few hours of daylight were left, so he moved swiftly along, dodging branches and low limbs in an attempt to see where the man might have gone. It took some doing. While still trying to stay out of sight, he made occasional visits to the edge of the tree line and checked the view. At last he saw something just at the edge of a barn. A few more feet and maybe...

Dakota stood and stared. In a remarkably picturesque setting sat a large, low farmhouse and a huge barn. The buildings were in fine condition, and as he watched, it looked as though a child was running in the yard, a little girl with flowing blonde hair.

Tying Eli up the hillside a bit, Dakota dug his field glasses from his saddlebags and climbed a tree. With enough light to still see things clearly, he methodically went over every building and scrap of ground. No one was visible until a man emerged from what appeared to be a bunkhouse to throw out a pail of water. An outhouse stood beyond that structure, as did one for the main house.

Dakota was in the process of planning how to get into the barn when he saw her. The hair was the first thing to catch his eye, and then the field glasses did the rest. Never taking his eyes from her, Dakota watched Darvi stand at the corner of the porch, her gaze locked on the road that led to the ranch. A moment or two passed before she looped an arm around the porch support and leaned there.

Dakota was still watching when the little blonde girl appeared, held something out for Darvi to see, and then took her hand to lead her back inside. Dakota scanned the windows of the house but saw no sign of life. Shaking just a little, the big man climbed from the tree and moved to Eli. Once next to the horse, his arm went across the saddle and he buried his face. A sob broke in his chest as he prayed.

You knew she was here; You knew. Please help me. Please let me rescue this woman before she comes to any more harm. I want to ride down there and take her and defy anyone to stop me, but something isn't right here. I've got to go slow and use my head.

Dakota took some moments to compose himself before climbing back up into the tree. He watched until darkness filled the sky but caught no further sight of anyone he could be certain was Darvi. The decision to camp in the woods was no decision at all. Scouting the area for safety and privacy, Dakota settled down early. He didn't dare light a fire and was glad he'd eaten a large lunch, but in fact, his stomach was not really on his mind.

Not interested in lying down right away, he sat for a long time in the dark and thought about what might have gone on at the ranch. It seemed a good sign that at least one child appeared to live in the house. That didn't mean the adults in the situation could be trusted, but the child appeared happy and carefree as she played. And at least from a distance, Darvi looked all right. Dakota was thankful for that much, but he knew even without getting closer that she didn't want to be there. And for that reason alone he was intent on getting her out just as soon as he could manage it.

It was well and truly late by the time Dakota sought his rest, but it was a peaceful sleep. He hadn't been able to read his Bible, but he prayed off and on for hours. He also fell asleep with a plan. He would put it into action in the morning.

§-§-§

Darvi groaned a little as she bent over to pick up the spoon she'd just dropped. Nate had finished his breakfast but not cleared his place. Darvi stooped, and sticky as the utensil was, she managed only to lose it again.

"You sound stiff," Cassy commented.

"I am."

"Is it your mattress?"

"It might be," Darvi guessed, not having thought of it.

"Nate slept on that one for a time and said it was a bit lumpy."

Darvi decided not to comment. She didn't think it would do any good to complain about the mattress, but more than that, she had just noticed that Seth was in the room. She was not giving him the cool treatment or anything too dramatic, but if he was in the room, which was too often for her comfort, Darvi was careful with what she said and did.

"I'll check it for you, Darvi," Cassy now offered, thinking that her silence meant she was a bit unhappy about it.

"Thank you. Do you want me to do anything special with this water?" Darvi asked from her place by the sink.

"Why don't you just dump it? I'll send Nate for fresh."

Seth had learned not to take things from Darvi—he knew she did not want him to coddle her—but that didn't stop him from following her outdoors. He stayed well back when she poured the water on the flowers at the side of the house but was right close when she turned.

"You can always try my mattress," he said gently, his gaze tender and inviting. "It's not lumpy at all."

Darvi barely hesitated before drawing her foot back and kicking him in the shin. Her foot hurt with the impact, but having him double over with pain was well worth it. Darvi didn't speak until his red face came up again.

"Where I come from," she gritted, "a gentleman does not make such suggestions to a lady! If you ever say such a thing to me again, I'll not only repeat the kick, I'll slap your face until your ears ring." This said, she turned on her heel and stomped into the house.

"Good girl," Dakota Rawlings found himself saying aloud from the tree he had staked as his own. As he watched, the man—not the one from town—straightened up and put a hand to the back of his neck, his face thoughtful. When he did move, limping slightly, he didn't go into the house but toward the barn.

Dakota planned to hit town while it was still early and then realized it was Sunday. He would still try the telegraph office and the sheriff but thought later might be best. Witnessing Darvi in action gave him great hope that, at least in some ways, she was not completely at the mercy of others.

Gathering his gear and making his way back to town, all out of sight of the ranch house, Dakota washed up and then went looking for the sheriff. He was pleasantly surprised to find him alone in his office.

"Well, Mr. Rawlings, how is your search coming?"

"I found the person I was looking for. May I ask you a few questions?"

"On one condition."

"What's that?"

"You tell me who it is."

"It's just a friend," Dakota stated, still not willing to give Darvi's name. "I put her on the train in your station, thinking she was headed for St. Louis, and then I realized someone had other ideas. I've spotted her now, and I'm making plans to get her."

The lawman came to his feet. "You mean to tell me that a woman was taken against her will from the train?"

"Yes, I do."

"But how do you know? How can you be sure she isn't visiting friends?"

"She would have told me. Her plan was to head home and see her family. If she had even known anyone in Aurora, I would have been aware of it."

All idle curiosity about this woman melted away. "Ask your questions," the sheriff directed. He knew people thought he was soft when it came to crime in this town, but that wasn't true. He even suspected that some of his own men were dirty, but he had never turned a blind eye to it. He just couldn't move without proof.

"There's a ranch about five miles south of town. Who owns it?"

"Cassy Robinson."

"A woman?"

"Yes. She has two children, and her boyfriend lives with her, as does his brother, not to mention about six ranch hands who keep the place going. She has a good-sized spread." The man stopped and speared him with his eyes. "Why?"

"Because that's where she is. I don't want to shoot anyone to rescue my friend, but if I have to, I will. How many children did you say?"

"Two. The girl never comes into town, but I see the boy now and again."

The sheriff had much more he could add, starting with Seth and Eliot's connection with Jared Silk, but he kept this to himself. He had no way of proving if they were involved in an abduction, a pretty serious charge, and decided to refrain from comment, at least for the moment.

"I think I'll head out there tomorrow and see if Miss Robinson needs any more hands."

"It's Mrs. Have you done any ranch work? I have an undercover man I could send."

Dakota thanked him but explained that he would do fine. He asked the names of the men who lived there but kept the conversation short. He wasn't willing to discuss this overly much, and if he kept looking for answers, the man might expect him to return the favor.

"I will tell you one more thing," Dakota said as he moved toward the door. "I want whoever is behind this to answer for it, but not until I have my friend at a safe distance. If I get a chance, I'll take her and run, but you can bet I'll be back in town at some point."

For a moment the sheriff was put off but then realized this was the very thing he wanted in his own men: determination to see justice done and a concern for the innocent.

Unfortunately, before he could comment one way or the other, Dakota had gone on his way

❦ ❦ ❦

"He's dead?" Cassy asked in disbelief. "You can't mean that."

"He is, Mrs. Robinson. We all slept in 'cause he didn't wake us, so when Timmy woke first and didn't find any coffee to clear our heads, he checked. I checked too. Q is gone."

Cassy was in shock. Q had been cooking for this ranch since her husband had been a little boy. A more loyal, hardworking cook she couldn't imagine. She knew he had been tired and worn out lately but thought that her offering to take the big meal on Sunday and evening meals during the week would be enough.

"Mama," Nate said from beside her, and she turned to find both children with very large eyes.

"Wake Eliot," she said softly. The children were swift to obey.

The next few hours were spent confirming the news, comforting the children, going for the preacher and setting up a time for the funeral the next day, and going about the day's activities and chores in quiet shock. The men were very subdued, many still feeling the effects from Saturday-night drinking, but the family was also quiet. The children tried to attach to Eliot and Seth, as all Cassy wanted to do was lie on her bed.

Darvi felt at a complete loss and wandered around as lost and confused as everyone else. She could offer no words of comfort. She hadn't known the man; in fact, she'd only seen him a half-dozen times. The children were very upset, and she wondered if it was over their mother's distress or if they had known and cared for the old man as well.

"Are you all right?"

Darvi turned to see Eliot. She nodded.

"How are Cassy and the children?"

"All resting on the bed. Lindy is almost asleep, and Nate is drifting."

"Did the children know him well?"

Eliot smiled. "If they knew he was cooking hotcakes and their mother was only serving oatmeal, they would eat as little as they could get away with and make a visit to the bunkhouse. That, and he always had something sweet for them."

Darvi only nodded, again at a loss for words.

"Well, I guess he's in a better place."

Darvi had all she could do to keep her mouth shut. Why did people always say that? Why did people who gave God absolutely no place in their life on earth assume that someone dead was now at peace and rest? Darvi wanted to comment or at least ask what he meant, but she didn't think this was the time to attack the man's views.

She was doubly glad she'd kept her mouth shut when she looked up to see that Cassy had come from the bedroom. Eliot went to her. They spoke quietly for a moment and then Eliot went to the bedroom and shut the door. Cassy approached.

"You don't believe that, do you, Darvi?"

"Believe what?" Darvi asked, a bit afraid of the answer.

"I heard what Eliot said. I saw your face. You don't believe that Q is in a better place."

Darvi's head cocked a bit in genuine confusion.

"Tell me something, Cassy, why do my beliefs mean so much to you?"

The blonde woman shrugged. "I don't know," she admitted, "but they do. I'm so cut off out here. The days just tend to run together. Not until Eliot reminded me that the preacher wouldn't be available until after church did I even remember it was Sunday. I mean, I knew it was Sunday because of the extra cooking, but not because it was the Lord's day. We didn't actually attend church, but I was still raised differently. Your being here has reminded me of that."

Darvi nodded but didn't reply. Cassy was not put off so easily.

"You didn't answer me."

The women's eyes met.

"Do you think," Cassy repeated the question, "that Q is in a better place?"

Darvi put a hand on the other woman's arm.

"There are a lot of things I don't understand in God's Word, Cassy, but this one I know. God says the way to Him is through His Son, Jesus Christ. When we humble ourselves and accept His free gift of salvation, then we are assured of a better place when we die. If, um, if this man—"

"Q."

"Q?"

"Yes. That's all we ever called him.

Darvi's nod was decisive. "If Q accepted God's gift to him, then yes, I think he's in a better place."

Cassy saw what she had done. Rather than start a debate about what she believed, Darvi had very neatly put the responsibility on Q.

And where else should it be? Cassy asked herself, knowing that the same reasoning applied to her own heart.

Cassy suddenly looked to Darvi and found anxious eyes studying her.

"You've given me something to think about, Darvi."

"I don't want to overburden you when you're hurting, Cassy. I honestly don't."

"It's all right."

Darvi wasn't sure that Cassy's words matched her eyes, but when the ranch owner gave her a small smile and moved to go outside, she knew that, for the time being, that was the end of it.

Fourteen

"THE LORD GIVETH AND THE LORD TAKETH AWAY. Blessed be the name of the Lord."

The preacher's final words fell hard on Darvi's ears, causing her to wonder what they actually meant, or rather, what the preacher had meant. She'd heard those same words many times, but as with Eliot's overused cliché about Q being in a better place, she wondered if the man speaking actually believed that God was to be praised, even in the midst of death and loss.

"Are you all right?" Seth asked her quietly as the few mourners broke up and started to move away.

"What does my face look like that everyone keeps asking me that?"

Seth hesitated before saying. "In truth, I'm not sure. If I knew you better I might have an answer, but you almost look as though you disapprove, and since I can't think why you wouldn't approve of giving a man a proper burial, I assume I've read you wrong."

Darvi was shocked. *Am I really so transparent?* She didn't want everyone to know that she didn't approve of the things being said. Her frustration had nothing to do with burying this man but with all the ridiculous concepts about God. Cassy had seen it in her face and so had Seth.

"You're right, you have read me wrong," she tried to say gently. "I'm not looking with disapproval because this man

176

was buried. I'm very sorry for your loss, but there are some things I find confusing."

Seth was on the verge of asking what they were but stopped himself. He was certain this woman was for him, but he was also certain if they talked right now, they'd disagree. His brother had hinted at Darvi having some strong religious beliefs. That was fine with Seth—she could believe anything she wanted—but he didn't want her knowing that he might not agree. Once they were married they could talk on all the issues, but not now, not when he was still trying to get close and gain her trust.

"We have a visitor," Darvi heard Eliot comment from behind her, but she didn't look up. She walked straight into the house and hoped that Seth wouldn't follow her. To keep from having to face him when she realized he had indeed trailed her in, Darvi picked up a cloth and began to wash the crumbs from the table. She would have dropped it in an instant if she could have seen the pleasure on the man's face behind her, so certain was he that her actions meant she was beginning to see this as home.

❧ ❧ ❧

"I'll handle it for you," Eliot offered as they watched a rider come up the road. His offer was born of compassion, as the running of the ranch was all Cassy's.

"It's all right," Cassy declined, squeezing his hand a little.

"Are you sure?"

"Yeah. Maybe you could just check on Lindy for me. She didn't eat much breakfast."

"Will do."

Cassy moved away from the porch and waited for the rider to near. He swung from the saddle, dropped the reins, and covered the distance between them on foot, removing his hat as he approached.

"Good morning, ma'am," he said even as he took in her mourning garb. "I think I've come at a bad time."

"It's all right. Did you need directions?"

"No, ma'am. I'm looking for Cassy Robinson because I'm hoping to find work. The name's Rawlings, Dakota Rawlings, and someone in town said Mrs. Robinson might need an extra hand."

"I'm Mrs. Robinson, but I don't need more hands right now."

Dakota nodded respectfully but did not have to feign his disappointment.

"We'll be eating in about an hour," Cassy offered hospitably, "if you care to join us."

"I appreciate that, ma'am. Thank you."

Cassy began to turn away but stopped abruptly and faced Dakota again.

"Can you cook?"

"Yes, I can. I do better as a ranch hand, but I can cook."

"All I need right now is a cook."

Again Dakota gave that humble, polite nod. "If you're willing to try me, I'll do my best."

Cassy was won over in a heartbeat.

"Where're you from, cowboy?"

"Originally, St. Louis, but lately I tend to roam around."

Cassy smiled at him. "Come on in. I just need to check on something, and then I'll show you the bunkhouse and introduce you to the men."

Dakota did as he was told, glancing back to see that Eli was watching him and ready to follow right up to the house.

"Stay put," he ordered the horse as he would a dog. Then he walked into the ranch house, heart pounding and praying at the same time.

"Thank you," he said when Cassy held the door for him.

"I'll be right with you, Mr. Rawlings."

"Please call me Dakota."

Darvi, still bent over the kitchen table, became very slow in her movements. She heard the door behind her, Dakota's voice, Cassy's voice, Cassy's footsteps, and then quiet. But even knowing that no one else was in the room, she knew better than to turn around. Working at keeping all expression from her face, she returned the washcloth to the counter and found the solace of her room.

Hands shaking as they came to her face, Darvi sank onto the bed, her heart pounding beneath her dress.

He's here! He's actually here. I didn't know how You were going to do this. I couldn't imagine how I would ever be rescued.

Darvi was so overcome that she couldn't move. She sat on the edge of the bed and worked to muffle her sobs. Not until she saw Cassy come from her own room, saying a word to Eliot before she shut the door, did she think to stand up and shut her own bedroom door, thankful that the other woman hadn't even glanced her way.

The door finally shut, she stood still and tried to assess her emotions. It came to her that she could not just go to him. Even though the men who slept in the bunkhouse had eaten at the dinner table every night, Darvi had had literally nothing to do with them. She had exchanged a few words with Cassy, Seth, or Eliot, but rarely did she even look at the men. It wasn't anything personal, just her constant attempt to keep some distance from the situation.

Darvi heard voices and turned toward the window. Moving the sheer curtain just a bit, she watched as Cassy, now changed into a cotton workdress, walked Dakota to the bunkhouse. Darvi watched until they were out of sight before sitting back and praying, her mind coming to grips with one main fact.

His being here doesn't take care of everything, Lord. Help him to be wise and not get hurt. I know he's here for me. I know You sent him, but this won't be easy. You've brought us this far, Lord. Please help us all the way out of here.

❧·❧·❧

"Gentlemen," Cassy spoke quietly after she knocked on the bunkhouse door, heard someone's call to enter, and then stepped inside with the new cook, "this is Dakota Rawlings. He's going to be cooking for us."

Dakota watched five men either come to their feet or turn to look at him.

"This is Timmy," Cassy began. "Next is Scooter, then Roy, Adam, and Gordie."

"Howdy," Dakota said quietly and watched the men nod or utter a quiet greeting. No one looked particularly glad to see him, but neither did he feel threatened.

"Plan to join us for lunch today," Cassy said, turning back to the ranch's new cook. "Then you can get started tonight."

"All right."

"Your bunk is around here," Cassy directed him, taking him through an open doorway to the kitchen area. It appeared to be a well-stocked kitchen, and across from the stove was a bed and a small dresser. Dakota thought the space must be too hot for sleeping when it was mid-summer and a meal had been cooked, but he didn't plan to be there next summer, so that was the least of his worries.

"I have an account at Dawson's General Store. When you need supplies, make a list and let me check it, but Dawson's is where you'll head for nearly everything. Breakfast is at 6:30, lunch at noon, and dinner at sundown or when the men come in. At times you'll need to cook on the range. For those times there's a cook wagon in the barn. Any questions?"

Dozens was Dakota's first thought, but he said only, "I'm sure I'll have some, but for the moment I'll just settle my horse in the corral and have a look around. Oh! I guess I'd better ask how you want me to work the meals. Do I decide what we have?"

"In the future, yes, but Q had meals set up for a month in advance. He kept a list—oh, yes, here it is—nailed to the pantry door. If you follow it, you'll probably have all the supplies you need. However, keep in mind that this list was for noon dinners. You'll probably run short since you'll be cooking evening meals too."

Dakota moved with her and saw the schedule.

"Thank you."

"No problem," Cassy said quietly, having been affected just by seeing the dead man's handwriting. She moved slowly back to the doorway. "You and the boys all come in for lunch—maybe 30 minutes."

"Thank you."

Dakota wasn't far behind his new boss when she exited, walking slowly back to the front of the house to get Eli. The horse was within five feet of where Dakota had left him and came to him like a big dog as soon as he spotted him.

Not until he had Eli settled and was headed back to the bunkhouse with his saddlebags did Dakota think about how hard this was going to be. He didn't want to stay here, and he didn't want to work here. He wanted to walk into that house, take Darvi, and ride as fast and far as they could go.

Still praying for patience and wisdom about how to act and when, Dakota hung around in the kitchen of the bunkhouse until it was time for lunch.

❧❧❧

When she first realized Dakota had come for her, Darvi had been sorry that she'd never developed any kind of relationship with the ranch hands, but now that fact was standing her in good favor. It would have been nothing short of disastrous if she had even allowed herself to gaze in Dakota's direction, but since she never looked at the ranch hands, she didn't have to do any pretending.

The men usually ate rather quietly in the evening, but today, during the noon meal, they were doubly so; everyone was. It had to have been Q's death, and Darvi didn't blame them. At the same time, Cassy hiring Dakota as cook probably meant that the men wouldn't be in for supper. Darvi wondered when she would ever have an excuse to speak to the man when she realized Seth was addressing her.

"Were you speaking to me?" she asked to give herself time to school her features.

"Yes." Seth looked amused. "Do you want pie?"

"Yes, please." Darvi took dessert for the first time, wanting to be close to Dakota for as long as possible.

Seth's gaze became rather hopeful. He took this as another good sign. Darvi usually ate and started on the dishes or disappeared into her room as soon as she was through. He passed her a large slice of pie and then tried to engage her in conversation, but she wasn't going for it.

"Are you upset with me about something?" he finally asked.

"You know I am," Darvi said plainly. "I've never made a secret of it."

"I mean other than the obvious."

"The obvious is all that matters to me right now," she said quietly, not wanting to draw attention. A glance into Seth's face told her that he wanted to say more but was hesitating. She shouldn't have been surprised that he wanted to speak with her almost as soon as the meal was over, but surprised she was.

"I'm helping with the dishes," she explained.

"You help with them every day. I want to talk with you."

"Go on, Darvi," Cassy urged her. Cleanup wasn't that bad, and right now she didn't want Seth to be sad. She didn't want anyone to be as sad as she was. If Q's death could somehow open a door for Seth and Darvi, she would be thrilled.

"Lindy can help me," she added. "You go on."

Darvi did so reluctantly. She laid her towel down and preceded Seth out of doors.

"Walk this way," he directed and started toward the woods. The last time she walked to the woods with him, he tried to kiss her, but Darvi was not going to be caught out this time. She kept her distance as well as a watchful eye.

"I've noticed that you've stopped asking me to let you go," Seth began, making Darvi's mouth open in surprise and then shut before he could notice. "I know you didn't want to come here originally, but I guess I'm hoping that your silence means you're getting somewhat adjusted."

He stopped talking, and Darvi realized his head was turned to look at her. He was doing it again, watching her with such tender anxiety that Darvi was amazed. She shook her head a little and tried to think.

"Seth," she began but got no further.

I'm going to have to tell him. I'm going to have to share my belief and not worry if he tries to emulate it for the wrong reason.

"I can't give you any hope, Seth." Darvi put it on the line. "I don't even know if I'm supposed to be married, but—"

"That's ridiculous," Seth cut in with quiet conviction. "Do you have any idea how envied I am?"

Darvi blinked, not having expected this.

"Do you really not know how much you're meant to be cherished, Darvi? It's so clear to me, I just assumed you would understand."

"It's not that simple, Seth. I want to marry a man who shares my beliefs."

"How do you know I don't?"

"Because you've abducted me, Seth!" she said with some heat. "It doesn't take a genius to figure it out."

"But if I had met you some other way, it wouldn't have been like this."

"But you still felt you had the right, and you don't."

Seth looked slightly discouraged and spoke softly, almost to himself.

"Why can't we ever talk about things?"

"I'll tell you why," Darvi spoke up, not caring if he'd really asked her or not. "You can't steal a person and then expect to find her reasonable. It's reasonable to me that you return me to town this instant, and your idea of reason is that I fall for you because you're handsome and polite."

"You think I'm handsome?" he asked with such great hope that Darvi threw her arms into the air.

"I'm done!" she announced, turning and striding toward the barn.

"Darvi, come back."

"No! Leave me alone, and I mean it."

"Darvi!" he tried again, but she kept walking.

Darvi was so angry she thought she could spit. All the excitement over Dakota being there to rescue her had drained away. She thought she would go crazy if she had to spend another moment on this ranch.

Willing to be anywhere but in the house, Darvi stalked into the barn and stopped suddenly to let her eyes adjust in the dimness. She heard movement at the rear, but before she could investigate, she glanced over and spotted Lindy.

"Hello, Lindy," Darvi said softly, always wishing to be kind to the little girl. "What are you doing?"

Lindy looked up at her and then toward the rear.

"Is someone working back there?"

The little girl nodded.

"You want me to go with you so you can see?"

Lindy nodded at once and slid off the barrel she'd climbed onto.

As Darvi half-expected, Dakota was doing something with the cook wagon. Still angry at Seth, Darvi didn't find it too hard to keep her other emotions at bay. Earlier she'd have burst into tears and sobbed out her whole story, but not now.

"Hello," she said as they neared. "We came to watch you work."

"You did?" The Ranger came out with a smile, wiping his hands on a handkerchief. "Who's this?" he smiled down at Lindy, his attention entirely on her.

"This is Lindy."

"Hello, Lindy."

"She doesn't say too much with her mouth, but her eyes and hands do a lot of talking."

"I'm Dakota." Dakota put a hand out and smiled hugely at her when she shook it. "It's nice to meet you, Lindy. Are you Mrs. Robinson's daughter?"

Lindy nodded, her cheeks dimpling in delight before tugging on Darvi's hand. After observing a few hand movements, Darvi turned to translate.

"I think she wants to know what you're doing."

"I'm just looking at the cook wagon today in case I need to make a meal for the men when they're out on the range. Have you ever eaten out on the range, Lindy?"

The little girl shook her head no.

"It's pretty fun. Especially if you get to sleep out under the stars."

Lindy smiled and moved to climb up onto the wagon. Dakota helped her, and Darvi stayed to the side. She listened as he talked and explained things, but suddenly Darvi's breath quickened. What if they didn't make it? What if he couldn't figure a way to get her out? Darvi wondered if she might need to be the one to put together a plan; after all, she'd been there longer.

Her mind raced with what might be the best method: full confrontation or slipping away quietly after dark? Now, or when everyone had been lulled into thinking Dakota was a real cook? Darvi was so intent on her ideas, she didn't even hear Nate calling his sister but suddenly saw Lindy run past.

"The thing to remember—" Dakota's voice came softly to Darvi, and she looked up to find him bent over the back of the wagon, not even looking at her, "is that there will be no heroics. Some night when I tell you, you'll climb out your window, I'll be there, and we'll leave for Kinkade. No shooting. No one chasing us. We'll just leave."

This said, Dakota tucked things away, moved toward the rear door, and exited the barn. Darvi stood with her mouth open, wondering if she might have imagined the entire episode.

"Darvi?" Eliot called from outside.

"I'm in here," she answered, hoping she sounded normal.

Eliot came to the double doors and stopped.

Watching him, Darvi waited for him to speak. She almost began to question him, but he was finally ready to talk.

"When are you going to stop running from Seth?"

Darvi found her mouth open again in shock. She shut it swiftly in irritation.

"Don't you start with me, Eliot McDermott! Don't you do it!" Darvi spat out her words with instant vehemence. "You know as well as I do that it was wrong for him to take me. And I've made it very clear to everyone that I wish to leave. So don't you dare stand there and tell me to be nice in order to put his or anyone else's mind at rest."

"Have you heard him out?" Eliot asked.

"Regarding what?"

"How he feels about you."

"Eliot." Darvi tried to temper her voice. "He's just infatuated, that's all. The man barely knows me."

"If you knew him better, Darvi, you'd see how wrong you are. He's in deep."

Darvi only shook her head, knowing it was pointless to keep up this line of conversation. She wanted to sigh in frustration but thought she might be doing a little too much of that lately.

Eliot, on the other hand, did a little sighing of his own and then admitted, "The truth is, Darvi, I'm getting married a week from Saturday, and I want it to be a happy day."

Darvi blinked. "I didn't know that. Cassy said you didn't have a date."

"Well, we do now."

His tone and face spoke volumes. Darvi's hands came to her waist and she went to him, her eyes hard and determined.

"There's a simple answer to your problem, Eliot, and we both know it. You can return me to town so we can all get on with our lives."

He was shaking his head, and Darvi's brows lifted.

"You have some nerve," she said quietly, "coming and asking me favors when you're just as much to blame for this as Seth is."

As Darvi stepped around him and moved toward the house, she wondered what would happen if she just started walking down the road. Then she remembered Dakota's words.

I must be patient.

Rounding the house, Darvi found Seth on the porch, his facing lighting up at the sight of her. Darvi knew that more prayers for patience would be forthcoming.

3·3·3

Having left the interior of the barn, Dakota was still leaning against the side, fixing a boot that was just fine but hearing enough from inside to put a few more pieces into this puzzle. Right now he hoped for one of two things: a chance to either get Darvi out or run low on supplies and have an excuse to head into town and hopefully see the sheriff. He found he had a few more questions for that man.

Fifteen

"COME AND GET IT," DAKOTA TOLD THE MEN that evening, thinking he would have to start some bread; they wouldn't miss it tonight since he'd made biscuits, but they would surely expect it in the morning.

The men were slow to join him, but in time they gathered around the table at the far end of the kitchen area, no more talkative than they had been at the noon meal; that is, until they tasted the food.

"This is good," Gordie said, shoveling in more spoonfuls of the beef, potatoes, and thick gravy.

"So are the biscuits," Roy added.

Dakota reminded himself to thank Katy when he got home. She was the main reason he knew his way around the kitchen.

"You boys worked here long?" Dakota now felt free to open some conversation.

The answers varied, one man as many as ten years, the others somewhat less. The youngest of the group, Dakota remembered his name to be Scooter, said that Q had been on the ranch the longest, way back before Mrs. Robinson had married her husband.

"So this is his ranch, but he lets her handle it?" Dakota asked, thinking about the man he'd first seen in town.

"Robinson's dead. You're thinking of Eliot McDermott."

188

Dakota nodded as though that explained everything. It didn't, but he still refrained from asking any more questions.

He was sitting quietly over his own plate of stew when Roy announced to the group that he was going to ask his girl to marry him come Saturday night. Dakota knew that a longstanding joke was in play because his comment brought gales of laughter, something he could see they all needed.

"Will we be invited to the wedding?" Adam asked. "I'll polish my boots if you let me dance with the bride."

Dakota had to put up with a few comments about the other things Adam wanted to do with the bride, but overall he could see that the men respected each other. He also caught a note of respect for Mrs. Robinson and the others living in the house.

Thinking of the house shifted Dakota's thoughts back to Darvi. Though he didn't know it, he was experiencing some of the same emotions she had struggled with, especially that of not wanting to get too close to these people.

What's the balance here, Lord? I want to be a witness for You, but I've had to come here under pretense to get Darvi. What is my main role?

The answer was not obvious to Dakota. The men thanked him and left him to the cleanup. Dakota was glad to be on his own.

ॐ·ॐ·ॐ

"Is there anything else you need from town, Mrs. Robinson?"

"No, Dakota. I didn't think you'd need to be going this soon, but I'm low on flour too," Cassy said, standing next to the wagon. "No, Lindy, you can't go." The mother directed this to her daughter, who was tapping her and looking up with pleading eyes. Cassy looked back to Dakota. "Why don't you grab a little candy or something?"

He smiled. "I'll do it."

Dakota put the team into motion, finding he wasn't enjoying this at all. From what he could figure out, Darvi's predicament all revolved around the wants of one man. He didn't know his name yet, but clearly the man wanted Darvi.

At moments like this Dakota had to remind himself that the other people at the ranch might have been able to help her escape. He needed to think this way to keep things in their proper perspective. Most things could not be blamed on just one person. The man, a brother to Eliot McDermott if their looks could be trusted, must have instigated the abduction, but Cassy Robinson was a capable woman. If she had wanted to help Darvi, she would have.

Dakota pushed these thoughts aside. He was determined to speak with the sheriff but knew that at least one of the men and the boy had gone into town earlier. It could get a bit tricky. He was thinking about how to handle it when he realized he was on the edge of town and had better look for Dawson's. Then something wonderful happened. About a block from his destination he spotted Joe Laverty, who had spotted him as well. They had managed just enough eye contact to give Dakota hope, and sure enough, when he was almost through with his list, the law man appeared at his side.

"Is there somewhere we can talk?" Dakota said without introduction.

The sheriff was right glad to see this Ranger after so many days. Without a word he moved toward the back room. Dakota waited a moment and followed.

"I thought you might have moved on by now."

"No, but that's my plan for the end of the week."

"And you need me," the sheriff said with some satisfaction.

"In a way I do. Can you answer some questions for me?"

"Maybe," he said thoughtfully, not wanting the younger man to sense his need to be needed.

"Is there a woman in town who works for the newspaper named Ann Bell?"

"Her name's Annabelle. Annabelle Hewett. She writes for the paper every week."

"What contact does she have with the men from the Robinson ranch—Eliot McDermott and the other man?"

"The other man is Seth Redding, and they're half-brothers. They work for Jared Silk, a banker whose dealings are called into question by Annabelle on a regular basis."

"But the brothers themselves," Dakota went back to them. "You've never brought them in for anything?

"No, they always have airtight alibis."

"What kind of things do you suspect of them?"

The sheriff's smile was bitter.

"That's the problem. They don't often get their hands dirty, and neither does Silk. The brothers have connections who give them what they want and still let them come out smelling like a rose. I've never heard of them having someone murdered, but I'm not too sure they're above much else."

Dakota nodded, but the sheriff wasn't about to provide information without gaining some in return.

"Now it's your turn. What does this have to do with the woman you're after?"

Dakota knew it was time. "Her name is Darvi Wingate, and she's a near mirror image of Annabelle Hewett."

The sheriff let out a low whistle. "Abduction is not the brothers' style, but it sounds as though they tried it and grabbed the wrong woman."

"And decided to keep her," Dakota finished. "Do you think this banker is behind that?"

"I don't know, but I'm going to find out."

"I would appreciate your sitting on that until I get Miss Wingate out of there."

"I can do that."

A creak in the floor caused the men to cut the conversation short. Dakota left the room first, and the sheriff hung around just long enough to let him get on his way.

Neither man noticed the way Nate Robinson kept behind the shelves, his eyes peeking just above the large sacks of meal as he watched the men's mouths move and listened to their words. He eventually left the storeroom as well, but by the time he got out front, both men were gone.

☙ ☙ ☙

Darvi opened her window very slowly, listening for creaks and groans. Not hearing any this night or the previous nights, she pushed it all the way up and settled back into bed. The first two nights she'd done this, she'd heard other noises in the house and even someone outside, but not now. Whoever was checking on her must have figured that she was just sleeping with her window open, which was partly true.

She had started opening her window the day after Dakota had arrived, all the while hoping not to draw suspicion. After Dakota's words that day, she acted the scene out in her mind. It all worked beautifully until she thought of opening the window with a loud creak and bringing the entire house down on her head.

Darvi stiffened suddenly when out the window she heard a door open and close. Was tonight the night and had she missed it? Another door, farther away, opened, and Darvi knew someone was using the outhouse.

She made herself breathe normally and tried to pray. At moments like this she wondered if she was going to make it. Helplessness and frustration had begun to be the norm in her world as Seth would not listen to reason. Now all of that was replaced by tension and fear. She didn't think anyone was noticing—Seth and Eliot both went off to work as usual, and Cassy and the kids had nothing but the wedding on their minds—but inside Darvi felt like a tightly stretched thread.

Doors moved again, and Darvi knew all would be quiet now. One of the children shifted in bed, and Darvi was once again set to wondering how she'd come to be in this place. It was all so unreal at times, and altogether too real at others. Sleep finally came, but not before Darvi muffled unexpected tears. Dakota had come to rescue her; she was still so amazed over that fact that she could hardly believe it would happen.

⁂⁂⁂

When the plan hit his mind, Dakota wanted to laugh. It was so simple, and yet it took some days to perfect. He had discovered that every man in the bunkhouse went to town on Saturday night. Dakota would simply join them. He knew they all drank, visited friends, or played cards and came back with great hopes that their horses could find the way. It couldn't have been more perfect if he had planned it with them.

Dakota had meant what he said. There would be no guns fired nor anyone chasing them, not even Seth Redding. That the man was besotted with Darvi was more than obvious, and Dakota had no doubt he would take action to keep her, but the Ranger wasn't going to give him that chance.

Letting Darvi know had been tricky. He hadn't been certain just how he would do it, but burning the biscuits and needing to have all doors and windows open gave him an excuse to be outside by the barn and available when Lindy came to see about the smell. Even Mrs. Robinson had checked on him. The single word *tonight* had been easier to pass than he'd figured, and the brief moment of eye contact with Darvi told him he'd been understood.

Now as he made his way to town, having told the men he would bathe last and to go on without him, it felt like child's play to cut off the road and double back through the woods to the place near the ranch where he'd spent that first night.

Even though it was dark, Dakota still climbed the tree, field glasses in hand, actually quite pleased with so little moon. He couldn't see much, but sound carried well, and it would be easy to count the men as they returned. The hours would be long, possibly until two or three in the morning, but in the end Darvi would be safe. Right now that was all that mattered.

$$\text{\&-\&-\&}$$

Darvi could feel sweat breaking out all over her body. It didn't help to be under the covers with her clothing on, but she was sure it was more than that. The first sounds she heard outside caused her to gasp in fear, and she knew she was going to have to keep still or ruin the whole thing. Had the men come in so noisily on the other Saturday nights? Darvi had never noticed, but right now each sound of hooves, each low voice or laugh, made her feel as though she were being struck.

And the children were more restless too, which eventually told Darvi that a closed window had been keeping the noise out. She didn't want them to waken, but neither would she shut that window. Darvi had to force herself not to think of them. Against her will she had come to care for them. She had to leave here—there was no other option— but she didn't think she would ever forget Cassy and the...

"Darvi."

It was said so quietly that she almost missed it, and for a moment she hesitated before reminding herself that no one else would be calling her name. Reaching for the satchel that was packed and ready next to the bed, she sat up and started to put it through the window. Her heart nearly came out of her chest when she felt Dakota take it.

On legs that would not stop shaking, Darvi stood on the bed and leaned out, wondering how she would stay quiet and climb out at the same time. She need not have worried. Dakota's strong arms were there and almost before she could guess his intentions, he lifted her and stood her against the side of the house.

Taking her cue from him, she stood very still beside him. She thought that all might be quiet, but her breathing was so labored she couldn't be sure. However, Dakota must have been. He suddenly took her by the hand and began to walk with her across the field. They were more than halfway to the woods when Darvi realized her other hand was empty.

"My bag," she said on a soft gasp.

"I have it."

And on they went, right into the trees, Dakota leading the way, ducking and moving branches from her path. Then suddenly, when they had climbed several dozen feet, he stopped. Darvi couldn't stop shaking and jumped nervously when he whistled. Again she had to stifle a gasp when something moved and started toward them. The next thing she knew, Dakota's horse had drawn abreast of them, and Dakota was lifting her. Climbing into the saddle behind her, he maneuvered Eli through the woods.

Darvi had no sense of time. She tried to listen for the sounds of pursuit but could hear only the horse and the sound of her own breathing and pounding heart. She said nothing. A thousand thoughts rushed through her mind at once, but not one would stop and make itself heard. For a time she thought she might sleep, but the pounding inside was giving her a headache, so she sat very still, Dakota's chest at her back, and tried not to give in to the temptation to cry hysterically or leap off the horse and run.

She knew some relief when they came from the woods and began moving down the road. She wished she knew where they were and hoped Dakota did, but as with the other questions, she kept this one to herself.

At last the sky began to lighten. Darvi was not glad to see it. The darkness made her feel safe; it made them untraceable. She had not been afraid of the people she'd been forced to live with for these weeks, but having them pursue her and take her back was nothing short of terrifying.

All these tempestuous thoughts took their toll. Darvi was near to bursting by the time Dakota pulled off the road and into a wooded area. He climbed down and brought Darvi down after him. It was light enough for him to see that she was deathly pale, her eyes huge. He had wanted to give her time, knowing her stay had to have been traumatic, but he needed to check on her before they went another step.

"Are you all right?"

"I think so," she said softly, eyes looking up at him in amazement. "You came for me." Her voice held wonder. "I can't believe you came for me."

A nearby falling branch caused her to start and move toward him.

"Is that him?" she asked in panic.

"No." Dakota's voice was soft and reassuring as he watched her keenly. "No one is following us, and even if someone was, I wouldn't let him have you."

Darvi couldn't hold back. She wanted to be so brave, but she couldn't do it much longer.

"Please don't let him, Dakota," she said on a soft sob. "I'll do anything you ask, but please don't let Seth or anyone take me back."

Dakota's heart couldn't stand it. He moved and wrapped his arms around her, not at all surprised when the dam burst forth. Dakota didn't remember ever hearing anyone cry like Darvi did. She choked several times, but not even that stopped her. Not until she seemed too weary to make a sound did the tears stop, and by then she was like a limp rag. Dakota felt her legs buckle and bent to lift her in his arms. Darvi worked to catch her breath, looking up at him through swollen eyes.

"Do you want something to drink?" he asked, not letting his mind dwell on all she'd been through; it wasn't time for that yet.

"Not right now."

Dakota took her back to the horse. It occurred to him after they'd started back down the road that she might have wanted a few minutes of privacy, but he didn't check with her. She would tell him if there was a need. And no doubt they would stop at some point, but home was just a few hours away. Darvi didn't know where they were heading, but Dakota found it comforting beyond words. No matter what had happened, no matter how awful things had been, he would take her home to the ranch and take care of her. He couldn't think of a safer place in all of Texas.

ॐ-ॐ-ॐ

Kinkade

"Cash, I think you'd better come," Katy called out, interrupting the rancher's newspaper reading at the kitchen table. They had not been home from church that long, and Katy was still preparing Sunday dinner. She had been in the kitchen with him but suddenly left. Cash now followed her through the house and into the front yard.

Dakota rode toward them, a woman in the saddle in front of him. He came to a stop before Katy, and Cash could see that the woman was asleep. Both Dakota and Darvi looked very spent.

"Darvi," Dakota said softly, but she remained limp in his arms.

Cash stepped forward, and Dakota handed her down to him. The moment his feet were on the ground, however, he took her back. Katy led the way through the house and to an upstairs bedroom. Dakota had just stepped across the threshold of the guestroom when Darvi woke up. She started violently and reached for the front of his shirt. There was no disguising her panic.

"Where are we?"

"In my home in Kinkade."

He started to bend down a bit.

"I'm going put you on your feet, and Katy will see to you. All right?"

Darvi nodded, working hard to clear the webs from her mind. She felt Dakota let go of her and put her arms out to steady herself. His hands were instantly back.

"Are you there?" he asked, a small smile in his voice. Darvi looked up into his familiar face and felt peace stealing over her.

"Yes, I'm here. Did my bag make it?"

"Right here," Cash said from the door, his eyes not missing a thing.

"Darvi," Dakota began, "this is my brother Cash, and behind you is Katy."

"Land sakes! I don't know why they can't just introduce me as the housekeeper. That's what I am, and proud of it, but you would think they're afraid to say the word. Land sakes!"

Katy smiled at the woman and got just what she wanted: a smile in return.

"Now you boys get," she ordered. "Miss Darvi and I have things to do, and we don't need you. Cash, you check that meat if I don't get down soon. I will not have that dinner ruined."

"I will," he said with an amused smile.

"You do that. Keep an eye on the top."

Dakota caught Darvi's eye one more time before they exited and was pleased to see her looking a little more normal. However, he didn't get far down the wide hallway. After exiting and shutting the door, he leaned against the wall. Cash stood with him.

"Do you want to talk about it?"

"I would," Dakota admitted, "but I don't know anything, at least not much. It seems a man in Aurora got it into his head to keep her. I think it started with a case of mistaken identity and then rolled into a full-blown abduction. She didn't seem to be abused by them."

"Them?" Cash frowned, working to follow.

Dakota slowly shook his head. "It's one of the strangest things I've ever encountered." His voice died off, and he stood there.

"Come on," Cash ordered. "Let's get you cleaned up and fed."

Dakota went willingly, but his mind was still in the room with Darvi. He knew she was in good hands, but he felt rather helpless right now. If they could talk he might be able to reassure her about any remaining fears, but if he knew Katy, she was probably tucking her into bed at this moment.

Thank You, he suddenly remembered to pray. *You got us out of there, Lord. I know this. Thank You that Darvi's all right. Help her to heal and be at peace in the days to come.*

"By the way," Cash began once they had reached the downstairs, allowing Dakota to go ahead of him to the washbasin in the corner of the kitchen, "you got a telegram from Brace."

"Did you read it?"

"Yes. He was just checking on you."

"Any mention of Darvi?"

"No. I assumed her family hasn't missed her yet."

Dakota shook his head. "I'd almost forgotten about her family."

"How long did it take to find her?"

Dakota's shirt was off, and he lathered his face and neck while he spoke.

"Not long, and I'll tell you something, Cash, the only explanation for how things went is that God led the way. I was sitting in a hotel when I saw this woman who looked like Darvi. Then I noticed a man watching her, so I followed him. I ended up asking for a job at a ranch where the cook died the day before, and I was hired. That led to waiting until late last night while the men were coming home from town. I took Darvi out a bedroom window and we walked away."

Cash was silent with thanks over what Dakota had just revealed. He'd prayed the whole time his brother was gone, thinking for part of the time that he might have sent him on a wild goose chase. He was so relieved that Dakota had been there for Darvi that for a moment he couldn't speak.

"She refused to be babied. I'm trying to mother her, and she won't have it!"

Katy's words preceded the woman herself, who was closely followed by Darvi.

"Did you check this meat?" she demanded.

"Six times," Cash told her with wide eyes.

Katy turned away toward the oven so as not to be caught smiling. Slipping into a clean shirt that Cash had handed him, Dakota headed to see Darvi, who was still in the doorway.

"How are you?"

"I'm okay. I keep thinking about my Uncle Marty and family. I need to send word."

"Brace has been in touch." Dakota told her, "and it doesn't sound like anyone has missed you. Did your family know when you were headed back?"

Darvi looked surprised. "As a matter of fact, I didn't say, but I would like to wire them."

"We'll go to town tomorrow and take care of it."

Darvi nodded. She still looked a bit under the weather, but he could see that she was coming along.

"Hungry?" Cash stepped forward and asked.

"Very. Is there anything I can do to help?"

Something akin to a growl escaped Katy's throat, and Cash only shook his head.

"I think that means no. Why don't you come on through here and get comfortable in the living room? We'll eat in no time."

Cash led the way, and Dakota brought up the rear. They took Darvi to the large living room, warm with earthy colors and deep, comfortable furniture. Darvi sank down in the first chair and thought she could lay her head back and go to sleep.

"Go ahead," Dakota directed.

"Go ahead and what?"

"Sleep. I can see you want to."

Darvi smiled at being so transparent. "I am tired, but it can wait. It feels too good to be awake and know that I'm not trapped anymore."

"When you're up to it, I really would like to hear what went on."

"Well, I'll tell you, Dakota, as soon as I've had a little something to eat. I'll tell you everything."

As though on cue, Katy called them to the table. No one needed to be asked twice. And Darvi was good at her word. Before her plate was even half-empty, she began to talk.

Sixteen

STARTING WITH "THEY THOUGHT I WAS a woman named Annabelle Hewett," and ending with hearing Dakota's voice in the ranch house, Darvi chronicled her adventure. She grew emotional at times, but as they shared a wonderful Sunday dinner, Darvi explained the details she could recall.

Listening to her, Dakota knew his own range of emotions. At some times he thought he could string up Seth Redding, and at other times he felt Cassy and Eliot were to blame as well. That they hadn't harmed her physically was a remarkable relief, but it didn't get them off the hook. He would see to that personally.

"It's your turn, Dakota," Darvi finally said. "How did you find me? How did you know?"

Dakota smiled. "I have Cash to thank for that."

Darvi looked to the tall redhead and waited for someone to explain. When Dakota did, she was as amazed at his story as he was at her own.

"So this woman, this reporter, does look like me?"

"Remarkably so. I had all I could do not to ask her where she'd been the day you boarded the train, thinking I'd made a complete mistake."

Darvi shook her head a little. "That day feels like such a long time ago."

"It was," Cash said gently. "Not in actual chronological days, but in events, and those are far more emotionally draining than just time moving along the clock or calendar."

"I can't honestly say that I've ever thought of it before, but I think you must be right. I don't know when I've been so tired."

Not having meant to hint, Darvi was surprised when both men pushed back their chairs.

"Head out, Darvi," Dakota spoke to her surprised face. "Go get some rest."

"I didn't mean for you..." But they didn't give her a chance to finish.

"I'll look forward to talking with you later, Miss Wingate," Cash said, his voice and expression very warm and kind.

Darvi looked into his eyes and smiled.

"Thank you for a wonderful meal and for allowing me to stay with so little notice."

"Well, don't hurry off. I think you'll find Kinkade and the Rawlings Cattle Company very much to your liking."

Cash went on his way then, and Dakota came to get her chair.

"I'll walk you up," he offered, and Darvi allowed herself to be cared for. As her legs took the stairs, however, they began to feel weighted. By the time she reached her room, she was nearly wobbling.

"Will you get some rest too?" she couldn't help but ask before going into the room.

"We take it pretty easy around here on Sundays, so I'm planning on it."

Acute disappointment sprang into Darvi's eyes.

"I missed church again," she said with a small shake of her head. "It feels like it's been forever."

"It's over now," Dakota told her very gently.

"You're right," Darvi agreed, a part of her heart still trying to process this.

"Come on down to the living room when you're ready. We'll ride out and see a little of the ranch."

"All right. Thank you, Dakota, for everything."

"My pleasure."

Dakota turned for the stairs, hearing Darvi's door close behind him. He sought out his favorite chair in the living room and reached for Cash's Bible. He was asleep before he could read five verses.

※※※

"And this," Dakota pronounced dramatically as they rounded the trees, "is the pond."

"Oh, my," Darvi breathed. "It's beautiful."

"We think so."

The two sat astride their horses and took in the scene. The pond was almost a perfect circle, a good 300 feet across, bordered on two sides by pecan trees.

"Do you want to walk awhile?" Dakota asked, all the time trying to gauge how she was doing.

"That sounds nice. Where shall we leave the horses?"

"Right here. We'll tie Toby, but Eli will stay put."

Darvi looked at him. "You whistled for Eli in the woods, didn't you, just like a dog?"

Dakota smiled. "That about describes him. He's always been like a big puppy. If you look behind us right now, you'll find him watching me, as though he doesn't want me out of his sight."

Darvi did as he suggested and laughed out loud at how accurately he had called it. Dakota loved hearing the sound of her laugh and joined her when her face began to turn red.

"And you say he's always been like that?"

"Yep."

Darvi bit her lip to keep from laughing again. She didn't know if it was that funny or if she was still tired. She was trying to figure it out when she spotted a half-circle of wooden benches that sat around a fire pit and gave a perfect view of the pond. Going to a seat and getting comfortable, Darvi let her mind drift back. It didn't take much coaxing. The people she'd left, most especially Cassy and the children, were never far from her thoughts.

"It was strange," Darvi began as though they'd already been speaking of it.

Dakota had taken a seat across from her, but she hadn't looked at him. He watched and listened in silence.

"Cassy and the children were so sweet, and even the men were kind, but Seth would not see reason. I woke up every morning shaking my head that this had happened. I just didn't think such a thing could go on in this day and age, and certainly not to me."

Darvi finally looked at him, and Dakota asked the question he dreaded, fearing that the answer would make him want to shoot the man in question.

"Did he hurt you?"

"No. I didn't feel threatened in any way."

Darvi suddenly frowned.

"He wanted to kiss me. I wouldn't let him!"

"You did the right thing."

"One time I kicked him."

"That was good. Your kisses are yours to give, not someone else's to take."

Darvi melted a little. It was such a nice thing to say, but as she was finding, memories continued to flood back.

"He said I had an upside-down mouth."

Dakota looked at her.

"It's a very kissable mouth."

Emotions chased across Darvi's features in rapid succession: first surprise, then pleasure that softened her features as she looked at the man across from her. But before long that softness was replaced by a look of uncertainty and then another frown.

"Dakota Rawlings," she said in soft rebuke "a gentleman does not tell a lady that her mouth is kissable."

Dakota wished he'd kept the thought to himself.

"You're right. I'm sorry I said that."

An uncomfortable silence fell over them, neither looking at the other. The water proved to be a helpful neutral point, and both took advantage of it.

Several minutes passed. A breeze stirred the trees, and as always, the low sound of cattle could be heard from the distance. Not certain how she felt about what had just happened, Darvi did not like sitting there with a strain between them. She was the first to chance a peek and was glad the Ranger's gaze was on the water. She transferred her own gaze back before saying, in as normal a voice as she could manage, "I've been meaning to ask you, Dakota, how are your bullet wounds? Has all of this mess with me kept you from going back to work?"

"No, it hasn't. My wounds are fine. I feel I could go back at any time, but Brace said he didn't want me for another month after I dropped you off."

"How long has it been?"

"Let me see. I think I had dinner with you and Brace in Austin just four weeks ago yesterday, and after that we were in Stillwater with Calder and Merry and then in Aurora, so that makes it about two and a half weeks ago."

"We were in Austin just a month ago?"

"As far as I can figure."

Darvi stared at him, looking upset.

"Is that right?"

"Yes. You can check the calendar when we get back to the house."

"That means I haven't been home for more than a month."

Dakota, who was on the road most of the year, understood completely. At times he missed home so much he ached. Darvi's face told him she ached right now.

A bell rang in the distance.

"That's for us," Dakota told her as he stood. "Katy must have supper nearly ready."

By the time they reached the horses, Eli was rather anxious, starting Darvi's laughter all over again.

Dakota listened in silence, hoping to find other ways to hear her laughter in the following days. In his opinion, she'd been frightened and sad for much too long.

❀ ❀ ❀

"Are you just a little bit amazed by it all?" Cash asked kindly. Dinner was over, and they were having coffee in the living room. "I mean, I thought about it most of the day, and it's almost too outrageous to be true."

"I was just telling Dakota that very thing. Even in the midst of it, I could hardly believe it."

"I don't find it so hard to believe," Dakota stated calmly.

The two other occupants of the room stared at him.

"You don't know her, Cash, but things have a way of following Darvi around."

"Things?" Cash questioned, even as he caught the gleam in his brother's eye.

Dakota shook his head in pity. "Yes, things. They just mange to follow Darvi around. I'm not sure why, but there's no doubt about it."

"Do not believe a word he says, Cash," Darvi finally cut in, having gotten over her shock to see she was being teased. "Dakota is very imaginative; that's all there is to it. Those other incidents were just circumstances beyond my control."

"Following a stranger down the streets of Austin?"

"I knew you were a Ranger," Darvi defended, trying not to laugh.

"Then there were the men in Stillwater who just *had* to talk with you and wouldn't let you pass?"

"I think," Darvi responded, growing as outlandish, "that they were wanting to ask directions to the sheriff's office, and we didn't give them a chance."

"The snake?"

Darvi shook her head, her expression one of pity over his shortsightedness.

"The snake simply misunderstood the time schedule and that it was my turn at the creek. It's all very easily explained."

Dakota gave a huge sigh of mock exasperation and looked back to his brother.

"You see, Cash. Things happen to Darvi, so I'm not at all surprised she was mistaken for another woman. She just can't seem to help herself."

"And if that wasn't bad enough," Darvi added, almost taking Dakota's side against herself, "even after those people realized their mistake, they decided to keep me."

"That's the part!" Cash came forward in his seat and exclaimed. "I can't get over that—I can't imagine what they must have been thinking."

"It was more Seth than anyone else. If it had not been for him, the others would have let me go."

"Are you angry about that?" Cash asked.

Darvi had to think on it.

"Not exactly angry, but amazed—like you are. Seth's and Eliot's jobs are not aboveboard, and the fact that they believe they can do things outside the law leaves them open to any whim. They have their own standard, which they feel gives them the right to take someone."

"Did this Seth really think you would eventually wish to stay?" Dakota now asked.

"That's exactly what he thought," she replied, shaking her head, and suddenly wanting to laugh a little more. "Did I tell you that I tried to sneak out in the wagon?"

Both men smiled but said no.

Darvi nodded. "I did, but Seth caught me, and Cassy went to town without me."

"Tell us about Cassy, Darvi," Cash urged her. "Did she not have trouble with what the men were doing?"

"Actually, she did. In fact, my telling her about my faith somehow prompted her into marrying Eliot. They just set a date after being together for five years."

Both men gawked at her.

"You had a chance to witness to this woman?" Cash asked to be sure.

"Yes. We were talking, and she was saying how sorry she was that I'd come to be there under those circumstances, but that Seth was a fine man. I told her I didn't want him, and thinking that I meant he wasn't good enough for me, she became angry. I had no choice but to lay it on the line. She took it very well. It actually got her to thinking. The next time she went to town she bought a dress to be married in and showed it me. Then later I heard they'd set a date."

"When is it?"

"Let me see. The days were so full and anxious at the same time that they tended to blend together, but I think it's this Saturday."

Dakota looked thoughtful, and Cash was the first to catch on.

"She's going to have to go back, isn't she?"

"Eventually, yes, but I think it can wait until after she goes home."

"Why do I have to go back?" Darvi asked with a sinking heart.

"Because anything that happened to you is hearsay without your testimony." Dakota looked at her. "You do want these people to answer for this, don't you?"

Nate's and Lindy's faces sprang into her mind, but she still nodded her head yes.

"I can't say that I'm thrilled to return, however."

Dakota caught her eyes and told her plainly, "I'm not going to let anything happen to you."

"You'll be there?"

His brows rose as though he'd been insulted, and for a moment they only looked at each other.

"But first," Cash cut in, "you'll get in touch with your family and tell them you're spending the rest of the week here resting up before starting for home." Cash paused and smiled at her. "At least that's what I hope you'll do."

Darvi smiled back. "I would like to rest a little before traveling again. Are you sure I won't be imposing?"

"Very sure."

"Does the train run from Kinkade?"

"Twice daily. You'll connect at Dallas and then be on your way."

"I'll telegraph tomorrow."

"I'll take you in," Dakota offered.

At that point the evening came to a very quiet close. Darvi found herself watching Dakota yawn and needing to do the same. Cash rescued both of them and said he was turning in.

Darvi lay down in bed just a short time later, hardly able to remember that she'd taken a nap. She thought she might lie there for long minutes, still in wonder over how God had used Dakota to rescue her, but the strange sounds and surroundings took little time to fade.

❧ ❧ ❧

"So when did you tell them you'd be home?" Dakota asked when Darvi was finished in the telegraph office. He saw her inside but took a seat to give her privacy.

"I'm going to take Cash's offer and stay until Friday or Saturday."

"Why not Sunday or Monday?"

Darvi looked up at him. "I don't want to wear out my welcome."

Again she received that look; Dakota's brows went up as though he was insulted for his brother.

"I told them to look for me sometime next week," she admitted.

Dakota smiled complacently and offered to show her around town, pointing out the bank and the new hotel. Kinkade had a fairly good-sized school, and Dakota told her all about it.

"I love Texas," Darvi mentioned at one point.

"Why is that?"

"The diversity. Some areas are huge and flat; others are hilly and dense." She looked up at him. "Uncle Marty even took me to Houston one summer and down to the Gulf of Mexico. It was so exciting."

"I've never been," Dakota admitted.

"Oh, you've got to go, Dakota. It's beautiful."

"I think I'll do that sometime," he said with quiet conviction.

Watching him, Darvi noticed for the first time how handsome he was. His eyes were very dark and oftentimes serious, but when he was smiling or amused, they were beautiful. She took in the square line of his jaw to the thick black hair atop his head. His features were strong, something she found very appealing. Suddenly feeling shy with him, Darvi dropped her eyes, hoping he had not caught her gawking.

"I just spotted someone I need to speak with, Darvi. Come on over with me, and I'll introduce you."

Feeling rescued, Darvi looked up to see they were in front of the general store.

"Would you mind very much, Dakota, if I stopped in here first? I'll come find you afterward."

She watched him hesitate but didn't know why.

"All right. I'll come back for you, okay?"

"Okay."

Dakota waited until she went inside before crossing the street. Darvi didn't look back but headed inside with good intentions. Unfortunately, they didn't last very long. She wasn't in the mood to shop, just in the mood to think about this new awareness of Dakota. She wandered the aisles of the store for a time but couldn't keep it up. With a smile to the proprietor, she exited.

There was no sign of Dakota. Darvi was getting ready to sit on one of the empty benches out front when she spotted a small dog as he went limping into the alley. She changed her mind and trailed after the stray.

"Hey, there," she said softly when she found the dog had gone just halfway down the alley and stopped against the mercantile wall. The dog's tail thumped at the sight of her, but he still held his right foreleg close to his body.

Darvi approached without fear and stroked his small head. He didn't look to be more than a pup. Nevertheless, she knew she would need help. Darvi made a swift trip back out to the boardwalk and immediately spied a pair of teenage boys. She stopped them with a word.

"Excuse me."

The boys stopped and came to immediate attention; this lady was pretty, and she had spoken to them first.

"There's a dog in the alley that seems to be hurt. Could you tell me where I could take him?"

"We'll help you," the taller of the two boys said.

Darvi didn't know why they did this but still showed them the dog. It was no trouble for the first one down the alley to lift him, and Darvi was glad to see that he was gentle.

They took the dog to Dr. Wilcox, whose sign Darvi remembered seeing earlier. His speciality was people, the boys told her, but he had compassion for dogs. That was enough for Darvi.

She was a little surprised that the boys did not drop off the dog and leave, but she didn't mind the company as long as the little dog was helped. Darvi was still sorting through some of her thoughts when the doctor joined them in the waiting room.

"What can I do for you?" Dr. Wilcox asked.

"I found this dog in the alley," Darvi explained. "His leg seems to be hurt."

The wise doctor took in the scene at a glance before kneeling down to examine his canine patient.

"I think this is Rickmans' dog. Why don't you boys run down the street and let them know he's here?"

The youths agreed readily enough, but neither one moved. Darvi had been too busy watching the dog to notice.

"So what's your name?" one of the boys now asked.

The strawberry blonde answered without looking up. "Darvi Wingate."

"Darvi. That's a nice name. You new in town?"

Darvi finally caught on. She looked up to find keen interest in both sets of young eyes. Hers had been for the dog; theirs were for her.

"I think I should tell you, gentlemen, that I'm old enough to be your, well, your older sister."

They both smiled at her.

"Where do you live?" was the next question, telling Darvi they were not put off.

Darvi's chin came up, but she turned away from them, opening her purse as she moved.

"I'd like to leave payment with you if I could," she said to the doctor and held out a coin.

"Thank you," he said graciously, "but I'm sure Mr. Rickman will be happy to take care of it."

Putting her money away, she asked, "Will the little dog be all right?"

"He'll be fine. We'll have him wrapped up and back to his owner in no time."

"Thank you," she said to the doctor and then to her helpers.

As she moved to the door, she heard the physician say, "Stay here, boys." With that she moved outside and almost into Dakota's chest.

"Oh, Dakota, I'm sorry I couldn't tell you. I found a dog in the alley and he was hurt. We just brought him down here."

"Is the dog all right?"

"He's going to be fine. The doctor is taking care of him."

"Are *you* all right?" he asked, thinking she looked a little flushed.

Darvi nodded quietly, and Dakota was willing to let the matter drop, but he'd caught the word we and noticed the two young men who stood at the doctor's office window watching them.

"Ready to head back to the ranch?"

"Yes, please."

Dakota saw her to the wagon, but before he could assist her, she stopped and looked up at him.

"There were two young men who helped me. I think they were more interested in me than the dog."

Dakota nodded, his eyes telling her he cared.

"I think you might be right," she said in a soft little voice. "Trouble seems to follow me around."

"It's not your fault, Darvi. If I know you, you didn't do anything improper. Their interest is not your doing."

"Why were they interested?" she asked in genuine confusion. "I'm clearly no longer a teen, and they don't even know me."

"You're very pretty and very sweet, and that's a combination most men can't resist."

Darvi smiled a little at the compliment and allowed herself to be helped into the wagon even as her heart asked, *What about you, Dakota Rawlings? Can you resist?*

Seventeen

THE NEXT FEW DAYS BROUGHT AN EASY routine with them. Cash and Dakota worked for a good portion of the day while Darvi worked around the house with Katy, read, prayed, baked, took naps, or sat thinking about the changes in her life.

Come late afternoon and evening, the men would return, clean up, join Darvi and Katy for a wonderful meal, and then spend the evening visiting or playing games. Darvi couldn't remember when she'd had such a restful, peace-filled time. Both she and Dakota accompanied Cash to a Bible study he attended on Tuesday nights, and the three spent the next two days talking about the passage they'd studied in Genesis.

In fact, they were still doing this on Thursday night when someone knocked at the door. Cash rose to answer it. On his doorstep he found a remarkable sight: a refined woman, not young but elegantly dressed, whose eyes betrayed worry. She also bore a startling resemblance to Darvi.

"Good evening," Cash began, telling himself not to gawk.

"Good evening. I'm so sorry to call on you without notice, but could you please tell me if Miss Darvi Wingate is here?"

"Yes, she is here."

The woman's eyes closed momentarily in relief.

"May I see her?"

"Certainly. May I tell her who's calling?"

The woman hesitated, the fingers of one hand coming up to her mouth in uncertainty.

"Please excuse my horrid breach of manners, but I would really like to introduce myself."

Cash smiled and stood aside.

"She's right in here."

"Thank you."

Cash followed the woman back to the living room and watched as Darvi looked up at her.

"Aunt Renee?" the younger woman exclaimed, coming to her feet.

"Hello, Darvi," the older woman said, her voice thick with emotion.

The nearly identical strawberry blondes met in the middle of the room in a huge embrace.

"How did you know I was here?" Darvi asked in astonishment. "And what are you doing here? Mother had a fit when she couldn't find an address for you, so she could tell you about the wedding."

Darvi's aunt held her at arm's length.

"You're getting married?"

"Not anymore."

Renee's brows rose.

"It's a long story."

The two women stared at each other.

"My mother used to tell me that I looked like my father's sister," Darvi said, "but it's been so many years since she's mentioned it, and I just lost track."

The older woman smiled. "It's all right, Darvi. As long as you're safe from Seth Redding."

"You know about that?"

"Darvi," her aunt returned, becoming very serious, "I'm Annabelle Hewett."

Darvi's hand came to her mouth. "Oh, no. You're not serious."

"I'm very serious."

"So that's why..." Darvi began, but she had already started to laugh. Renee joined her.

The men stood and stared as both women collapsed with laughter onto the davenport. They didn't know if they should stay or go; both were too fascinated to move. Darvi finally noticed them standing side by side across the room.

"Oh, I'm so sorry," she began and stood. Renee followed suit. "Dakota, Cash, this is my aunt, Renee Comstock, or should I say Annabelle Hewett?"

"As long as you don't call me Aunt Renee in Aurora, I don't care."

Renee was now poised and gracious as she faced them.

"I'm so sorry to have come in this rude way, gentlemen. Please forgive me."

In the next few seconds, official introductions were made all around, and then the four sat down to talk.

"How did you know Darvi was here?" Dakota had to ask.

"Sheriff Laverty. I guess both Eliot and Seth came tearing into town on Sunday morning, acting and looking as though they'd lost a trunk of gold. Because you had told the sheriff your plan, he wasn't too surprised. I came in wanting the story for the paper, and he told me." The woman looked at her niece. "I nearly fainted when he said the name Darvi Wingate."

"And I wouldn't have thought that Annabelle Hewett was related to me in a million years. What are you doing in Aurora?"

"You knew that Sam died, didn't you?"

"Yes. Mother told me. I'm sorry."

"Well, he left me in a very comfortable position, so comfortable that I could have sat back and had ladies in for tea, and little else, for the rest of my years. I didn't want that. I wanted to make a difference. I found a way to do that very thing through the paper. It's been the most fascinating experience of my life."

"But you're not married again?"

"Not yet. I became engaged about two months ago to a man who lives in Kerrville, but we haven't set a date."

"I'm glad," Darvi told her sincerely. "I know it hasn't been easy."

Renee smiled. "Now that was your mother talking."

Darvi blinked. "Why? What did I say?"

"You said it's been hard for me. That's the type of thing she would say to explain away the embarrassing behavior of the black sheep of the family. If I'm off acting wildly for no reason, they must not talk about me, but if I'm getting things out of my system because of grief over losing my first husband, then there's no family shame."

Darvi sat back and crossed her arms. "I had no idea anyone else had Mother so well figured."

The men took their cue at that point. Unnoticed by the women, they rose and quietly left the room, going out the front door and onto the porch. The sun was setting fast, but there was still enough light to see each other.

Dakota took the large rocking chair, and Cash sat on the double swing.

"I wonder how the sheriff knew to send her down here," Cash pondered aloud.

"He knew my name was Rawlings, and the Rawlings Cattle Company of Kinkade, Texas, is pretty well known."

"Maybe. I'll have to ask Darvi's aunt."

Dakota's chair creaked as it moved, the swing giving off its own low groan.

"It wasn't that long ago I was teasing you about finding a woman, Dak," Cash said thoughtfully. "Mother would be awfully glad to see you two together."

"What two?" Dakota asked in genuine confusion.

"You and Katy," Cash replied sarcastically. "Who do you think?"

Dakota gawked at his older brother and then shook his head.

"I don't know anyone who does ranching better than you do, Cash, old buddy, but you need to stick with cattle."

"I don't think so."

"Cash," Dakota began again, this time his voice very serious, "Darvi is one of the sweetest women on the face of the earth, but she's like a sister I want to protect. I assure you, there's nothing more."

"Dakota, old buddy," Cash said, taking on the same tone as Dakota, "You can deny this all you want, but I've seen you two. Darvi Wingate may be a lot of things to you over the years, but a sister isn't going to be one of them."

Dakota had no reply. Cash had been utterly serious. His mind reeled with the implications, and he shook his head a little. He'd told Darvi her mouth was kissable and meant it with all his heart. He'd also said she was very sweet and pretty and meant that too, but not in a romantic way—at least he didn't think it was. In truth, having Darvi smile and be lighthearted was something he'd very much come to enjoy. Being with her was just plain fun.

"You riled at me, Dak?"

"No, just thinking."

"I'm right, aren't I?"

"I don't know, Cash. I honestly can't tell you right now."

"Do you mean you really haven't seen it?"

"Seen what?"

Cash was silent for a moment.

"You two have something special going. I know you just rescued her, and I can't say that that's not what I'm seeing, but she looks at you with hope and confidence. And I know you're used to taking care of people and wading into the fray to see justice done, but there's something different where Darvi is concerned. Mother saw to it that she raised three gentlemen, Dak, but what I'm seeing is above and beyond the call of duty."

Again the men fell silent, each alone with his thoughts. Cash prayed for this brother he loved so much, somewhat afraid he'd said too much. Dakota prayed for understanding and wisdom over these new thoughts and feelings.

He was rather drawn to Darvi, but did that mean he was falling in love, or did it just mean that he'd spent some time with her? He was not made of stone. He had held her in his arms a few times and even dried her tears, his heart deeply affected by her emotions. Were his own emotions more involved than he suspected? And what did she feel? Was Cash really seeing interest on her part? Dakota wondered how he could possibly know, wishing he could see her right now but knowing it would have to wait. She was still talking to her aunt.

ٷ-ٷ-ٷ

"So you were engaged," Renee prompted after they'd talked for some time about all that Darvi had been through.

"Yes. His name is Brandon Young."

"What happened?"

"I've gone through a lot of changes in the last few months, and I knew that Brandon was not the man for me."

"What kind of changes?"

"Spiritual ones."

A cynical gleam entered Renee's eyes. "So, you found religion. Your parents must be having a fit."

"I did not find *religion*," Darvi corrected in a firm voice. "This is different. This has been life-changing for me."

Renee took the reproach very well. The cynical gleam disappeared, and she only nodded.

"How did you know my parents would be upset?" Darvi questioned, suddenly hearing what she had said.

"Well, maybe not both your parents, but I knew your mother would be."

"Why?"

"Because your mother's world is perfect. By your needing God, you're saying she did something wrong."

"Oh, Renee," Darvi said softly, "that perfectly describes the situation. You would have thought I had committed murder. She wouldn't even let me discuss it with her."

"Your mother is a wonderful person, Darvi, and I'm so glad my brother married her, but her standard is higher than God's."

It was a very irreverent thing to say, but Darvi had to bite her lip to keep from laughing.

"Family is everything," Renee continued. "A good face must be put on at all costs. You must marry well. You can grieve someone's passing, but in a quiet way. And whatever you do, remember the ancestors!"

Darvi thought she could become very depressed at the moment. She found herself praying very hard for her mother, thinking that if she could please her mother, she would have an opportunity to share her new faith. She prayed for Renee as well, and in the midst of that, the men returned.

"I'm sorry we chased you out of your own living room, Cash," Darvi said.

"Not at all," he replied dismissing her words.

"Well, I'm glad you came back. I was just about to ask my aunt about her connection to Jared Silk."

Renee gave an unladylike snort.

"That man," she spoke as both Dakota and Cash found seats. "He calls himself a banker. I think before this is over, his entire operation will be disclosed. At least I hope it will be."

"How did you get onto him?"

"I used to bank with Jared, and I would see the most interesting people coming and going while I would be in his building, men who were not known for abiding by the law. I did a little snooping and found out that he wasn't always honest in his dealings. I pulled my money from his bank, and it's been war ever since."

Renee glanced over just then and found her niece smiling rather hugely at her.

"What are you grinning at?"

"You. And thinking about my father's reaction to your new life."

Renee shuddered. "We might have to have a talk, my dear little niece. There are some things the family does *not* need to know." Renee shifted her gaze to the men. "Do you two have a younger sister?"

They both shook their heads no.

Renee did a little head shaking of her own. "It's not fun. It doesn't matter that I've been grown and gone for years—I'm still Stanley Wingate's baby sister."

The people in the room laughed at her aggrieved expression, but each one also caught a bit of longing in her eyes. She might fuss and fume about her sister-in-law's views on family, but family was important to her too.

"I hope you'll stay with us," Cash suddenly said. "I hope Darvi invited you."

"She didn't, but I would appreciate the offer. When I arrived I didn't even look around to see what the hotels were like."

"How did you find us in the first place?" Dakota asked.

"I got as much information as I could from Sheriff Laverty. Then my boss at the paper knew of the Rawlings Cattle Company, and I came down with great hopes."

"And here I was," Darvi said with a smile.

Renee became a bit emotional but hid it very well. She hadn't known she had such a beautiful niece. Darvi was in the same boat. She had only seen an old photo of her aunt as a younger woman and heard of their likeness over the years.

But Renee didn't have to leave until the next afternoon, so the two renewed old family ties. In fact, Darvi was so caught up in her aunt's visit that the time rushed away. Her aunt had been gone only an hour when Darvi remembered that she had decided to leave on Saturday, which happened to be the very next day.

♣·♣·♣

"Are you all set, Darvi?"

"Yes. Thank you, Cash, for everything. And please thank Katy for me too. I tried, but she only shooed me away with the towel."

The two stood on the train station platform while Dakota went to the ticket booth. Cash laughed at Darvi's description, knowing it had to be very true.

"If she let you say goodbye, she might become emotional, and we can't have that."

Darvi smiled in understanding.

Dakota joined them in short order, and Cash gave Darvi a hug. She turned to Dakota, who smiled and hugged her as well.

"Thank you for everything."

"You're welcome. Here's your ticket. Have you got everything?"

Darvi nodded, her throat suddenly very tight.

"I hate goodbyes, so I'll just go."

Not even waiting for them to reply, Darvi turned and went on her way, swiftly taking the conductor's hand and boarding with her satchel. So she wouldn't think about the men behind her, Darvi made herself think about where her trunk might be after all these weeks.

Having watched her out of sight, Cash turned to his brother.

"Why didn't you tell her you were going?"

Dakota gave him a quick glance.

"The truth?"

"I wouldn't expect anything else."

"I wanted to hug her."

Cash had all he could do not to shout with laughter.

"Go on, Dak," he said with a chuckle and a slap on Dakota's back. "Chase her down until she catches you."

The men embraced, and Dakota, bag in hand, one that Darvi hadn't even noticed, went to board the train. It wasn't hard to find the person he was determined to sit with; she was on the opposite side from the platform, face to the window. Dakota stowed his bag up top, his eyes on Darvi as he worked. Not until he sat down did she turn, her eyes so full of vulnerability that he immediately apologized.

"I'm sorry I didn't tell you I was coming. I didn't mean to startle or deceive you."

"Why are you, Dakota?" she asked, honestly needing to know.

His eyes shifted away, but he still answered.

"It bothered me quite a bit to have you taken off the train like you were in Aurora. When I think of how long ago you started home, and you're still not there, it upsets me even more. As much as it's within my power to do so, I'll see to it this time that you arrive safely in St. Louis."

Darvi put a hand on his arm for a moment before once again turning back to the window. Dakota let her have the silence. He was more confused than ever about almost everything—his feelings and his job as a Ranger, just to name two. But right now he didn't need to dwell on those. He had a goal, and it was not complicated: Get Darvi home. Once he had done that, he would wait and see what the future might bring.

&#x3-&#x3-&#x3-

The telegraph for Darvi actually arrived a few hours ahead of her. Completely sealed in an envelope, it was from Annabelle Hewett, telling Darvi when she would be needed back in Aurora as a witness in Jared Silk's trial. It was all very businesslike and proper, allowing Renee to keep her cover yet still remain in contact with her niece.

Darvi, however, did not know this as the hired hack pulled up in front of her house and she listened to Dakota tell the man to wait. She stood on the sidewalk while he fetched her bag from the rear and proceeded to walk her up to the front door of the large, blue two-story house that loomed above them. Darvi went to that door and opened it without hesitation.

"Mother," she called as Dakota brought up the rear, closing the door behind him.

"Darvi!" a deep male voice came in reply, just moments before a tall, well-dressed young gentleman rushed to the front door and took Darvi in his arms.

"You're home! You're home!" the man kept repeating as he appeared to be squeezing the life out of her. He let her go for a moment but then snatched her right back into his arms.

Darvi caught Dakota's eye and tried to communicate her helplessness, wishing at the same time she could read his expression, which was very bland.

"Brandon," Darvi got out at last.

That man stepped back and looked at her.

"Where are my parents?"

"Your mother had to run uptown for a minute. And your father is at work."

She nodded and put a hand up so he could not hug her again.

"Brandon, I'd like you to meet Dakota Rawlings. He's the man who brought me home."

Brandon turned with a huge smile.

"Thank you so much, Mr. Rawlings." His hand came out for a shake. "I can't begin to tell you how I've missed her."

"My pleasure," Dakota assured him as they shook hands. He then turned to the strawberry blonde, who was watching his every move.

"Well, Darvi, I'd best be on my way. You take care of yourself."

Darvi's mind screamed that it wasn't supposed to be this way. Brandon wasn't supposed to be there. She and

Dakota had just spent two and a half more days together, and Darvi was more taken than ever. He couldn't leave now, not before meeting her parents.

"Thank you" was all she could manage, her voice coming out in little more than a whisper.

"It was nice to meet you," Dakota told Brandon before giving a last goodbye that encompassed them both.

Darvi watched in shock and amazement as he went to the door, exited, and shut it behind him.

Out on the sidewalk, Dakota returned to the waiting hack, spoke to the driver, and climbed on board. Not even after he'd taken a seat and the driver put the horse into motion did he look back at Darvi's house. His gaze swung here and there as they moved, but for the most part, his eyes were down the road.

The driver navigated a few turns, and some three blocks later, Dakota finally spoke.

"The big white one," he said quietly.

"Yes, sir."

Just moments later the driver halted again. Dakota alighted this time, paid the man, reached for his own bag, and went up yet another sidewalk. Much like Darvi, he too opened the front door without hesitation, stepped inside, and closed it softy.

Across the wide foyer stood an elegantly dressed woman, hair perfectly coifed, face turned to the housekeeper as they studied a list together.

"And you found two broken chairs?" the lady of the house inquired.

"Yes, but Croft is fixing them right now. It shouldn't be a problem."

"What about the glasses? Any more broken?"

"Not a one. That new girl from down the street is a marvel. She has the nicest touch of any girl you've ever hired."

"Good, good," the lady said absently, her eyes once again on the paper. When she glanced back at her housekeeper, however, she found her eyes on some distant spot, a smile on her lips.

Virginia Rawlings turned to the front door for the first time, her own smile bursting forth.

"Dakota," she said softly.

"Hello, Mother." That man's smile mirrored her own.

"You're home," she spoke again, this time moving forward.

The two met in a warm embrace, Dakota's heart echoing her words.

Yes, Mother, I'm home.

Eighteen

"HOW ARE YOU?" VIRGINIA FINALLY ASKED. At first she hadn't talked. She just wanted to hug him, not caring the reason he was suddenly in St. Louis and not Texas.

"I'm doing fine. How are you?"

"Worried about you."

"Why?"

She looked him in the eye.

"The last I'd heard you had five bullet holes in you."

Dakota grinned. "And you thought that might slow me down?"

Virginia only shook her head.

"Mother," he said, changing subjects quickly to what was on his mind. "Have you had your fall fling yet?"

"If you mean my Autumn Garden Party," she told him patiently, "no, I haven't. It's in 18 days."

"Can you invite the Wingates?"

His mother's brow furrowed. "Three blocks over, the large blue house?"

"That's the one."

"Why?"

"I want to see a little more of their daughter."

After dropping that tidbit of information, Dakota started for the stairs.

"Oh, and Mother," he now tossed over his shoulder, "can you send for the tailor? I need a new suit."

A moment later the bell rang at the front door.

"Dakota James Rawlings," his mother said in a no-nonsense way, "you come back here this instant!"

Dakota turned with a smile. "I've got to clean up if I'm going to be fitted for a suit."

"That can wait. Tell me about this girl."

"Get the door, Mother," he teased her, turning to go on his way.

Virginia had all she could do not to laugh. He was a rascal, just like his father, but she adored him.

The matter at the door only took a moment, and the second she was free Dakota's mother made a beeline for the stairs. Long before she reached his bedroom, she heard Dakota and his father talking. Not bothering to even knock at the door he had only partially closed, she barged right into her son's room. Dakota was already shirtless, bent over the washstand, Charles Rawlings Sr. talking to his back.

"So how's the ranch?"

"Doing great," Dakota spoke as he scrubbed. "I worked with Cash the days I was there. Everything looks fine. I think he's got a sale coming up soon."

"I've been following the prices. He should do well at market right now," Charles commented.

"How can you be talking about the ranch at a time like this?" Virginia demanded, arms akimbo.

"At a time like what?" Charles questioned in confusion.

Virginia pointed to Dakota. "The boy is in love."

"He didn't tell me he was in love," Charles stated. He then mumbled, "No one tells me anything."

"Of course he didn't tell you he was in love, you're only interested in the price of beef. Did you even ask about your mother?"

Charles looked sheepish, and both Virginia and Dakota had to fight smiles as they looked at him.

"How is your grandmother?" he ventured at last.

"I didn't get a chance to go see her, but as far as I know she's doing fine."

"And Cash?" This came from Virginia.

"Great. I've been at the ranch quite a bit these last few weeks. He's doing well."

"Slater and Liberty?"

"I haven't seen them, but I think everything is fine."

"Good. Now, about this girl," Virginia started. "What's her name?"

Dakota grinned but still said quietly, "Darvi."

Virginia's eyes widened with memory. "Darvi Wingate? Isn't she engaged to Brandon Young?"

"Was engaged," Dakota corrected.

"Did you have something to do with the breakup?" Charles asked.

"No. It all happened before we met."

Virginia was frowning again. "Before you met? She's Marty Bracewell's niece, isn't she? You've known each other for years."

"Met again," Dakota explained and waited for the barrage that wasn't long in coming. His mother wanted to know everything. Dakota did not volunteer every detail but gave his parents a fairly clear picture of the situation. His mother was stunned into silence, and he was rather relieved. It had been an emotional time.

"Is she all right now?" Charles asked kindly.

"Yes. She's doing very well."

"Good. I forgot to ask how long you can stay," Charles continued, reading his son's face very easily.

"I should head back to Aurora tomorrow, but I'll return for the party. The timing hasn't been right to talk to Darvi about some of what I'm feeling, and I may never have a chance, but I wish to do my own talking."

Both parents nodded in agreement, understanding completely.

"I'll get an invitation out today. I'll also send for the tailor, or if you'd rather, you could go to him and speed the process a bit."

Dakota nodded. "I'll do that. Thank you, Mother."

Virginia went to hug him again. "It's good to have you here, scars and all, even if it's just for a day."

Dakota looked over his mother's head to see his father looking pleased. It was at that moment he realized he'd missed a vital opportunity. This was the first time he had seen his parents since coming to Christ. By coming in and mentioning Darvi he had lost his chance, at least for the moment, of bringing up the changes in his life.

His parents left him alone, and Dakota prepared to go uptown. As he did so, he prayed for yet another opportunity to share his faith. If not now, then in a few weeks when he returned to St. Louis.

$$\text{৯-৯-৯}$$

Darvi would eventually kick herself for not making the connection, but they had never socialized with the Rawlingses before, and she simply gave their last name no thought.

Accompanying her parents to the party, she wore a dress of dark apricot. Made for her, it was lightweight and full-skirted. It fit perfectly, displaying her lovely shape and slim arms and neck. She didn't go for too many ruffles or much lace, but her gown was elegant.

A group of six arrived just ahead of Darvi and her parents, Stanley and Clarisse Wingate, forcing them to wait in line for just a few seconds. Nevertheless, the moment Darvi caught sight of Mr. Rawlings, her mind began to work. She didn't have time to develop any ideas—they were inside more quickly than she expected—but as soon as she spotted the man who had occupied many of her thoughts for the last two and a half weeks, it all made perfect sense.

Dakota was slightly taller than his father, who was an older version of the Ranger, and Darvi's eyes drank in the sight of him in a formal suit. His shirt was a snowy white, a black tie at his throat, and to Darvi he looked taller and larger than ever.

Her parents went through the receiving line first, and almost before she was ready, she was standing in front of him. Dakota held her eyes as he bent over her and kissed the back of her hand.

"May I see you on very short notice?"

"Yes." Darvi's soft tone matched his own.

"This evening? After the party?"

All she could do was nod. She thought it might be time to move away, but Dakota still held her hand. Her mind scrambled for something to say.

"I've heard from Annabelle Hewett," she got out.

"She told me she'd been in touch."

Darvi's eyes widened. "You've seen her?"

"I just got back."

Darvi nodded, even as her heart sank. "And that's why you want to see me."

Dakota studied her face.

"Are you seeing Brandon again?

Looking surprised, Darvi said no.

Dakota couldn't stop his smile. More people were coming in the door, so Dakota turned to his mother.

"I'm going to walk Darvi to the punch bowl. I'll be back shortly."

Virginia sent a beaming smile at the small strawberry blonde, who smiled in return. Dakota offered his arm and led her away.

If Darvi expected more of his time, however, she was to be disappointed. Dakota walked her directly to the punch table, got her a glass, and bent slightly to catch her ear.

"What time may I call for you later? I thought we might go for a walk."

"What time are you available after the party?"

"I think about six."

"Will seven o'clock work then?" Darvi asked, wishing it could be now.

"I'll be there."

Darvi forced herself not to watch him walk away. Most people knew she was no longer engaged, but she hated it when people talked about her.

There was someone talking about her right now, but had she known about these two and how kind their words were, she would have relaxed.

"Is Darvi all right?" Virginia asked as soon as Dakota was back at her side.

"Why do you ask?"

"She was clearly surprised, Dakota, and she looked rather pale."

"I noticed that too. I'll be seeing her later and hopefully I can clear everything up."

More guests arrived, and they went back to work. They spent another 20 minutes receiving people and then joined their guests in the huge garden at the rear of the house. It was a large group, but Dakota had little trouble finding Darvi with his gaze. He forced himself not to stare at her, much as he wanted to, but to mill around and talk with his parents' guests, some of whom he hadn't seen for years. And he enjoyed himself. He was even able to have a brief conversation with Darvi's father, who watched him rather closely but did not seem to object to him as a person. Dakota's heart, however, could not see seven o'clock coming fast enough.

☙ ☙ ☙

"Did you have a good time at the party?" Dakota asked when they were barely out Darvi's front door.

"Yes, I did. Your parents are very nice." She glanced sideways at him while they walked. "We've never been invited to anything at your parents' home before."

"Haven't you?"

"No. Did you have anything to do with today's invitation?"

"Yes, I did."

Darvi stopped and turned to him. "Why, Dakota? Why did you never tell me you're from St. Louis?"

"Because I'm not," he began, but seeing how stunned she was over that statement, he didn't go on. He glanced down the sidewalk just then and saw they were almost at the park.

"Would you mind if we sat down?"

"No, that's fine."

A few minutes later they took opposite ends of a bench in the middle of the park so they could turn and see each other. Darvi said not a word but waited and hoped that this man wasn't about to hurt her. She worked to keep her emotions from showing, hoping he would explain everything.

"The first thing I need to tell you is that I've never intentionally kept something from you. I knew you were from St. Louis, but where I was born just never came up."

She looked confused, so Dakota tried again.

"I left St. Louis when I was five, Darvi. My home is Kinkade, Texas. I'll always think of it that way. My father worked the ranch until just six years ago, when he and my mother moved back here. I'm 26 years old, and for most of those years my parents lived in Kinkade. My grandmother is still in Texas. She loved it so much she didn't want to move back, even though her only son did.

"On top of that, St. Louis is a sprawling city. If you had looked at my face when we pulled into your neighborhood and then up to your house, you would have seen that I was stunned to see how close you lived to my parents."

"Why didn't you say anything then?" Darvi asked. It was not an accusation, just an honest appeal for understanding.

"I was all ready to meet your parents, Darvi, but they weren't there. Brandon was. I could see that you didn't want him hugging you, but for all I knew he'd had a life-changing experience of his own, and the two of you would be engaged again by the time we next saw each other. I wasn't even convinced that he might not be with you at the party today."

For a moment they stared at each other, and then Darvi looked at her lap. She fiddled with the folds in her skirt before speaking.

"He didn't understand. He offered to take me to church every day if I wanted, but he just couldn't see how our not sharing the same beliefs could make that much difference. It took two days to convince him, and now I think he hates me." Darvi paused, her voice growing thick. "It also didn't help to have my parents just as confused. My mother is barely speaking to me."

"What did they have to say about the abduction?"

Darvi shook her head a little. "In order to protect Renee's privacy, I didn't go into much detail. I'm not sure that's fair to them since I don't think they understood the full gist of what happened, but I didn't know what else to do." Darvi paused before adding, "Not that I'm sure it would matter. All my mother seems concerned about right now is my breakup with Brandon."

Dakota's face clouded with compassion, and Darvi tried not to cry. Instead, she shifted her attention to Dakota.

"How did your parents take the news of your conversion?" she asked Dakota.

"We haven't discussed it. I wrote them as soon as I was able to sit up, and Mother mentioned it in her letter back to me, but when I got home, I didn't bring it up. I was gone less than 24 hours later and just arrived back yesterday."

"And you've been in Aurora?"

"Part of the time, yes. Jared Silk has been charged for money laundering, fraud, and embezzlement, but so far Seth and Eliot are still at the ranch. Something tells me they are behind Silk's arrest."

"But they're not in jail?"

Dakota shook his head no, even as he read the worry in her eyes.

"When does your aunt suggest you come back?"

"Suggest?" Darvi exclaimed. "She says I'm to *be* there by the twenty-eighth."

"A week from today."

"Yes."

"There's no point in my going all the way there and back. I'll just stay and go with you."

"You don't have to do that."

They stared at each other.

"I have a lot of things going on inside of me right now, Darvi," Dakota confessed. "But it's only fair to warn you that I'm not a St. Louis type of person. I love Texas."

"I love Texas too, but it's only fair to warn you that I've never been so confused about anyone as I am about you."

Dakota laughed a little.

"It's good to hear that someone else is in the same boat."

Darvi smiled, and again they found themselves regarding each other.

"Aunt Renee's telegraph was at the house when I arrived," Darvi said quietly. "I read it and remembered your telling me you were going to be in Aurora with me. I didn't see how that was possible, since you'd just left."

"If I had it to do over again," Dakota said, "I'd have asked to see you a moment before I left, so you would have known of my plans to return to Aurora."

"Would you have told me about your parents too?"

"That one's a little harder, Darv," he said comically. "I can never remember when Mother has that fall garden thing of hers, and for all I knew, she and my father were on a trip somewhere. They don't exactly check in with me."

Darvi had to laugh, and not just at Dakota's expression. She was beginning to see that he was from a different world. He teased her about trouble following her around, and she knew she was somewhat sheltered, but never once had he treated her like a child the way her parents and

Brandon were wont to do. She was just a year younger than Dakota, but he'd been out of the nest and on his own for ages. She, on the other hand, was still treated like a little princess, one who had suddenly discovered her wings and was not living up to the life her parents had planned for her in the palace.

"I should get you home," Dakota said. "It's getting dark."

Darvi sighed. "I feel terrible that I'm in no hurry to go home."

"I feel bad about that too, but I'd feel worse if your reputation suffered because of my keeping you in the park too long." Dakota had a sudden thought. "Would you like to stop by your house and ask your parents if you could spend the evening with my family?"

Darvi perked up but then thought better of it. "Won't your parents be rather tired?"

"Yes, but we always play cards when we're home on Saturday nights, even when everyone is weary. You could be our fourth."

"I would like that," Darvi said. Dakota stood and offered his arm, his heart swelling over the chance to spend more time with her. He still didn't know if that meant love, but he was enjoying every moment of it.

And his parents enjoyed it too. Darvi's parents were willing to let her go, and Dakota's parents were delighted to see her. They brought her in and made her feel very welcome, even going so far as to tell her how sorry they were for all she'd been through. Dakota's heart squeezed with thankfulness for their kindness and hospitality. It was a fabulous evening, and Dakota had all he could do not to take Darvi's hand when he eventually walked her home.

To Dakota's surprise, his parents were still up when he got back. They called him into the living room when they heard the door.

"I thought you'd be asleep by now, Mother."

"I should be, but the game perked me up a bit."

Dakota sat down, kicked his shoes off, and put his feet on the ottoman.

"She's a sweet girl," Charles opened. His shoes were off, his feet up as well. "A lot of fun."

"Yes, she is," Dakota agreed, his eyes a little distant.

His mother then proceeded to astound him.

"Have you fallen for her because of her beliefs, Dak?"

Dakota had all he could do to answer in a normal voice.

"That has played a part, Mother, I'm sure of it, but that's not the only reason." He stopped and looked at her. "Have you heard something?"

"Only that she broke it off with Brandon, not the other way around, and that the reason had something to do with religion."

Dakota nodded but didn't know what to say. Was this the opportunity he had been looking for?

"Your grandmother wrote to us, Dak," Charles put in. "She made no secret of her excitement over what she calls *your salvation*. This is the third, no fourth, time we've heard this. First Cash, then my mother, then Slater, and now you. I don't know what you think you all have that the rest of us don't."

Dakota was no longer left wondering. There was no getting around the fact that his parents were ready to talk. But was he prepared to tell them? With a quick reminder that he was only responsible for what he knew, he tried to start.

"No one's ever wanted you to feel left out, Father. I hope you understand that. And I know in the past you've said you've been to church all your life." Dakota paused. He was already starting to ramble. He took a breath and began again. "There's so much I don't know or understand, but this much is clear to me: I was lost in my sin. It took awhile, but I finally saw that I *do* sin, and that my sin separated me from God."

Dakota looked into their faces, encouraged that they were listening so closely.

"You've seen my scars, and I know Cash wrote you. I nearly died. When that happened, I knew I wasn't ready to die. If I had been forced to face God in person at that moment, I would have had no excuse. Cash and Slate had both told me that my sin separates me from God, and that the only way to cover the separation is through His Son, Jesus. I accepted Jesus as my own Savior, and I no longer fear death or judgment." Dakota's eyes met those of his father's. "It's not about going to church all your life or being a good person. It's more personal than that."

When they said nothing, he went on.

"And to answer your question, Mother, the same thing happened to Darvi. Brandon wanted no part of it, so she broke it off. Darvi and I didn't fall for each other because of that, but knowing that we believe the same lets us explore this relationship. If she didn't share my belief, I wouldn't have a choice but to ignore my feelings, no matter how much it might hurt."

"But you do think you're in love with her?"

"I don't honestly know, but I'm willing to find out."

Again, they silently regarded him.

Dakota suddenly hated this. He had never known such peace as he had now, but not having his parents being in one accord with him was very painful. They had raised him to be independent and think for himself, so he knew they would never be harsh with him over this or any decision, but he wasn't sure they had the slightest inkling of what had happened to him.

"Well, Dak," his mother finally said, although her tone was sober. "We're glad to see you home and safe. Any little difference in our beliefs is nothing in light of your being safe. That's all we care about."

Dakota held his tongue. The "little difference" his mother spoke of was nothing short of a life-and-death matter, but Dakota knew there was no sense arguing. Reminding himself to stay respectful, Dakota kept praying and asking God to work in their hearts and open doors of opportunity.

Nineteen

"WHAT IF HE'S RIGHT?" CHARLES ASKED Virginia after they had retired.

Dakota's mother turned from the bottle of lotion she had been reaching for and stared at her husband.

"About what?"

"About facing God. Can I honestly say I'm ready?"

"Of course you're ready, Charles. You're a good person. What more can God want?"

He stared at his wife. Had she not heard what Dakota had said? Had *he* misunderstood?

"Charles?" Virginia ventured, her voice so tentative that the senior Rawlings wondered what his face looked like.

"I'm going to go ask Dakota something. I'll be right back."

Virginia was stunned. What had he been thinking? Her brow furrowed with deliberation. She didn't like the children coming home and upsetting things. If Dakota left chaos in his wake, it would put such a damper on his visit. Confrontation was the last thing she wanted.

Down the hallway Charles' thoughts were far different. His heart almost in dread over some of the things his son had said, he knocked on Dakota's door, working to remember what Cash and Slater had shared as well. Dakota answered before anything came to mind.

"Are you going to church tomorrow?" Charles asked without preamble.

Dakota nodded. "I was going to go early in the morning and get a note to Darvi to see if I could attend church with her."

"What about your mother's and my church?"

"In truth, Dad, I don't know anything about it, but because you don't agree with my beliefs, I'm assuming there won't be anything there for me."

"And what do you hope Darvi's church will have?"

"Some type of message and challenge from God's Word. Something I can learn from and put into practice in my life."

"And that's all part of not being afraid to die?"

"My peace about death does not come from a sermon I might hear, but from knowing that I have a relationship with Christ. However, salvation is only the beginning. There's a whole life to be lived, and I won't know how to live it without study in the Word."

The older Rawlings studied his boy's face, their eyes meeting and holding.

"I'll go with you! Your mother too!"

Dakota blinked. "All right," he said slowly. "But I'm not sure what Darvi will say. I mean, I haven't checked with her."

"What if," Charles began, his pride rubbing him a bit, "it turns out she goes to our church, and the preacher explains it just like you did?"

"Then I'll wonder how you could have been missing it all these years," Dakota replied before he thought.

Charles wasn't happy with this disrespectful statement, and his eyes communicated that with ease.

"I'm sorry, sir. I shouldn't have said that."

"No, you shouldn't have, but it's what you believe, isn't it?"

Dakota dropped his eyes before admitting, "Yes, sir."

Charles didn't like the shame he felt over the way he'd gained the upper hand. It was true that he had taught his boys to respect him, but he had come knocking on Dakota's door, not the other way around.

"It's all right," he said quietly. "Sleep well, Dakota."

"Thank you. Goodnight."

Charles made his way back down the hall, unaware of the way Dakota stood and watched him retreat into the darkness. He gained his own room, where Virginia still had a light on, and floored her with his announcement.

"We're going to church with Darvi and Dakota in the morning."

"What church?"

"I don't know yet, but we're going."

Her mouth opened a little. "You don't mean that."

"I do mean it."

"Charles, what will our neighbors who go to our church say?"

"I don't care."

Virginia knew very well how true that statement was. Charles Rawlings Sr. never did anything because someone thought he should. She watched him settle into bed, not at all comfortable with his plan. The lantern was still on, so Charles caught her gaze on him when he turned on his side. Virginia dropped her eyes and reached for the lamp, but his hand stopped her.

"Ginny," he said quietly, "he's got me to thinking."

"About what?"

"I'm not a kid anymore."

"You're not old, either."

"Neither was Ben down at the bank, and he dropped without warning."

"So that's what this is all about," she said in a mothering tone. "You've just realized you're not going to live forever."

"Exactly."

Virginia had not expected him to agree. She had even used a tone with him that usually angered him.

"All right, Charles." She gave in more out of confusion than anything else. "I'll go with you."

Charles had not thought anything else. Virginia went nearly everywhere with him. But her answer gave him pause. Would he go if she refused? It took some time before

Charles fell asleep, but even then he wasn't sure he would go without her.

ॐ-ॐ-ॐ

"I'm sorry to call at your back door at such an early hour," Dakota said to the woman at the Wingates' kitchen door. "I didn't want to disturb anyone, but could you please get this note to Miss Wingate as soon as possible?"

"I will, sir. Is there anything else?"

"No, thank you."

That was how the morning had started. Dakota had awakened early and gone swiftly to Darvi's, hoping she would get the note as he directed, and she did. Just an hour later a return note arrived from her, telling Dakota what church she attended and that if he liked, she would come for him at ten o'clock. One more message from Dakota established that his parents would be along and also offered to include her in their carriage.

Now, Dakota, Charles, and Virginia rode in silence to the Wingate home. Virginia was tense, her mind filled with uncertainty over this outing. Charles seemed so certain, and Dakota was calm, his expression relaxed, but she felt completely out of her element.

It helped to have Darvi join their group. That young woman began a conversation with her the moment she took a seat, and Virginia actually relaxed a little before they arrived at the church.

"I want you to meet a friend of mine," Darvi continued to talk as they walked up the steps, the younger woman having taken the older woman's arm. "Her name is Mrs. Beacher, and she's such a dear. In fact, she lives just a few blocks from you."

"Martha Beacher?"

"Yes!"

"We've known each other for years. She goes to your church?"

Darvi smiled. "This is her church. She was the one who introduced me."

Virginia relaxed a little more. Martha Beacher was a wonderful woman, always kind and ready to lend a hand. Up to that moment Virginia had not known what to expect, but suddenly she wasn't worried, at least not about meeting the people. However, the sermon, or whatever the service entailed, still had her somewhat concerned.

🌸🌸🌸

"Can you tell what your parents thought?" Darvi asked Dakota as they walked in the garden behind the house.

"Not exactly." His voice was deep and soft. "I think my father understood, but I'm not sure what Mother was thinking."

"How is it that they wanted to come?"

"My father decided. I'm not sure he gave Mother much choice."

"Does she do everything he says?"

Dakota smiled. "What do you think?"

Darvi smiled back. "I think the Rawlings men are used to getting what they want."

Dakota looked very innocent. "I can't imagine what you're talking about."

"Of course you can't." Darvi's voice was indulgent. "You always *ask* me and give me lots of choices. You never *tell* me to do anything."

Dakota worked at not smiling. "Regarding what?"

"'By the way, Darvi, we're not going to make the next town. Would you like to camp here for the night?'" she began to tease him. "'Darvi, you've been through a lot. Would you like to lie down and rest awhile?'" Her brows rose in a way that told him she was very pleased with herself just then. "You're used to giving orders, Dakota Rawlings, and I suspect your father is the same way."

"You little pill," Dakota growled playfully and began to reach for her. Darvi darted away from him and around a bush.

"Did I hit a little close to home, Mr. Rawlings?"

Dakota told himself not to laugh as he came around the bush toward her. Darvi evaded him nicely and slipped across the paved path around an arbor. She peeked through and watched him approach. She was about to dart off again, but he stopped. Bending just a little to watch his face, Darvi waited.

"I just thought of something," he admitted, his eyes on hers. "I can't really do anything if I catch you."

Darvi's smile grew rather wide, her expression downright smug.

"On second thought..." Dakota reconsidered and started forward again.

Virginia chose that moment to call from the kitchen door, telling them she was serving coffee and cake in the living room.

"We're coming," Darvi took advantage and answered, her eyes gleaming with amusement as she sauntered triumphantly up the path.

"You're an impudent piece of baggage, Miss Wingate," Dakota growled close to her ear as he drew up beside her. Darvi smiled for a moment but suddenly stopped and turned worried eyes up to his. Her brow lowering in concern, she studied him a moment.

"You knew I was teasing just now, didn't you, Dakota? I mean, you do know how much I appreciate everything you've done, all your care and such?"

Dakota's finger swept through the soft tendrils of hair that refused to stay off of her forehead, pleased when her brow softened a little.

"Yes," he said softly. "I do know that you're thankful. You've told me in dozens of ways."

Darvi's head tipped to the side in a way Dakota found irresistible.

"What kinds of ways?"

In a flash Dakota was back on the roadside, having rescued Darvi from Cassy's ranch. He had stopped to check on her and soon found her sobbing in his arms. Never had he felt so needed.

"Let's just say," Dakota began, working to dispel the image, "in your own special way you've made it very clear."

Darvi studied him. "Will I ever get a straight answer to that question?"

Dakota could feel himself falling, his heart squeezing and filling all at the same time as he looked into eyes that held such trust and honesty.

"I hope so" was all he was willing to say just then, and Darvi understood. She smiled a little and nodded.

They walked on to the house, Dakota doing all he could not to place an arm around her slim waist. He hadn't been glad to see Brandon at the house a few weeks back, but he couldn't say he blamed the man for trying.

※ ※ ※

"Have you been at church this whole time?" Clarisse Wingate spoke rather primly the moment Darvi walked in the door. It was almost two o'clock.

"No, the Rawlings asked me to lunch, and I accepted. I didn't think you'd mind."

"And does my minding mean anything to you these days?"

"Of course it does, Mother. I thought you enjoyed the Rawlingses and approved of them."

Her mother sniffed, not wanting to admit that her daughter was right. Another tact was needed.

"You've certainly transferred your affections swiftly enough."

"Swiftly?"

"Yes, swiftly! You just broke off with Brandon a few weeks ago."

Still managing to keep her voice kind, Darvi said, "I broke up with Brandon early this summer, but no one would listen to me."

Her mother shook her head. "I don't know you anymore."

Darvi felt cut to the quick but stayed quiet. Why her mother would want the "old Darvi" back was unimaginable. The old Darvi pouted if she didn't get her way. The old Darvi was never happy, constantly wanting more things, parties, or excitement. The new Darvi was very glad to be rid of her.

"Did I see Mr. and Mrs. Rawlings in the carriage earlier?" her mother asked next, working hard to sound as though she didn't care.

"Yes."

"Does Mrs. Rawlings go to that church?"

"She did this morning."

Her mother's face was so stiff it looked as though it might crack.

"May I tell you something, Mother?"

Clarisse Wingate nodded but looked no less unyielding.

"Our ancestors are so important to you, but I can't remember half of them. I'm your only child. If I don't remember, who will?"

"You could make more of an effort."

"I suppose I could, but even you have forgotten some of them, and when that happened, I finally understood that we do not carry on through our ancestors."

Her mother's face went from stony to livid.

"How can you say such a thing? Why, you were named after your dearly departed Uncle Darwin and Uncle Virgil!"

Clarisse stomped away at that point, leaving the foyer area and retreating to her small sitting room on the south side of the house. It was her sanctuary, her leave-me-alone spot, but Darvi did not take the usual hint. She followed right behind.

"Please, Mother. Please discuss it with me."

"I will not! I've never heard such nonsense. You're going against everything we've ever taught you."

But her mother did turn to her, and even though her eyes did nothing but accuse, Darvi tried again.

"I have so much I want to share with you and Father, so much in my heart. But it seems to me that you only want to look good on the outside, not take time to see inside to the real person."

"You will not speak to me in such a way!"

The words were all but shouted, and Darvi retreated in defeat. Her face a mask of pain, she uttered her final words. "Uncle Marty told me I could live with him anytime I needed. I leave Wednesday for Aurora. I think I'll just go on to Austin from there."

Darvi waited for her mother to ask her not to go, to order her or demand that she come right home, but nothing was forthcoming. Feeling as though her insides were breaking into little pieces, Darvi took her pain over this rejection to her room, where fighting tears of horrible pain and confusion, she began to sort through her things and pack.

3·3·3

"I want you to do me a favor," Virginia said to Dakota the moment he came home from returning Darvi. Setting her book aside, she turned a little to face him squarely.

"All right," Dakota said as he sat down, watching his father put his paper aside and figuring that he was in the dark as well.

"When do you leave?"

"Tuesday or Wednesday."

Virginia nodded. "I want you to write me a letter."

Dakota forced a dozen questions to stay inside.

"You can write it now and leave it here for me, or you can write it after you leave and mail it."

Dakota only looked at her; Charles did the same.

"In the letter, I would like you to explain to me what that man was talking about this morning. What does he mean when he says we have to be born again?"

"May I ask you a question?" Dakota put in before she could go on.

Virginia gave a brief nod.

"Why can't we talk about this face-to-face?"

Virginia looked away and kept her eyes averted while she answered.

"I haven't told anyone how much it bothers me that all of you boys have something with your grandmother that I don't have. And now your father is interested, and I'm going to be left all alone."

"I would never leave you all alone," Charles said quietly.

"Not physically—I know that—but this is bigger than our living together, Charles. You must see that."

"Yes, I do," he admitted out loud because she was still not looking at either one of them.

"But why a letter, Mother?" Dakota persisted.

"Because I need time to think. I feel rattled when you start to talk of this, and I want to panic and run." She finally turned to him, and Dakota was shocked to see tears in her eyes. She managed to speak, but her voice was filled with self-deprecation. "Wouldn't the women in town be amazed to find the invincible Virginia Rawlings all shook up over her son's religious convictions?"

"I'm not sure I agree with you there, Mother. If you were to get any of them alone to talk about their own mortality, I think you might see something different. Maybe all the parties and committees are a way of covering their own fears."

"But you and that pastor honestly think I deserve to go to hell, don't you?"

"*I* deserved to go to hell," Dakota countered. "Why God saved me from that I'll never know, but that's what He did, and I know He's waiting to do the same for anyone who will call on Him."

Virginia's heart lightened within her. She had felt so helplessly condemned, but Dakota's tone had been understanding and humble. And she did want to comprehend, but it was frightening to her as well. At the same time, he had made it sound as though there was hope.

"So you'll write the letter?"

"Absolutely. I'll leave it in my room."

Virginia wanted to cry in earnest then. He was so much like his father: used to taking charge but sensitive with those he loved. She didn't know why she'd expected the worst, but she had.

Stifling a yawn, Virginia suddenly felt very weary. Not getting her son's wrath or scorn was so relieving that all she wanted to do was sleep.

Having been married to her for 30 years, Charles detected the signs. She had yet to look at him, which told him she was either embarrassed or still felt betrayed, but even in profile he watched her lids grow heavy over the pages of the book she had reopened. Before long she was trying to read with her head laid back, finally giving up and placing the book in her lap. Moments later her eyes were closed.

Father and son were on their own, but neither spoke. Dakota had questions but sensed they should wait. His father hadn't looked his way before going back to the newspaper, but Dakota had watched the way he'd studied his wife. It came to him without warning, and he was not sure his parents were aware of the fact, but Dakota saw for the first time that God had certainly blessed their marriage.

Dakota didn't join his parents in reading or napping just then. He was too busy wondering how he'd never seen this before. Not moving an inch from the living room, Dakota talked the whole thing out with God and determined to ask Cash the next time he saw him whether God blessed those who wanted nothing to do with Him. Dakota thought He must, but that wasn't good enough. The Texas Ranger wanted verses to prove it.

కు-కు-కు

"How are you today?" Dakota asked quietly as he and Darvi walked from her front door on Monday evening.

"I'm fine," she said quietly.

"Was your mother a little cool just now," he asked before getting to the carriage, "or did I imagine things?"

"Frozen better describes her," Darvi said so quietly that Dakota let it drop. He had asked her to join him for dinner and knew that this conversation would wait for the restaurant.

They rode in silence; Dakota at the reins, Darvi beside him. Thinking as they moved along that Dakota was one of the most restful persons she'd ever known, Darvi felt not the slightest anxiety whenever she was with him. If he looked at her a certain way, her heart would pound and her pulse race, and his nearness affected her no small amount, but never did she know danger or fear. It was an amazing thing.

Sitting beside her, having already pulled the carriage over to the curb in front of the Grayson Hotel, Dakota studied Darvi's profile and waited. He smiled just studying that captivating mouth and little-girl-turned-up nose. She was in a far-off place right now, but the half-smitten Ranger saw no reason to disturb her. Not even the horse's shifting brought her attention around, and Dakota waited several minutes in silence. When he saw her noticing where they were, he just waited for her eyes to swing to his. Darvi smiled as soon as they met.

"We're here," she grinned a little.

"Yes."

"How long?"

"I didn't keep track."

"But we didn't just get here, did we?"

"No."

For a few seconds they just watched each other. Dakota's heart felt a little fuller every time he was with her. Darvi's was doing the same.

Dakota climbed down at last, moved to her side, and assisted Darvi to the walk. Offering his arm to her, he said, "May I escort you to dinner, Miss Wingate?"

"Yes, please," she said.

Dakota led her inside. It was going to be a wonderful evening.

Twenty

"I WAITED FOR HER TO TELL ME I COULDN'T go to Uncle Marty's, but she was silent. She's been silent ever since."

"Oh, Darvi, I'm sorry it's gone like that. Is it the same with your father?"

"No," Darvi said with relief. "I think he's a bit upset with Mother. In fact, he talks to me more than he has in years. He's nonstop at the dinner table and in the evenings. He even asked me to breakfast this morning. We had a wonderful time."

Darvi bit her lip suddenly, and Dakota let the subject drop. They had enjoyed a sumptuous meal of veal cutlets, baked potatoes covered with dill and cheese, baby peas, and dark rye biscuits. Now they had hot coffee in thin porcelain cups with French pastries headed their way. The gas lighting was soft, and the table was set in a horseshoe booth. There were couples on either side, but all voices were quiet, the waiters moving silently over the brightly colored rugs, making the setting more elegant.

"Will it work for you to leave here tomorrow afternoon instead of Wednesday morning?" Dakota inquired.

"I think so. Is there some problem?"

"No, but we have to go back through Kinkade, as I need my horse, and it might be nice to have a little extra time on the other end."

"Would it be easier if we split up at Young Springs?" Darvi made herself ask. "I could go on to Aurora on my own and meet you there."

"I'm not letting you out of my sight," Dakota said bluntly.

"But then you'll have the trouble of getting whatever horse I ride back to your brother's."

"I'm sorry I didn't tell you, but I planned for us to ride the train. I'll just pay the price to put Eli in with the stock. You won't have a horse to worry about."

Much as Darvi wanted to bask in the warm glow of knowing that he had planned all this to take care of her, she couldn't get Eli from her mind. She bit her lip to keep from smiling, but it didn't work.

"What's that for?"

"Eli."

Dakota rolled his eyes.

"What will he have done all this time without you?"

"Probably driven Cash crazy. My brother has better things to do than entertain my horse, but Eli will be keeping a close eye out for me, and as compassionate as Cash is, he will have probably ridden him a time or two."

Darvi suddenly smiled. "Admit it, Dakota."

"Admit what?"

"You miss him too?"

Dakota grinned but didn't have to answer; the pastries had arrived. They talked for another hour, eating slowly and enjoying endless cups of rich coffee. It was like a dream come true for both of them as they covered various subjects and beliefs, some held very dear and others still under inspection. They talked about their moments of salvation again, both reflecting on the way God had been working behind the scenes and how obvious that was now. Dakota told Darvi nearly every word of the letter he had written to his mother and appreciated her encouragement. After hearing about Dakota's letter, Darvi thought she might write to her own mother and wondered if that might not be easier for her to take.

"Dakota," Darvi asked as they finally rose from the table to go, "would you mind giving me the Scriptures you wrote to your mother, the exact ones?"

"Not at all. Do you want them tonight, or can I bring them tomorrow?"

"Tomorrow is fine. I think I need to put some distance between us, so I won't write until I get to Texas."

Her words had the strangest effect on his heart. He didn't say anything, but knowing she was returning to Texas with him and that she was so matter-of-fact about it filled him with hope and happiness. Though she was deeply affected by this fallout with her mother, he still wanted her with him. He wanted her close, not just to protect and keep an eye on her, but to be with her, to hear her voice, listen to her laugh, watch her smile, and talk with him about a thousand different subjects. He was afraid to let his heart move too fast, but at times it was so hard.

Such a moment came upon him when he dropped her off. He wanted to spend more time with her. He wanted to hold and kiss her but knew that such actions at this time would be a mistake. Instead he held her hand for a moment and lightly kissed the back of it, much like he had done at his parents' house that first afternoon. He looked up to see Darvi's smile.

"Is something funny?"

"No, it's just a little hard to remember the Ranger when I see you dressed like this and using manners one would expect to find only in the city."

"Well, we are in the city," he teased a little. "I thought it appropriate."

"Is that the only reason you did it?"

Dakota's white teeth gleamed as he smiled, but no answer came to her question.

"I'll see you tomorrow. I'll be here around one o'clock, and we'll take the 1:45 train."

"All right. Thank you for a wonderful evening."

"Thank *you*" was all Dakota said, and he moved on his way.

Darvi's father was in the living room, but she was glad he was busy with a newspaper. She wanted to be alone and to cherish the memories of the evening.

❦ ❦ ❦

They were silent for the first time in hours. The conversation that had started at dinner in St. Louis the night before only continued as the train moved south and west. Dakota had been good at his word: He had brought the list of Scriptures he'd put in his mother's letter for Darvi. Darvi's mouth was dry, and she was tired of talking, but her brain was still moving faster than the train. Dakota had put his head back and fallen asleep, but Darvi took her Bible from the satchel at her feet and turned to the first verse.

The list started with Romans 3:23: *All have sinned, and come short of the glory of God.* Next was Romans 6:23: *The wages of sin is death; but the gift of God is eternal life through Jesus Christ our Lord.* Dakota had also written some notes. One was about the jailer in Acts who had asked Paul and Silas how he could be saved. Darvi found their answer in Acts 16:31: *They said, Believe on the Lord Jesus Christ, and thou shall be saved, and thy house.*

The book of Ephesians came next with 2:8,9: *By grace are ye saved through faith; and that not of yourselves: it is the gift of God, not of works, lest any man should boast.* Romans 10:9,10 went on to add: *If thou shalt confess with thy mouth the Lord Jesus, and shalt believe in thine heart that God hath raised him from the dead, thou shalt be saved. For with the heart man believeth unto righteousness; and with the mouth confession is made unto salvation.*

Second Corinthians 6:2 left no doubt as to the urgency of the decision: *I have heard thee in a time accepted, and in the day of salvation have I helped thee: behold, now is the accepted time; behold, now is the day of salvation.* The last verse Darvi looked up was from John 20:31: *These are written, that ye*

might believe that Jesus is the Christ, the Son of God; and that
believing ye might have life through his name.

Thank You, Lord, Darvi's heart now prayed. *Thank You for*
saving me and showing me all of this. Help me to write to my
own family. I want them to have this hope. I want them to know
and believe.

Darvi felt tired now. She hadn't slept all that well in the
night and had woken early, hoping her mother would offer
an olive branch before she left. No such offer was made.
Darvi had said goodbye to her father and mother, but only
her father had replied. Her father had started to scold his
wife even before Darvi was out of earshot, but that hadn't
made her feel any better.

Quite suddenly Darvi wasn't certain if the letter was a
good idea. She had already said enough. What she needed
right now was for her mother to speak to her. Anything she
said short of that time would surely fall on deaf ears.

Thinking she would have to discuss it with Dakota, and
hoping that he hadn't written all of those references out for
no reason, Darvi drifted off to sleep.

꙳ ꙳ ꙳

Never had Texas looked so good. Dakota had sent word
from Dallas that they were on their way, but not until he saw
Cash on the platform was he certain the telegram had
arrived.

The brothers embraced just before Cash hugged Darvi.

"Welcome back," he told her with a huge smile.

Darvi would have replied, but Dakota stepped over and
hugged her too.

"What was that for?" Darvi asked, even as she wished
he would do it again.

Dakota looked innocent. "I was adding my own welcome to Texas."

"But you came with me," Darvi pointed out, eyes just
short of laughter.

Still managing to look innocent, Dakota asked, "So does that mean it doesn't count?"

"Come on you two," Cash cut in, his voice dry. "Dakota needs to visit a certain horse."

"How is he?"

"Completely depressed. He must think you're dead."

As they moved to the wagon that would take them to the ranch house, Dakota could only laugh at the description; he knew it had to be all too true.

∂·∂·∂

"How was your trip?" Cash wanted to know as soon as Darvi had returned from freshening up in her room.

"It was fast. Very few delays. We stayed over in Oklahoma City one night but otherwise just slept and ate on the train."

"Where did you stay in Oklahoma City?"

"The big hotel. I can't recall the name."

"The Oaks?"

"That was it," Darvi said with a smile. "You've been there?"

"Several times. Oh!" Cash remembered. "A package came for you."

"From whom?" Darvi asked as Cash moved to his office and came out again.

"I don't know."

Darvi took the package from Cash's outstretched hands, her movements somewhat cautious. Cash offered his pocketknife, and a moment later the strawberry blonde had it open. A letter came first and then, surprisingly enough, a black-haired wig.

Darvi read the note, her eyes growing huge just before Dakota came in the front door.

"You're not coming in here," he said sternly to Eli, who had clopped right onto the porch. "Now get back before I put you in the barn."

With this he shut the door, but a glance out the window told Dakota that the horse had stationed himself in the yard, where he could see inside. The Ranger only shook his head and joined the others, surprised to see Darvi looking rather sober.

"What's going on?" Dakota asked.

"She wants me to wear this wig."

"Who wants you to wear a wig?"

"Aunt Renee. She wrote, reminding me that Jared Silk is locked up but Seth and Eliot are still free men. She doesn't want Seth to recognize me and get it into his head to snatch me again."

Dakota shook his head a little. "That's not going to happen."

Doubts assailed Darvi in a horrible rush. It was so easy in this place, at this ranch, to forget how helpless she'd been, but for a moment the memories came flooding back. A shudder ran over her as she pictured Seth's calm, implacable face. He had been completely serious about keeping her until she fell for him.

Seeing her uncertainty, Dakota sat next to her, his head turned to watch her. Cash had quietly left them alone. Darvi did not look at Dakota, so Dakota sat a moment, giving her time to think.

"I tell myself you won't let anything happen, but in truth, Dakota, you can't be with me every moment."

"That's true."

Darvi finally looked at him.

"But you're still sure he's not going to get me, aren't you?"

"Yes, very sure."

She looked so troubled and confused that he took her hand.

"Listen to me, Darvi. I'm not trying to play God here, but I'm very good at what I do. I assume your plan is to stay with your aunt, and I'm hoping that will work out, but if we need to take rooms in the same hotel in order for me to be close by, that's what we'll do. Seth Redding is not going to take you against your will again."

Tears filled her eyes before she whispered, "I didn't like it, Dakota."

"I know," he said softly before reaching up with his free hand to touch her cheek. "We'll be thinking very clearly; we'll take all the necessary precautions; and in truth, I just don't think he's that stupid. As soon as he spots me, he'll put the situation together."

Darvi looked surprised. "He will, won't he?" she said in soft amazement.

"I certainly think so. He's not a fool, or he wouldn't be working for Silk. In fact, they probably know now. After all, we both disappeared at the same time."

Darvi shook her head. "Why didn't any of this occur to me before?"

"I don't know, but there's no point in worrying. We're going to do everything we can to keep a lid on this. I'm not expecting any trouble." Dakota reached for the wig, his mouth just beginning to smile. "Your aunt is quite a character." He fingered the hair for a moment and then looked at her again. "You might look good with black hair, but I prefer what you have."

Darvi smiled but didn't reply. She wanted to say something about the way he looked too—his size, his handsome face, his gentle manner—but she thought someone might be headed their way.

Dakota watched her, wanting to speak as well but holding off for the same reason. Dakota didn't know when the time would be right, but it wasn't now.

"I've got dinner on," Katy called from the edge of the room.

"Thanks, Katy," Dakota responded and stood with Darvi. "Are you all right?" he asked as soon as Katy turned away.

"Yes, thank you. I can't say that I'm looking forward to it, but I think I'll be fine."

Dakota took her arm to escort her to dinner, thinking she was the most courageous woman he knew.

He would have laughed if he could have heard Darvi's prayer at the moment: She was asking God to give her strength and to help her be brave.

⅊-⅊-⅊

"It's almost completely dark now," Darvi commented, her head tipped back a little. Dakota followed her gaze.

"I love a Texas sky," he said quietly. Having eaten dinner, he and Darvi had taken a walk. The sky was clear this night—huge and full of stars.

They were silent for a moment, both still looking up and trying to take it all in.

"There's a man who runs the general store in Shotgun where my brother lives," Dakota began. "He's huge. He has to duck for every doorway, and if he's coming through, no one can walk beside him. Not too long ago I read in Isaiah 66 where it says that heaven is God's throne and the earth His footstool, and I thought about what a big God He is. I love a Texas sky. I think it's the biggest in the world, but even at that, God has to duck His head to enter my world, because He's so huge." Dakota looked down at Darvi, who was staring up at him in the shadowy light. "But that is what He did for me, Darvi. He ducked His head and entered, so I could be saved."

"Oh, Dakota," was all she could say.

He reached out his hand and she took it, finding comfort in his touch. Darvi was not at all looking forward to returning to Aurora, not even to see her aunt, but Dakota's hand and words reminded her that she was not alone. Dakota wasn't all that thrilled himself, but he wanted closure to the situation so Darvi would not have to look over her shoulder in fear.

And the sky only helped. If God could create a universe this big and perfect, He could surely handle the relatively small court case that awaited them in Aurora.

᠀᠀᠀

"You still awake?" Dakota asked Cash after bedtime that night, barely taking time to knock.

In truth Cash had just dropped off, but he was able to wake swiftly.

"What's up?" he asked as he threw the covers back and swung his legs out to sit on the edge of the bed. Dakota sat down as well.

"I haven't had a chance to tell you what happened with the folks."

"Why, what happened?"

In great detail Dakota explained the way Charles had shown interest in the things Dakota shared, his visit to Dakota's room that night, and the way they had attended church together. Dakota recounted almost word for word the letter he had written to his mother while Cash sat in stunned silence.

"They went to church with you?" the older Rawlings clarified in wonder.

"Yes. Mother was not happy about it, but you can tell she's thinking. Father, for all his interest, is not asking too many questions. I'm not sure if Mother's lack of enthusiasm has tempered his response, or if the whole thing was a flash in the pan."

Again, there was silence in the darkness. Cash had been praying for his parents for years, but the door had never opened as it had for Dakota. Of course, the change in Dakota was more drastic, so it wasn't hard to see that this might have had an effect. Still, the whole thing took some getting used to.

"Tell me something, Cash," Dakota went on.

"Okay."

"Is the folks' marriage blessed by God?"

"Certainly."

"How do you know that?"

"Matthew 5 says God allows the sun to rise on the evil and on the good. He sends rain on the just and the unjust. What made you think of that?"

"Seeing Father and Mother…they love each other more than they ever have, but they haven't had the Lord to lead them. I can't imagine making a marriage work without God."

"But God does bless those who want nothing to do with Him, Dak; that's the kind of God He is."

Dakota nodded.

"I take it you've been thinking about marriage lately."

Dakota looked at him.

"I don't know what I'm thinking exactly, but I do know I've never met anyone before Darvi who actually made me think about giving up the Rangers."

"And you're certain you have to give up that job if you marry?"

Dakota's nod was decisive. "It's no life for a family man. I'd never be home."

"What would you do?"

Dakota smiled.

"I rather like this ranch."

Cash could only laugh.

"I won't tell you I could use you or you'd be welcome, little brother. I expect you to already know."

The two looked at each other.

"I'm going to bed," Dakota announced as he stood.

"All right. I'll see you in the morning."

Cash waited until the door closed and slipped back into bed. He didn't let his mind drift too far, but it wouldn't hurt his feelings to have Dakota around more often. Thinking that Darvi would be a nice addition to the picture too, he fell back to sleep.

Twenty-One

DAKOTA AND DARVI HAD TALKED FOR THE first part of the
journey to Aurora, but now both were silent with their
thoughts. Darvi was fine when she was distracted by conversation, but alone with her thoughts, she felt something
akin to panic creeping up on her.

Part of her mind simply could not accept the fact that she
was headed back to Aurora. And not just to the town, but to
the very train station where those two men had taken her.

A glance at Dakota's profile told Darvi he was as confident as any man could be in his ability to protect her, but
going back to Aurora was causing her no end of anxiety.
And the wig in her bag didn't help!

She shook her head at her aunt's scheme. What could
the woman be thinking? Darvi hated pretense. She honestly didn't know how her aunt stood such a life. A spark
of anger flashed inside her, and it was all directed toward
her aunt. Darvi knew it was wrong and worked for the
remainder of the journey to calm down.

*I'll just explain when I get there that I didn't want to wear the
wig,* Darvi finally calmed and told herself. *Aunt Renee will
understand. I don't have a thing to worry about.*

❧ ❧ ❧

"Where's your wig?" were the first words out of Renee's
mouth.

Darvi's mouth opened a little with hurt and surprise and for a moment she lost her train of thought. When she recovered, she was glad to hear that her voice was normal.

"Are you going to ask us in, Aunt Renee?"

"Oh, yes." The older woman was momentarily flustered by being caught off guard, and the result was a breach of manners. "Come in. I'm sorry. You took me by surprise."

Renee invited them into her living room. Moving silently, Dakota and Darvi entered and, when directed, sat on the comfortable red sofa. Most of the furniture was red or pink, but it wasn't gaudy as Darvi might have expected had she only heard about it. The room was warm with family photos and bits of lace and ruffles here and there.

"Why aren't you wearing the wig?" Renee asked as soon as she had taken a seat across from Darvi. She had known her own anxieties concerning the pending court case, and having Darvi show up looking like her wasn't helping.

"It's in my bag," Darvi told her quietly.

"You didn't feel you needed it?"

"No. I think Dakota is all the protection I need."

"What about my privacy—did you think of that?"

Darvi hadn't, but didn't say that. Why had she thought her aunt would understand? They had gotten on well at the ranch in Kinkade, but in truth, they didn't know each other at all. Working not to lead with her emotions, Darvi spoke.

"There's something I need to tell you, Renee. If, when I'm done, you want me to wear the wig, then I will, but I hope you'll hear me out."

"I will, Darvi," Renee said sincerely, seeing that she had come across rather strongly.

"Thank you," Darvi replied. "I think that even if I wear the wig, people will be able to see that we're related. I don't think it can be helped. I know you value your privacy, but at what price?"

"What do you mean?"

"I mean, if you believe in what you're doing here, it shouldn't matter. It shouldn't make any difference if people know that Annabelle Hewett is an assumed name. Everyone comes from somewhere. Surely people know you have family."

Renee blinked at her. Never had she looked at it that way. She then looked slowly at Dakota to gauge his reaction, but his face was unreadable. Watching her, Darvi thought Renee looked so surprised that it made her feel guilty.

"I'm sorry, Aunt Renee," She said quietly, sorry that she had even tried to explain. "I hate subterfuge, and having to wear that wig scares me more than taking my chances on the street. I couldn't even tell my parents the whole story because they would have wanted to know who this woman was that looked just like me. If you're hurt, I'm truly sorry, but I did mean what I said: Why must you hide who you really are?"

Renee looked upset, her fingers coming to her lips.

"I never thought about your not being able to tell your family, Darvi. Honestly, I didn't. Please tell them. If I had a daughter who had been through what you've experienced, I would want every detail. Tell them whatever you need to."

Darvi nodded, and in the moment Renee thought she looked very young and vulnerable. She also looked a bit pale. She wanted to speak more on the issue, but Dakota had a question of his own.

"There's something else bothering you, Darvi." Dakota's deep voice rumbled out, his head turned to study her. "What is it?"

Darvi closed her eyes for a moment and then looked at him.

"This whole thing—the trial, having to see Seth and Eliot again...all of it." Darvi glanced at her aunt. "I know you can't wait to see Jared Silk pay for his crimes, but in truth, I don't even know the man."

"You should still want to see justice done," Renee stated plainly.

"I do, but in the process I'm sure others are going to be hurt. I don't feel good about that at all."

"What others?"

"Cassy Robinson for one."

"Cassy's no child, Darvi." This time her aunt's words were blunt. "She knows exactly what type of man Eliot McDermott is."

"Be that as it may," Darvi went on quietly, "she loves him and so do the children. You may want justice served so badly that nothing else bothers you, but I can't make the same claim."

Renee sat back in her seat. She wanted to tell her niece to grow up and stop walking around with her heart on her sleeve, but maybe Darvi had a point. For the first time in a long time, Renee wondered if she might have become a bit hard.

"So, what is it you want to do, Darvi?" Dakota surprised both women by asking. "For that matter, what is it you want your aunt to do?"

Seeing that he was right, Darvi sighed very quietly.

"I guess I want her to do just what she's doing. Jared needs to answer the charges against him, and she's right, Cassy's made her choices with her eyes wide open." Darvi's gaze dropped to her lap. "Nevertheless, it still hurts my heart to be involved in all of this."

As Dakota had gotten in the habit of doing, he reached for her hand and held it tenderly.

"I'm glad to hear that, since this whole thing should hurt your heart," he assured her softly. "Justice is a must, but there are ways to go about it. There's nothing I hate more than coming across a Ranger who's lost his compassion, one who's mean and thoughtless. He gives the rest of us a bad name."

A distinct whinny outside the house suddenly set Dakota's gaze to the window.

"I'm sorry, ladies," he said with genuine regret. "I have to see to my horse. Would you please excuse me for a moment?"

"Certainly," Renee offered graciously, and a moment later she was alone with her niece.

"I appreciate all you've said, Darvi, and I plan to think on it."

"Thank you."

"I also don't want you to wear the wig. I think your point is very valid."

Darvi nodded with relief, as they both heard Dakota's voice outside. Darvi glanced that way, and when she looked back, her aunt was smiling.

"I certainly hope you're not going to let that one get away."

Darvi surprised her when she only smiled. Renee waited a moment for her to reply, but it didn't happen.

"No comment?" the older woman prompted, and Darvi laughed.

"Aunt Renee, I think you might be one of the most private people I know, but you expect me to bare my heart to you."

Renee grinned. "It's the reporter in me. I can't stand not knowing something."

Darvi smiled back, and Renee's eyes widened when she realized her niece wasn't going to answer. The older woman actually moved to the edge of her seat, reminding Darvi of a six-year-old.

"So tell me, how do you feel about him?"

Darvi laughed and watched her with amusement.

"Darvi Leigh Wingate!" She was very stern now. "This is your aunt speaking, and I expect an answer."

Darvi hadn't even opened her mouth when they both heard the front door. Dakota was returning. The younger of the two women had all she could do not to laugh at her aunt's aggrieved expression.

3·3·3·

"So you've never attended this church?" Darvi asked Dakota the next morning as they walked toward the end of town.

"No. I've never attended any church in Aurora." He glanced down at her and then back up the street. "I found myself looking for a certain strawberry blonde when I was last here. I'm afraid I thought of little else."

Darvi studied the firm, clean-shaven line of his jaw from a shorter vantage point and knew she'd been complimented. She shifted her gaze away again before speaking.

"My aunt seemed pleased that you asked her to join us."

"True. But if you'll notice, she's not here."

"No, she's not. She would say that my mother can't deal with the fact that I need a relationship with God, but I'm not sure she can either."

"It's easiest to be blind to our own sins."

Darvi silently agreed as the church came into view. The boardwalk would end in another 30 feet, and the church was still a block from there. They were nearing the end of the board slats when a horseman rode up. Dakota turned swiftly and brought them to a halt, but Darvi, whose hand was tucked in his arm, felt him relax.

"Sheriff," the Ranger greeted the rider.

"How are you, Rawlings?"

"Fine, and yourself?"

"I'm fine, thank you." With that the man tipped his hat toward Darvi. "You must be Miss Wingate."

"Yes," Dakota spoke up. "Darvi, this is Sheriff Laverty."

"It's a pleasure to meet you," Darvi greeted him.

"Your aunt tells me you're headed to church."

"Were you at the house this morning?" Dakota asked, his mind working so fast that he did not let Darvi answer.

"No, she came by my office as soon as Seth Redding showed up at her door looking for Miss Wingate."

Darvi's eyes grew large at this announcement.

"I'm not worried that he's going to try anything stupid," the law man went on smoothly, "but I'd just as soon not have you out and about today, Miss Wingate. In fact, if you wouldn't mind, the lawyer representing some of the bank customers was tied up yesterday when you came into town and would like to speak with you today. He's at my office."

"How did Seth know I was in town?" Darvi asked.

The sheriff's smile was lopsided. "Seth and Eliot seem to have eyes everywhere. Your coming in on the train would be no secret."

"And he was actually bold enough to go to my aunt's door?"

"Yes. She said he was very polite about it all, but that he seemed determined to speak with you."

From that point onward, Darvi's Sunday plans fell into a heap around her. Her expectation of spending some time in church and possibly fellowshipping for a time with the congregation was swiftly put aside. Knowing it was best to do as the sheriff asked, Darvi went with Dakota to a back room at the sheriff's office to meet with a Mr. Danby. He was a polite man, but all business. Some of his terms confused Darvi, but she asked enough questions to understand what her role would be the next day.

"All of this will be quite unnecessary," he said more than two hours later, his papers already in his case, "if Mr. Silk will simply admit to guilt—something we don't expect. But one can always hope."

Darvi could think of nothing to say to this, but something niggled at the back of her mind, even as the man stood, thanked her, nodded to Dakota, and went on his way. Dakota, good at his word, was with Darvi the whole time. He had been silent during the proceedings and was still quiet, giving Darvi time to think. A few minutes later she knew what was bothering her.

"This is all about Jared Silk, isn't it?"

"What do you mean?"

"No charge is being brought against Seth and Eliot for abducting me."

"Not at this time. Your testimony is about their involvement with Silk."

Darvi looked thoughtful and said with quiet conviction, "I'm going to have my say in that courtroom, Dakota. Even if none of the lawyers asks me about it, I'm going to tell them what happened to me."

Dakota smiled. "Go to it."

That smile was all Darvi needed until she had one more thought.

"Dakota," she asked, "why aren't Seth and Eliot in jail? Why is Seth allowed to roam the streets and look for me?"

"Because the law is imperfect, Darvi. I also suspect that his lawyer might have had something to do with it, along with the fact that you weren't here to file any charges."

Darvi knew she would have to be satisfied with this. She wasn't really content with it, but right now nothing could change her helplessness in the situation.

"I guess we'd better head back to my aunt's," Darvi was saying as the door suddenly opened.

"Oh! You *are* here," Renee spoke with relief as she entered. "I wasn't certain what could be taking so long, and I had myself convinced that Seth Redding had found you."

"He might find her," Dakota put in calmly, "but he won't take her."

Renee looked up at the Ranger's face and suddenly knew why Darvi was so trusting of him. Darvi's aunt liked Dakota—she liked him a lot—but there was no missing the steel in his eyes right now. Renee almost shook her head. She would not choose to tangle with this man if she was on the wrong side of the law. She thought anyone who did was a fool.

"Well, let's go home," she said quietly, simply wanting to see Darvi safe behind closed doors.

"That's fine," Dakota confirmed, "but if you don't mind, I'll answer the front door for the rest of the day."

All Renee could do was nod, but in her heart she was more determined than ever to see Darvi marry this man.

❧ ❧ ❧

Sunday turned out to be a very quiet day, which made the noise and crowded courtroom all the harder to take the next morning. It seemed that every person in town had turned out for this event, and Darvi knew that, as his witnesses, if the lawyer had not saved seats for them in the front row, they would have been outside with dozens of others who were denied entrance.

The courtroom was set up with a center section of seating flanked by two angled sections. Renee, Dakota, and Darvi had seats in the far right side. Once situated, Darvi settled her skirts around her, Dakota on her right and her aunt on her left, before glancing around. She had barely shifted her eyes when she spotted Seth in the far left section. The way the seats angled, they had nearly perfect views of each other.

He was looking straight at her, his eyes reflecting caring and interest. Darvi didn't look at him for long but shifted her own gaze back to the front. Dakota, on the other hand, kept watching.

The moment Darvi turned away, Seth leaned and spoke to a man—assumably his lawyer—who shook his head no. He then wrote a note and gave it to his lawyer. He read it, handed it right back, and once again shook his head no. At that point Dakota turned away, but not before seeing that Seth's eyes came right back to Darvi, who was still watching for the judge to enter. That the man was desperate to see the woman across from him was only too clear.

Dakota gave one more glance Seth's way, and that was when he spotted Cassy and the children in the front row of the middle section. All three looked pale and sober, and Dakota was glad for Darvi's tender heart. His own felt a little broken as well. He had chosen to deceive Cassy in order to rescue Darvi. Given a choice, he would do it all over again, but it wasn't something he enjoyed.

The judge finally arrived. He was a large man with stern eyes, and the audience was very quiet as he took his place and cast those penetrating eyes over the room. No time was wasted, however, and in less than five minutes, things were underway. Mr. Danby, whose strict business manner seemed to have melted into something a bit more dramatic, called many witnesses forward to testify, but the defense offered no cross examination until Annabelle Hewett was called to the stand.

Darvi watched her aunt move to the witness stand in graceful confidence. The defense was out to prove that the reporter's testimony, which was quite damaging, was nothing more than the rantings of an overemotional female. Their tactic fell very flat. Renee kept her cool, calmly answering all questions and putting holes in several theories. From her vantage point, Darvi thought Jared Silk looked angry enough to kill.

The day moved on slowly, and Darvi, to her surprise, wasn't actually called to the stand until the next morning. She thought she caught the softening of the judge's eyes at one point, but in her nervousness she couldn't be certain. She took the stand and tried not to feel the awful pounding of her heart.

"State your full name, please."

This came from Mr. Danby, and Darvi did as she was told.

"Darvi Leigh Wingate."

"Address, Miss Wingate?"

"49 Brighton Road, St Louis, Missouri."

"Thank you, Miss Wingate. Correct me if I'm wrong, but were you not taken against your will from a train in the Aurora train station on the sixth day of September?"

"Yes, sir, I was."

"And am I right in thinking that two men took you from the train?"

"Yes, sir."

"And am I also right in believing that those two men are in the courtroom today?"

Darvi's heart froze and then pounded on, making her feel breathless. She was certain she had told him this. Had he not heard her, or had he misunderstood?

Mr. Danby, who thought she would answer immediately, seemed to freeze as well. He looked at Darvi's stunned face and tried again.

"Would you like to me repeat the question?"

"Yes, please."

"Can you point out the two men who took you from the train?"

Darvi's heart sank. "No, I cannot."

Mr. Danby blinked.

"Maybe you need a little more time," he said, his face going slightly red, his eyes showing some strain. "Look around the courtroom again. Take all the time you need."

Darvi had all she could do not to look at Dakota and nowhere else, but she made herself take stock of the entire room. She had not been with those men for very long, but she was very sure they were not in the room. She looked back to Mr. Danby.

"Did you see them?"

Darvi began to shake her head no and then verbally answered.

"You're sure?" Mr. Danby tried again, but Jared Silk's lawyer had had enough and came to his feet.

"The woman has more than answered the question, your honor. What more could the man need?"

The judge waved him back down.

"Do you have another line of questioning, Mr. Danby?" the judge asked, his tone almost bored.

That man came just short of tugging on his collar.

"No, your honor," he admitted at last.

"Your witness, Mr. Robbins," the judge said to Jared's attorney.

"Thank you, your honor."

Darvi watched him come forward, a kind smile on his face, but it didn't fool her. She knew that all men had a right to a fair trial, but this man was out for blood.

"Now then Miss Wingate, there seems to be a bit of a misunderstanding here. You don't even know Jared Silk, do you?"

"No, sir, I don't."

"Have you even been into his bank or laid eyes on him before today?"

"No, sir."

"So anything you might have heard about Jared Silk is what you've read in the newspaper or been told by someone else. Isn't that right?"

"Yes."

The man's smile was just short of benevolent as he said, "That will be all."

"You're dismissed, Miss Wingate," the judge told her.

Darvi looked down just then and into Dakota's eyes. While he held her gaze, he raised his chin.

"Your honor," Darvi said a bit loudly, causing the judge to turn in surprise.

"Yes, Miss Wingate?"

"I would beg your indulgence, sir. I do have something to say, if I could just say it without having to answer questions."

"This witness has been dismissed!" Mr. Robbins nearly shouted, his calm face deserting him in a flash. Even Jared came to his feet.

"Sit down, both of you," the judge said in a frigid voice. "I want to hear what the lady has to say."

Darvi's eyes were huge in her pale face as she turned to face the judge, who was leaning toward her in full attention. Darvi made herself swallow and start.

"It's true, your honor, that I've never met Jared Silk, and that the men who took me from the train are not here today, but the two men who held me captive against my will are here today and have told me they work for Jared Silk." Darvi glanced their way and kept on. "Their names are Seth Redding and Eliot McDermott. I never saw the two men from the train again, but Mr. Redding and Mr. McDermott kept me in an apartment and made it very clear that I couldn't leave until I agreed to meet with Jared Silk."

"Why would they do that if you don't know the man?"

"They thought I was Annabelle Hewett, and even when they learned I was not, Mr. Redding decided to keep me. I was held at the apartment for two days and then taken against my will to Cassy Robinson's ranch. I had no idea where I was and no way to leave there."

"But you did get away?"

"Yes, a friend found me and got himself hired onto the ranch as a cook. We left one night after dark."

The eyes that the judge turned on the defense lawyer and Jared were colder than ever.

"Thank you, Miss Wingate. If there's nothing else, you may step down."

Darvi did so on shaking legs. She made her way back to her seat to the sound of the courtroom buzzing around her. Mr. Robbins was on his feet again, protesting the judge's interference and unorthodox behavior at the top of his voice. From their seats with the rest of the audience, the accused brothers and their lawyer had their heads close together, the lawyer doing all the talking. All three seemed to be completely unaware of the courtroom's state of pandemonium. The judge finally pounded his gavel to gain order and make an announcement.

"This court will adjourn until nine o'clock tomorrow morning, whereupon I will hear final testimony and make my decision. I will be available today until five o'clock for questions or further information."

With that he stood and exited the room. People talked even louder, babies cried, and in the midst of it, Dakota had Darvi's arm in a steel grip. Getting her outside as swiftly as he could manage, he moved her along through town, cutting off on a side street in hopes that it would be a shortcut to Renee's house.

In better time than he'd figured, the house came into view. Both still moving silently, Dakota took Darvi up the front steps, through the front door, and into the house, not even waiting a full heartbeat before he pulled her into his arms.

Twenty-Two

"YOU WERE WONDERFUL UP THERE," Dakota said softly, his arms still holding Darvi close.

Darvi let her head rest against the solid wall of his chest, thinking about how much she needed this man.

"I almost broke down," she said at last. "Could you tell?"

"No."

"It was when I caught sight of Nate and Lindy. I was so angry at Cassy for putting them in this position that I almost cried."

"You hid it very well, and you said everything that needed to be said. The judge was furious with Robbins." Dakota's chest vibrated a little with silent laughter. "You could see he believed every word you said, and Jared Silk looked as if he were going to explode."

Darvi put a few inches between them so she could look up into his face.

"I'm so glad you were there."

"I told you I would be," he said, thinking he wouldn't have missed it for the world. Seth Redding was still a free man, and for a moment, Dakota's thoughts clouded with all Darvi had been through and how much he wanted to protect her. He looked into her face and studied her eyes with tenderness before bending and kissing her very gently. Still holding her gaze with his own, he kissed her again.

"I was right," he whispered.

"About what?" Darvi breathed.

Steps outside drew them apart, and just after that, Renee came inside.

"How are you?" Renee asked Darvi as she came to hug her.

"I'm all right."

"You did so well. I was so proud of you."

"What do you think that judge will say tomorrow?"

"I think he'll end up throwing the key away where they're concerned. At least I hope he will." Renee hung her hat on the mirrored hat stand hear the door. "I've even heard that some of Aurora's crooked police will eventually be dragged into this." Smoothing her still-perfect coiffure, she finished, "Come to the kitchen. I'll make us some lunch."

Renee sailed ahead, clearly pleased with the way the morning had gone. Dakota brought up the rear, and as he held the door for Darvi, he bent and whispered close to her ear.

"Your mouth is very kissable."

By the time Darvi arrived next to the kitchen table, her face was the color of ripe watermelon. Renee turned to say something, took in that pink glow, and changed her mind. She went back to her lunch preparations with a huge smile on her face.

❧ ❧ ❧

"Are you going to try to see her?" Eliot asked Seth as he studied that man's back.

Seth stood at one of the windows in the apartment living room, his eyes on the street.

"I want to," he said at last.

"But you won't," Eliot guessed.

Seth turned. "No, I won't. I know this is our last day of freedom, but I can't take the chance that that Ranger will shoot first and ask questions later."

"He didn't do that when he was at the ranch."

"No, but jail time or not, I can't take that chance."

Seth turned back to the window. Eliot watched him in frustration. He hated this. It was never supposed to be this way. Jared was not supposed to mess up and get caught, bringing them down at the same time. And Darvi. She was supposed to love his brother and make him smile again.

A moment later Eliot told Seth goodbye and went on his way. They had just met with the judge. He had told them both to stay in town that night, but Eliot couldn't. If this was his last night of freedom, he wanted to be with the woman he loved.

೩·೩·೩

"I've made a decision," Darvi told Dakota that night. Renee had some business to attend to at the news office, so Darvi and Dakota were doing the dishes.

"About the trial?"

"No. Believe it or not, I've been thinking about my mother, and your mother is the reason."

"How's that?"

Darvi paused with her hands in the soapy water.

"You have such a wonderful relationship with your mother—she could even ask you about what you believe. I've so put off my mother by not marrying Brandon that she can barely stand the sight of me. I'm all ready to give her verses and share my faith with her, but she's barely speaking to me."

Dakota listened to the wonder in her voice and kept silent.

"I've been putting the cart in front of the horse. My next letter isn't going to say anything about Christ. I'm just going to try to get her to speak with me. What do you think?"

"I think you're right. Your mother is only going to see God as the problem unless you repair the relationship."

"I think so too. Our relationship has always been based on our pleasing each other. The moment one of us didn't do what the other wanted, we were in a fight. That's got to be fixed before anything else happens!"

With that Darvi went back to washing. Dakota watched her, not able to stop smiling.

You're like that to Your children, Lord—always giving us new insight and expanding our worlds with more knowledge, not just about You, but about how to live this life. I still marvel at how I survived without You, how I made a single decision on my own. But You must have been leading in those situations too.

And help my parents as they read my letter. Help them to see their need for You. Give Darvi just the words for her mother. Help her mother to read with an open heart and accept Darvi back.

"What are you thinking about?"

"I was praying."

"Oh, I'm sorry to interrupt."

"It's all right. Somehow I think God understands."

Darvi kept washing, but she looked very content. Dakota didn't think there was another place on earth he'd rather be than in Texas with Darvi.

※-※-※

For the third day in a row the courtroom was packed. From their front-row seats, Renee, Darvi, and Dakota noticed that things became very quiet when the judge entered, and in just a matter of minutes, the charges were read and the courtroom heard that Jared Silk was going to jail for a very long time.

On the adjournment, Darvi and Dakota stood, Darvi wishing that her abductors were going with Mr. Silk. She was still thinking this when a police officer approached with Seth Redding, his hands cuffed behind his back. Seth stopped and looked down at her, his eyes as warm and caring as always.

"Hello, Darvi."

"Hello, Seth."

He studied her a moment, and Darvi thought he would move on, but he spoke again.

"Eliot and I turned state's evidence against Jared. Our time inside will be very short."

He paused now, as though giving her time to think about it.

"Please tell me I can contact you when I get out, Darvi. I swear, I'll never hold you captive again."

"I can't do that," Darvi whispered, her heart in terrible pain over this whole ordeal. She shook her head and tried to find words. She ended up saying, "For so many reasons, Seth, it just won't work."

The temptation was very strong to say cruel things and make her feel as bad as he was feeling, but Seth couldn't do it.

"You're quite a lady, Darvi Wingate," he now said, a small smile in his eyes. "Don't ever forget that."

The officer led him away then, Eliot and another officer some ten feet behind. Seeing Eliot brought Darvi's eyes to where she'd last seen Cassy. That woman's devastated face was staring after the departing brothers. Lindy's face was buried in her mother's skirts, and Nate's little visage was nothing short of tragic. Darvi glanced up at Dakota, who nodded as he guided her in Cassy's direction.

"I'm sorry I had to deceive you, Cassy," Dakota said to the ranch owner the moment she looked at them.

"Don't be, Dakota." Her voice was resigned. "You only did what you had to do."

An uncomfortable silence fell over them as Darvi cast about desperately for something to say. She then noticed Cassy's dress. It was her wedding dress.

"Did you get married?"

Cassy actually managed a smile. "Yes, we did."

"Was it nice?"

The other woman nodded, her eyes softening in remembrance, before becoming direct as she looked into Darvi's face.

"I've been doing a lot of thinking, Darvi. I need to hear more. I've been trying to read my Bible, but I'm not understanding. I need to hear more about the way you believe. Will you write to me?"

"I'd be happy to meet with you, Cassy," Darvi volunteered. "I'll tell you anything you want to know."

But the blonde was already shaking her head. "No. I need to be able to read it and think it over."

Cassy's gaze dropped, her face looking tired and ashamed. She moved as though she would turn away and leave, but Nate was pulling on her arm.

"Oh, yes," she stopped to say, looking back to Darvi. "I almost forgot. Nate wants you to know that at the end he knew everything. He saw and heard Dakota talking with the sheriff, and he even heard you leaving out the window the night you left."

Darvi looked down at him.

"And you didn't say anything, Nate?"

"Not for a while," the boy told her. "Not until after you left, and then only to Mama."

"Why, Nate? Why didn't you wake the house?"

He shrugged a little. "You weren't happy. I know Seth wanted to keep you, but you were sad. And I didn't think you should have to cry in your bed anymore."

Tears flooding her eyes, Darvi took him in her arms. The little boy held on for dear life. When he let go, Darvi looked down and smoothed his hair. Lindy came next, hugging Darvi with all the sweetness she'd always shown her.

When at last they stood apart, Darvi knew that Cassy would have to make the move. Darvi's heart was ready to burst when Cassy stepped forward to hug her. She and the children then left without another word.

"I think maybe we should head to your aunt's," Dakota said quietly, and Darvi only nodded.

Halfway there, she had a thought and said, "Too often I can't see why God does things or lets them happen, but right now I'm willing to admit that I had to go through all of this to open a door between Cassy and me."

"I think you might be right."

"I'm going to use those verses you gave me for Cassy instead of my mother. Do you think that's all right?"

"I think that's perfect."

It was good to cover the rest of the way in silence. Upon arriving, both were surprised to find that Renee had reached home first.

"Aunt Renee," Darvi said the moment she saw her, "thank you for everything. It's been wonderful seeing you and getting to know you, but I'm going to leave for Austin tomorrow. I hope you won't think me rude, but I want to go see Uncle Marty."

Renee hugged her niece.

"That's fine, dear. I was hoping you could meet my James, but maybe another time."

"You could always invite me to the wedding."

Renee smiled.

"I'll do that, Darvi Wingate, just see if I don't."

The three spent the remainder of the day in relaxed pursuits. Renee took Darvi and Dakota out to dinner and spent the evening regaling them with stories of her reporting escapades. Dakota had plenty of his own tales, and they laughed until way too late.

Nevertheless, Darvi stood by her word. Dakota still acting as protector and guide, they left the next morning for Austin.

Epilogue

Austin
One Month Later

Dear Darvi,

THE CHILDREN LOVED THE LETTERS YOU WROTE just for them. You would not believe their excitement. They are working on letters back to you, but I wanted to reply first.

I can't thank you enough for your words to me. We miss Eliot terribly, Seth too, but your letter gave me some hope and peace for my own heart. I must admit that for a time I felt I'd sinned too badly to ever be forgiven by God, but the verses you gave me would indicate otherwise.

I think we are going to take your advice and start going into town for church on Sunday mornings. When I was shopping last week, I met a woman at Dawson's who was very kind. I don't recall ever seeing her before but found out that she's a pastor's wife. I know the church she goes to, and I thought if she was typical of the congregation, we might be welcome. I'm scared of such a move, but I'm more afraid of doing nothing.

Well, I've run out of words. Thank you again for the list of verses. The Bible does make it very clear; I just need to figure out what my heart should do. Take care, Darvi, and I'm sorry for all the pain we caused you. I wouldn't mind hearing from you again.

Sincerely,
Cassandra McDermott

Darvi lay her head back, her heart so blessed that she could barely think. She'd received four letters and hadn't known where to start. A little afraid of what her mother's letter might say, and certain that Merry's letter would be good news, she had put them aside in favor of Cassy's. The one from Dakota's mother intrigued her; nevertheless, she saved it until last, glad that after she read her mother's letter, she could tell her uncle it was good news as well.

᭡ ᭡ ᭡

Dakota was doing some letter-reading of his own. Having finally gone back to work on a job that put him under new command with a group of Rangers toward the south, he was just getting into Austin for his first leave. Upon his arrival he did two things: got a bath and checked to see if the post office had mail for him. A letter from his mother, which Cash had forwarded, awaited him. It was short. She thanked him, told him she would think about all he said, and went on to talk about some plans she and his father were making for the winter, possibly even a trip to Texas.

Dakota put the letter away with great hope. He didn't think he would belabor the point in his letters back to her, but she hadn't slammed the door in his face. His heart content, he heeled Eli toward Marty Bracewell's house. It had seemed like years since he'd ridden on official business, but in truth, once he was on the trail, it had felt like forever since he'd seen Darvi.

He used the kitchen door because he knew it would be open, and surprisingly enough found his boss sitting at the table reading his own mail.

"Well, Dakota, when did you get in?"

"Only just."

Brace smiled. "Your hair get that wet on the trail?"

Dakota smiled back. "It can get mighty hot out there."

Brace only laughed.

"Where is she?" Dakota felt he had waited long enough.

"In the living room. Her mother has asked her to come home for a time, so she's going next week, but right now she's reading a letter from your mother."

"*My* mother?"

"Yes," Brace responded, looking very pleased as he answered. "It was a pretty thick envelope. I suspect she's telling Darvi every rotten thing you did as a child. That would take more than a few pages."

Dakota had heard enough.

"Darvi," he called firmly as he moved that way, not missing the sound of someone scrambling and papers crackling. He went through the dining room, and sure enough, the living room was empty.

"Darvi." His voice was coaxing now, even as his eyes searched for some sign of her. He hadn't heard her on the stairs, and it took some doing to spot a bit of her skirt sticking out from the door that opened into the dining room. The door was open against the wall, and he could now see that she had scooted behind it.

He moved it slowly and tried not to laugh at her attempt at an innocent face.

"Dakota! When did you get in?"

He came close and put his hands on the wall on either side of her head.

"Just now."

"How nice," she said a little too brightly, all the while keeping her hands behind her back.

His eyes dropped down for a moment before coming back to hers.

"A little bird told me you got a letter."

"A letter?" Darvi appeared to think on this. "Now, let me see. Have I received any letters lately?" With that Darvi couldn't hold on. She laughed and brought out several pages.

"Is this really from my mother?"

"Yep," she teased him. "Every word. I'm learning an awful lot."

For a moment they just stared at each other. Darvi felt her cheeks grow warm and tried to divert his gaze with a question.

"Do you know when you head out again?"

"No."

"How about where you'll be going?"

"I don't know."

Darvi playfully shook her head.

"You don't know much, do you?"

"I know that I love you."

For Darvi, time stood still. She had never pushed this man to say those words, knowing she'd wanted it to be in his time and not her own, but she had been feeling love for him for a very long time.

"When did you decide this?"

"When I was near the river. It reminded me of the night we stayed on the trail and you met the rattlesnake."

"And that made you love me?"

He nodded. "It caused me to remember how many times I could have lost you. I don't want to lose you, Darvi. Not now—not ever."

Her heart filling her eyes, Darvi said, "I love you, Dakota Rawlings."

Moving very slowly and gently, Dakota leaned forward and kissed her. Darvi sighed when he pulled away. Dakota wanted to kiss her again but told himself that would have to wait.

"Brace tells me you're headed home next week."

"Yes, I prayed you'd get here before I left."

"I made it." He then added. "I'm glad your mother wants to see you."

"I am too, but I don't really want to leave Texas."

"But this time you'll leave knowing that I love you."

Darvi smiled. "And you won't forget my love, will you?"

"Not a chance."

This time Dakota didn't kiss her but took her gently into his arms. It was the sealing of a promise that both of them would keep.

About the Author

LORI WICK is a
multifaceted author of Christian fiction.
As comfortable writing period stories
as she is penning contemporary works,
Lori's books (6 million in print)
vary widely in location and time period.
Lori's faithful fans consistently put her series
and standalone works on the bestseller lists.
Lori and her husband, Bob,
live with their swiftly growing family
in the Midwest.

Books by Lori Wick

A Place Called Home Series
A Place Called Home
A Song for Silas
The Long Road Home
A Gathering of Memories

The Californians
Whatever Tomorrow Brings
As Time Goes By
Sean Donovan
Donovan's Daughter

Kensington Chronicles
The Hawk and the Jewel
Wings of the Morning
Who Brings Forth the Wind
The Knight and the Dove

Rocky Mountain Memories
Where the Wild Rose Blooms
Whispers of Moonlight
To Know Her by Name
Promise Me Tomorrow

The Yellow Rose Trilogy
Every Little Thing About You
A Texas Sky
City Girl

English Garden Series
The Proposal
The Rescue
The Visitor
The Pursuit

The Tucker Mills Trilogy
Moonlight on the Millpond
Just Above a Whisper
Leave a Candle Burning

Big Sky Dreams
Cassidy
Sabrina

Contemporary Fiction
Sophie's Heart
Pretense
The Princess
Bamboo & Lace
Every Storm
White Chocolate Moments